PRAISE FOR
A SECRET HEART

"This story was wonderful! Another Mail Order Bride romance, but packed with twists and turns that kept me hooked. I was rooting so hard for Ed and Rebecca! It's worth the wait to see it all unfold. And I can not wait for Isaac's story!"

—Jo Ruth, GOODREADS

"A wonderful, heartwarming enemies-to-more story with a strong faith theme set in wild Wyoming. Beautiful, engaging prose, a well-developed plot with enough action, danger, and romance, and characters you can't help but cheer for are a few things to enjoy in this book."

—Natasha, GOODREADS

"Very sweet mail order bride story. Romantic, heartwarming, and fun-to-read."

—Marianne, GOODREADS

"This is a fun book to read with an engaging storyline and well developed characters. It contains the right mix of romance, drama, relationship angst and action to keep you turning the pages and anticipating the story right to the very end."

—Catherine, GOODREADS

A
SECRET
Heart

Wind River Mail-Order Brides

A Secret Heart

Lacy Williams
Wendy Klopfenstein

sunrise
PUBLISHING

A Secret Heart
Wind River Mail-Order Brides, Book 3

Published by Sunrise Media Group LLC
Copyright © 2025 Sunrise Media Group LLC

Ebook ISBN: 978-1-963372-42-7
Paperback: 978-1-963372-41-0

This book is a work of fiction. Names, characters, places, and incidents are either products of the author's imagination or used fictitiously. Any similarity to actual people, organizations, and/or events is purely coincidental.
All Scripture quotations, unless otherwise indicated, are taken from the King James Version.

For more information about Lacy Williams or Wendy Klopfenstein visit their websites at lacywilliams.net and wendyklopfenstein.com.

Cover Design: Sunrise Media Group LLC

Wind River Mail-Order Brides

A Convenient Heart
A Steadfast Heart
A Secret Heart
A Dangerous Heart
A Forgotten Heart

To Mom. You are sorely missed.

"A MAN'S HEART DEVISETH HIS WAY:
BUT THE LORD DIRECTETH HIS STEPS."

Proverbs 16:9 KJV

One

June, 1893

H E'D MADE A MISTAKE.

Ed McGraw took two steps backward and pressed his foot on one of the new wood planks of the small porch of his Wyoming cabin.

Squeak.

There it was again.

Somehow, he must've missed catching a warped board. Now the spot squeaked when he stepped on it. That wouldn't do. Not for a would-be carpenter like him.

He paused just outside the door, glancing over his shoulder. The view of the radiant sunrise glinting across the Laramie Mountains made a man want to share it with someone, but Ed had zero prospects. And finding a wife was the last thing he had time for.

He needed to hurry if he was going to finish detailing the wooden cradle waiting for him inside his cabin-turned-workshop. Morning chores were finished, but his older brother Drew would have a list of work that needed doin' today the length of Ed's arm when Ed joined the family down at the main house for breakfast. Drew had kept the four McGraw brothers together after they'd lost both parents within two years, taking on the mantle of family patriarch, but there was always too much work to be done on the McGraw homestead.

Hoofbeats sounded. Too late to finish his project now.

"Uncle Ed!"

Ed lifted his head to acknowledge his fourteen-year-old nephew, riding past Ed's cabin on a pony.

With the awkward frame of a boy growing too tall too fast, David was the spitting image of Drew at that age.

David took a slight detour and reined in yards away from Ed's porch. "Pa wants me to check the water level in the little pond in the east pasture. And see if Uncle Isaac is up there."

If David was already riding out, that meant Ed had missed breakfast. His stomach growled a protest. He needed another hour or two's work on the wooden cradle before it'd be ready for delivery. Didn't seem like he was getting that hour today.

"Be careful," Ed warned his nephew. "Isaac's been tracking wolves around the high pasture."

Too much like his pa at that age, David lit up instead of appearing worried. "I'll look for tracks!"

And he was gone.

Ed cracked open the door long enough for a glance at

the unstained wooden cradle sitting along the wall before he closed the door with a soft snick.

A sigh slipped from Ed's lips. Would his family ever understand? He loved the feeling of a piece—chair, bed frame, shelf, anything—coming to life in his hands. He wasn't so fanciful as to think wood spoke to him, but when he sketched out a new item to build with pencil and paper, he felt as if some hidden part of him came to life. One at a time, his arms slipped through the suspenders hanging at his side as he started toward the worn path between his cabin and the main house. His fingers riffled through his hair, sending a fine layer of sawdust tumbling through the orange-tipped rays of sunlight.

The main house had been built by Ed's pa. After Isaac had joined the family, Pa had built onto the house, adding a second story and another bedroom downstairs. Ed had grown up running and riding all over this land, along with his older brothers Drew and Isaac and their youngest brother Nick. The McGraw spread was their legacy, a hard-fought family heritage.

Only, he wasn't sure he wanted it any longer.

The kitchen window was open, and once he got close enough, girlish voices floated from inside. Drew's daughters, at eleven and six, couldn't have been more different. Jo was a tried-and-true tomboy, wearing trousers more often than anything else. Tillie, never without a ribbon in her hair, loved playing family with her dolls.

Ed would do anything for them, but when he opened the door and stepped inside, his first urge was to turn back around.

"Don't pull!" Tillie whined. She sat in one of the straight-backed chairs, her face all screwed up.

Standing behind her younger sister, Jo scowled at the top of her head. "It's a braid. They're gonna hurt some."

Drew's wife Kaitlyn swiveled from gathering the dishes at the table, where Drew and Nick were still seated, to admonish her stepdaughters. "Stop arguing. The quicker you finish, the quicker you can head outside to the barn." That was directed at Jo. And the pointed words hit home. Jo focused on Tillie's braid, her tongue peeping out of the corner of her mouth.

Kaitlyn had only married into the family a few months ago, but she was whip-smart, and the children had taken to her. Now she glanced up and caught sight of Ed. He watched a minuscule grimace flit over her expression.

"I'm sorry. I forgot you were coming. I don't know how much breakfast is left."

Before he could say anything, she was already moving to the kitchen, bringing the dirty dishes with her. Ed scanned the table as Nick nodded to him. A strip of bacon remained. It'd go great with the last biscuit. No longer warm to the touch, but it was something. If he'd ignore the projects he kept hidden at his house, he might secure himself a big hot breakfast.

"Need a plate?" Kaitlyn returned from the kitchen. Evidence of her fancy upbringing slipped out again as she handed him a china plate and enough silverware for a four-course meal. She expected a level of societal propriety the brothers hadn't been used to abiding by before she'd shown up from St. Louis. She also brought more smiles to Drew's face than Ed had seen in a long time, so he guessed he could forgive her.

"I'm fine." No need for her to wash another plate for a piece of bacon stuffed in a biscuit. A cold biscuit. He tore off a bite as he pulled out a chair with his free hand to sit at the table, despite the wrinkle in Kaitlyn's brow.

His brothers eyed him while Drew kept talking. "Isaac needs to be here. He can't sulk alone forever."

Isaac had been with the U.S. Marshals for years before he'd come home a year ago, subdued and quiet—not the brother Ed had grown up with. And now they were having a discussion of how to draw his older brother in from the old cabin at the far end of the McGraw property. Why hadn't anyone bothered to wait for him to have this conversation?

"He'll come around." Nick leaned back in his chair, seemingly unaffected by their brother's absence. Always a peacemaker, he also possessed an uncanny understanding of Isaac.

"I'm not so sure." Kaitlyn put in her two bits from behind them. "The last time he came down for supplies, he seemed . . . lonely. As if he carried a burden and had no one to share it with."

Lonely? How did Kaitlyn figure that? More like Isaac went around as if he had lemon stuck in his teeth. Had ever since he'd hung up his hat as a marshal, coming home only to spend his time repairing the old cabin or moving the cattle from pasture to pasture. It would've been nice to have him show up for the planting, but that would've meant socializing with other people. Like his brothers. Like Ed.

With only a year between them, Isaac being the older,

they'd been close as boys until Isaac had started beating Ed at everything. And now Isaac had shut them all out. If he was lonely, it was his own doing.

Ed took another bite of biscuit. One with bacon in it this time. His eyes darted between Nick and Drew.

"Isaac will show his face when he wants to. When he's ready." Nick barely raised his voice.

"What if he had a wife?" Kaitlyn leaned in to grip the back of Drew's chair. "Someone to care for him, to come home to."

A gleam danced in Drew's eye. "Who do you suggest? Widow Mayberry?"

Ed chuckled before shoving another bite in. Even Nick grinned. Heart-breaking, tough-guy Isaac married to Widow Mayberry. She had to be twenty years older, and she talked nonstop. At least hard-nosed Drew's recent marriage to Kaitlyn had drawn out a bit of a sense of humor in him.

"Not funny." Kaitlyn pretended to bristle, then another spark lit her face. "What about Rebekah Edwards? She isn't married. Didn't you say she was sweet on Isaac?"

The biscuit lodged in Ed's throat. He choked back a cough. Not Rebekah. A quick wit and all those fiery red curls wrapped up in an annoying, although what some called "pretty," package. Ed would take anyone but Rebekah for a sister-in-law. It was bad enough he had to put up with her as a neighbor. The nagging crumbs in his throat threatened to break him into a full-blown coughing fit. He went for Nick's coffee. One swig and he set the cup down.

Nick gave him a sideways scowl.

"Rebekah's too busy working at the paper." Another

sip of coffee gave Ed time to pull his thoughts together. "Speaking of the newspaper, they're doing a special section for those mail-order bride ads now. You know, like the one you ran."

"An ad?" Drew raised a brow in question. While he had run an ad, it'd been a rough road and a twist of fate that'd landed Kaitlyn here as his mail-order bride. "Sounds good."

Drew sounded as if Ed had suggested a perfect idea when he'd only meant to divert the conversation.

"You'd post a matrimonial ad for Isaac?" Ed followed up. After all they'd been through with Drew's ad, he wanted to try this again? "Our Isaac?"

His brother obviously wasn't thinking straight. There had to be a better way to find Isaac a wife, if he even wanted one.

Nick shifted in his chair. "He doesn't need us poking our noses where they don't belong. Give him time to come around." Nick had always been close to Isaac. It wasn't a wonder that he was protective now.

"And if he doesn't come around? If he hides out the rest of his life up in that sorry excuse for a cabin? Or worse?" Drew fixed his eyes on Nick as he jabbed his finger at the table. "I can't even get him to tell me why he came back."

"Wouldn't be too bad to have his help around here either." Ed dusted the crumbs from his hands. All eyes fixed on him as if he were interrupting. "Might do him good to be around family more. That's all."

"A wife will do the trick." A dreaminess filled Kaitlyn's words. "Someone to love the rough edges away."

"He'll never go for it." Wise words from Nick. Surely

no one imagined Isaac would agree to their plan. It might even drive him further away. But Drew wasn't used to being questioned.

"We don't have to tell him." Ed finished the last of Nick's coffee. He rose to refill the cup from the pot Kaitlyn had placed at the other end of the table. Steam rose from the liquid. Even if breakfast hadn't warmed his belly, the coffee had.

"Good point." Drew ran a hand along his chin. "We don't tell him at first. We run an ad, evaluate the replies, then pick a woman or two that might fit him. We turn it over to Isaac from there."

Nick shook his head. "I don't know."

"He'll go for it when a pretty lady shows up," Kaitlyn said. She shared another glance with Drew. Obviously, the honeymoon phase hadn't passed yet.

Ed cleared his throat. Now was as good a time as any to tell them he'd be at his place working for a couple of hours. If he finished the cradle, he might have time to get it to town today.

"That's decided, then." Drew rose from the table before Ed got a word out. "Nick, are you ready to go see about that mare? Ed, I promised one of us would take the Boutwells to town. I need you to take care of that. Put in that ad while you're there."

What had led his brother to think he'd be available? Drew lived and breathed this homestead, thinking he needed to command them all like an army regiment. What if Ed refused? What if he dared to want more?

"I've got things to do here." Helping the Boutwells wasn't

so bad, but more than likely, he'd end up with Rebekah wanting to join them. She hadn't changed one bit from their school days, back when there'd been a little school on the edge of Heath Quade's property that all the neighbors had attended. Before Quade's wife had passed and he'd sent his younger girls off to boarding school, closing the local schoolhouse down. But that'd been after all the McGraws and Rebekah had graduated. Time with Rebekah still rubbed him wrong, like a sand burr stuck inside his boot.

Drew halted for the briefest second, then waved off Ed's faint complaint.

Ed swallowed back another protest. Wouldn't do him any good. The cradle would have to wait. He glanced at Nick. "You want to write the ad? You're the one with all the book smarts."

Nick rose to follow Drew without a look back. "I'll leave the ad to you two."

"Do the ad next trip. Time's a-wasting to get the neighbors to their train." Drew waved it off. Which meant Ed would get saddled with writing the ad too.

The sooner he got this over with, the better.

"I can always count on you, Ed." Drew's words settled heavy in Ed's chest as Ed stepped past his brothers on the way to the door.

One more thing added to the endless list of jobs everyone counted on him to do. All he wanted was a chance to prove his woodworking could be a means to bring in money. A reason for him to have the time to work on it. But how would he do that if he never caught a break to even finish this one project?

It simply has to be Isaac McGraw.

Rebekah Edwards stood at the kitchen window and strained her eyes to make out the identity of the driver approaching the farmhouse. Her heart beat out a fluttering rhythm. If Isaac drove to town, she'd add each minute of the long ride to her collective memories of every move he had ever made in her presence.

But the man's hat was down, and the morning sun coming through the kitchen windowpane blurred the figure on the wagon seat. He sat broad-shouldered, muscles flexing as he halted in front of the house.

If only his head would tilt to reveal Issac, his eyes the deep green of the pine trees and his dimpled smile so endearing. She hadn't seen him in town recently, but she was still holding out hope.

"Are you listening, Rebekah? I don't want to leave you here alone. Not with all the rumors about Quade's men." Aunt Opal's words pulled Rebekah's stare from the window. The men's voices were muffled through the wall.

Despite her excitement at the possibility of seeing Isaac, nothing in Rebekah relished being separated from her aunt and uncle. She'd lived with them on this farm since coming west over fifteen years ago at the tender age of eleven. While she stayed by herself in the loft over the newspaper office in Calvin during part of each week due to the distance, she'd never stayed on the farm alone. Rumors of Quade and his men harassing local farmers until they agreed to sell their land didn't help matters any.

"I can't leave the paper. It wouldn't make it a month without me." Rebekah leaned against the kitchen counter, cluttered with the meat and cheese her aunt was preparing for sandwiches, as she folded the checkered cloth around the loaf of freshly baked bread. Her statement held no bravado, only the bitter truth.

She'd worked at her beloved paper since the summer after she'd graduated from school, and it was struggling. If it didn't turn around soon, there'd be nothing for Mr. Sullivan to leave her. If she lost her paper, she'd lose her dream of independence.

Aunt Opal's brows knit together, further deepening the lines of worry as she layered the sandwiches together, working on the little counter space that remained. "I don't understand how you staying is going to make it better."

The yeasty scent of the bread tempted Rebekah as she shoved the loaf into the basket. How would she stretch it out for as many days as possible, this hug in a loaf? It would be all she had of her aunt's cooking for a long while. She stepped closer to Opal, looping her arm around the petite woman's shoulders. This woman who'd been closer to her than her own mother all these years.

"We've added a special section to take on more matrimonial ads. They're my specialty. Mr. Sullivan left them totally in my hands. I even convinced a larger paper to run them for broader circulation." She leaned in to give her aunt a squeeze in an effort to silence her arguments. Rebekah didn't need to add her aunt's concerns to her own worries about looking after the garden, the canning, and the endless list of chores inside the house as well as performing her duties at the newspaper. At least their closest neighbors, the McGraws, had agreed to help with the livestock.

Opal's weary smile faded. "Mind you, I don't want you talking to Quade while we're gone."

Rebekah suspected the fire in her aunt's voice hid a mountain of worries. For their homestead. For Uncle Vess. For Rebekah. Not to mention the trip east. It echoed Rebekah's own worries of staying here alone. The ones she'd been pushing aside for the sake of her dreams.

Opal cast another glance her way. The creases between her brows deepened as if she'd been reading Rebekah's thoughts. "And if he ever shows up here, you go get the McGraw brothers."

Heath Quade had been by more than once to make an offer on their place. The first one had made Rebekah whistle, which had garnered a scolding from Aunt Opal for being unladylike. The second one had come with a veiled threat. Rebekah hadn't heard it herself, but she had no reason to doubt Uncle Vess's word.

"I doubt Quade will come here while you're gone. I likely won't even see him unless he does something worthy of a news article." Not that Rebekah would mind going to get one particular McGraw, even if she could handle Mr. Quade on her own.

"You and that paper." Aunt Opal's weathered hands settled the sandwiches for her and Uncle Vess's train trip in another basket. "Make sure you weed the vegetable garden. Watch out for that hen that tries to slip out of the coop."

She glanced up from shuffling the sandwiches. "And lock the door at night."

All of Aunt Opal's talk meant more than the words she spoke. It meant she would miss Rebekah and worry about her. That she loved her. In a funny sort of way, the words wrapped themselves around Rebekah tighter than any hug ever could. She stepped closer to enclose the woman in her arms.

"What's all this?" Aunt Opal's words wobbled with emotion.

Rebekah leaned closer to her ear. "A little something to remind you of me while you're gone."

Aunt Opal gave Rebekah's arm a squeeze before backing away to swipe at a tear with the back of her other hand. "We'll be back, you know. Before you have time to even miss us."

"I doubt that." *I miss you already.*

Opal sniffed, then straightened. "Doesn't your uncle know it's high time for us to be leaving? I wish he wouldn't overwork himself walking all around giving out instructions. As if the McGraws don't know their way around a farm."

"Stop your worrying, Opal." Dear Uncle Vess leaned his lanky form into the doorway, blocking the view outside as another cough racked his body. "Everything is loaded but us. And whatever delicious-smelling bread you have there."

Rebekah's brow furrowed at his cough as she picked up the loaf and placed it in her makeshift bag. She had everything she'd need to remain in town for a day or two. Her regular trips to help oversee things at the newspaper office were usually a source of joy to her. If only her aunt and uncle weren't catching a train. The only source of joy today, putting butterflies in her stomach, was the hope of Isaac driving them.

She'd thought she'd grown out of the feelings she'd held for him back when she'd attended the one-room schoolhouse with Isaac and his brothers. Until the day she'd caught a glimpse of him returning to town after serving as a marshal. He'd still exuded all the manliness of a genuine hero, striding from the train station to meet his brother Ed. No one else lived up to the legendary Isaac McGraw. Not back in school. Not now.

Rebekah smoothed her dark woolen skirt with one hand as she grasped her bag in the other, then followed her aunt out into the sunlight. She angled her free hand under her hat to shield her eyes as the McGraw near the wagon turned to greet them.

"Morning, Mrs. Boutwell."

Not Isaac.

A lock of mahogany hair escaped beneath the edge of Ed McGraw's hat as he greeted Aunt Opal with a nod. Awkward seconds passed before he offered a faint "Miss Edwards."

Rebekah stiffened. *Him. Hmph.* Had no one else noticed the drop in his voice when he'd finally said her name? Did they ever notice his slights? Two weeks ago, he'd been by to change out a wagon wheel for Uncle Vess. She must have stood by the wagon for half an hour before Ed had acknowledged her only to refuse the lemonade Aunt Opal had insisted she take out to him. Infuriating man.

"I'll load that for you." He motioned to her satchel.

"I can do it." She attempted to pull her satchel back from his reach, but not before his fingers brushed hers as they tightened around the handle, leaving her bristling.

Ed tightened his jaw. He didn't glance her way as she let go. She knew that tic of his. He was none too happy to see her either.

"How is Isaac?" The words left her mouth unplanned.

Her aunt and uncle gave her a curious look.

"Haven't seen him in a few days." Ed flicked a glance her way as he pursed his lips. He placed her satchel under the seat with the other bags, then walked to the back of the wagon. He held out a hand to Aunt Opal. "I put in some hay to make the ride more comfortable."

"You are too kind to an old woman's aching bones." Aunt Opal stepped toward him and slipped her hand in his.

Ignored again. Rebekah rolled her eyes to avoid the distraction of his muscled arms hoisting her aunt into the wagon. The very arms she had so easily envisioned belonging to Isaac earlier.

Vess handed the basket of food to his wife once she was settled, then turned to face Ed. "You will look after Rebekah, won't you?"

"I'm a grown woman, Uncle Vess. I can look after myself." Rebekah's words fell on deaf ears as her uncle kept his eyes trained on Ed. Neither of them acknowledged her.

"My brothers and I will look after the place," Ed hedged.

She barely held in a snort. Uncle Vess might as well forget getting a promise out of Ed to look after her. Which suited her just fine.

Vess lingered by the side of the wagon, his hand running across the top board. "Promise me you'll be sure she gets to town and back safely. You're a man of your word, and I trust you."

"I'll check with Drew to see if he can spare me." Ed half mumbled the words, the way he'd always mumbled when the teacher had asked about missing homework back in school. He didn't want to drive her any more than she wanted him to.

"Rebekah is precious to me." Vess coughed again.

She swallowed hard, fighting the pull of concern over his illness that she'd been trying so hard to tamp down, at least until they got to the train. One quick turn of her head, and Ed's stormy glance her way stilled the rising swell of tears, filling her with resolve.

"Don't be silly, Uncle Vess. I'm perfectly capable of saddling up a horse and riding to town." Surely her assurance would ease his mind and end this.

Rebekah shot a pleading look at her uncle, but his focus held on Ed. A man-to-man sort of stare-down, as if Ed owed him this and he was calling in his favors. Ed broke the stare.

"You McGraws have been good neighbors to us. But it's not Drew's promise I'm after. I'd like your word, Ed McGraw."

Rebekah shifted her gaze from the men to the horses in an effort to control her rising frustration. Uncle Vess wouldn't settle for anything but Ed's promise.

A sigh from Ed filled the air. "No need to worry about a thing, sir. You have my word."

Tired of waiting for Ed to offer her a hand up, Rebekah scrambled into the back of the wagon herself. Her shin clanged against the edge of the wagon, and pain shot up her leg, deepening her annoyance. She caught the twitch of Ed's jaw before he nodded to a small container nestled in the hay. "Almost forgot. Kaitlyn sent a jar of jam for you."

Rebekah hugged the gift from her friend close, smiling as she placed the jar in her satchel and settled herself beside her aunt atop the hay. The wagon jostled, and she looked behind her to the front of the wagon. Her gaze connected with Ed's as he hoisted himself onto the seat. She felt her smile fading to match his expression, and she could almost read his mind.

It's going to be a long summer.

And for once in her life, she agreed with him.

<h1 style="text-align:center">Two</h1>

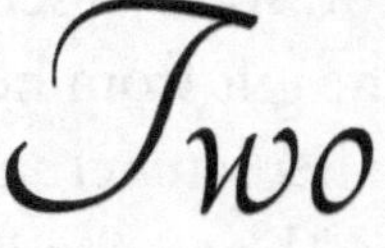

A LMOST . . . FINISHED!

It'd only been two days since Ed had dropped Rebekah off in town.

One more line of type to set before Rebekah would be done for the day. The click of metal letters sliding into the composing stick created a pleasant tune to her ears.

The clock tower at the train station chimed once.

A wagon rattled to a stop outside the newspaper office in Calvin. Right on time to take her home after two days of preparing the paper to go out. Too bad her work prevented her from peeking around the stacks of papers strewn across the desks to see out the window facing the boardwalk. The window offered a perfect view of the boardwalk, the shops across the dirt lane that made up the main street, and the pedestrians she loved watching. For now, she had to settle for listening to the clop of hooves and the jingle of harnesses.

If Isaac were sitting atop the wagon seat instead of Ed, her week would be perfect. For years, she'd tried to stop the wild moment of heart pounding every time Isaac approached. She'd begun to simply accept it as part of who she was. Ever since her first sight of him, when she was only eleven, she'd fancied him. Never could seem to help it, even now. If only it'd been Isaac who'd promised Uncle Vess.

The bell above the newspaper office's door jingled, followed by the even cadence of clomping boots across the planks of the printing office. A distinct pattern belonging to only one man in all of Calvin plunged her into the depths of disappointment. Twice this week, Ed had shown up where he shouldn't have.

Rebekah rescued the composing stick from crashing to the ground as she spun to face him. "If you can wait for a minute or two, I'm almost finished."

"Take all the time you need." His clipped words didn't hold the patience they implied. "If it's not too late, I have an ad for the paper."

She inhaled a slow breath of air in an attempt to ease her frustration before walking to the front counter. Any other neighbor might have asked about the weather or how she was faring with her family gone. Not Ed.

The sooty scent of the ink around her usually produced a calming effect of sorts, but it lost its power as the faint whiff of horse hung in the air. Isaac would have smelled like gunpowder, or so she imagined.

On her way to the front, she handed the composing stick to Mr. Sullivan. As she did, a curl escaped the pin holding her hair back. She dared not touch it for fear the ink on her fingers would color the tendrils. Her aunt was forever scolding her for coming home with ink-stained ringlets, telling her it ruined the glow of her beauty. For all Rebekah knew, another McGraw brother might be in town with Ed. That hope bolstered her spirits anew.

"An ad?" Rebekah arched one eyebrow as she spoke to Ed in a low tone. His white shirt bore scuff marks across the arms where he must have loaded items into the wagon earlier in the day.

"Morning, Mr. McGraw." Mr. Sullivan, the proprietor of *The Weekly Gazette* and Rebekah's boss, called out from somewhere behind her as the press clacked back and forth with the printing.

Spinning his hat in his hands, Ed nodded at Mr. Sullivan before focusing his attention back on her. The twirling hat stopped. "It's an ad for the matrimonial section."

"The matrimonial section? You?" Both her brows flew up with the corners of her mouth. If only she had the strength to keep from bursting out in laughter in the presence of Mr. Sullivan. He'd scolded her more than usual lately about professionalism with the customers. But maybe Ed hadn't taken notice of the incredulity in her tone.

Before her fingers could reach for a pencil to take down the ad, he pulled a folded-over piece of paper from his pocket. His jaw twitched.

"It's for Isaac." He slapped the paper on the desk, his gaze holding hers and his expression thunderous. He'd heard her all right. "I'll be back to take you home after I load up the supplies at the general store." His words were clipped.

Rebekah gulped back the aggravating tears pricking her

eyes as she held his stare. His face wore no emotion as he placed coins on the counter to pay for the ad, then spun on his heels. His steps echoed heavier than usual as he exited.

"What did you do now, Rebekah?" Mr. Sullivan moved in behind her.

Sullivan's words barely registered as Rebekah's fingers lifted the paper. A faint whiff of coffee mixed with bacon drifted to her nostrils. She carefully unfolded what appeared to be an envelope, worn with time. Words were scrawled across the width of the yellowing paper.

> *Rancher, tall with good manners, nice-looking, desires acquaintance with upstanding young woman, must cook well; object matrimony. Box 256, Calvin, Wyoming.*

A matrimonial ad for Isaac? Whatever pounding rhythm her heart had beat before, it slowed until the room spun.

Isaac wanted a wife.

"Rebekah?" Mr. Sullivan grasped the paper with one hand as he raked the other through his whitening hair. "Another rancher looking for a wife. We'll put it in the next edition."

"I can't." *I was supposed to be his wife.*

Mr. Sullivan made no indication he'd heard her over the clatter of the press. He surveyed her with a questioning crinkle to his brow, as if calculating why she stood so still. "Take it home with the other ads. Work it up. Make sure you run it in the next edition."

There was no way Mr. Sullivan had any idea of her feelings for Isaac. Since the humiliation she'd endured in the schoolroom, she'd kept her true feelings close, never sharing them with anyone. Most of her acquaintances had forgotten that long-ago debacle. Except for the boy—now man—who'd engineered it. Ed.

Her eyes roamed the room, at first to distract herself. The stacks of papers waiting to be tied with twine, the dusty desks, the ink on her own fingers—all reminders of what Mr. Sullivan had done for her. He trusted her with the ads. And she wanted more, so much more.

Rebekah breathed deep, this time letting the odor of printing ink settle her nerves. She had no choice but to print the ad. Isaac McGraw was a paying customer.

Her fingers worked to untie the leather apron that protected her light-colored blouse.

You could answer Isaac's ad.

The thought stopped her in her tracks as she climbed the stairs to gather her bag from the storage room above the newspaper office. Her well-worn satchel sat atop the cot that ran the length of the old newspaper stacks. Beyond them were boxes of filed papers, miscellaneous parts, and a lone window overlooking the street. She moved to the window. She'd wrestled with problems up here before, in the evenings when she stayed in town by herself. Mr. Sullivan's house was two blocks over on the residential street, and he let her lock the doors for propriety's sake.

Isaac McGraw couldn't marry anyone else.

Through the glass, she spied Ed returning with his wagon loaded. She must have lingered longer than she'd planned. Her fingers were still without feeling as she lifted her satchel. Or had her brain simply refused to acknowledge the motions of her own body while her heart went numb?

Rebekah descended the stairs. From the desk in the corner, she gathered up the stack of ads waiting to be sorted and placed for next week's edition. One particular ad glared at her from the top as she slid it into her leather workbag. What if it were to get lost in the busy news office? That was another option. Or a gust of wind might easily blow the ad away.

She finished gathering her work. With a wave to Mr. Sullivan, she spun to push the door with her back, lugging her satchel in one hand and the leather bag of ads in the other. As the door swung open, it met a thump of resistance. She turned to find Ed rubbing his nose. An apology stuck in her throat as he glared past his fingers at her.

"Ready?" The word came out clipped. He held out a hand for her things, but she brushed past him to put her bags in the wagon herself.

A swirl of emotions fought inside her. The last thing she needed was Ed's commentary on her feelings for Isaac. Or more of his snickering, which still echoed in the back of her mind, along with all the other students' laughter from that unfortunate incident years ago. She hoisted herself onto the seat, perfectly content if he didn't speak to her for the entire ride home.

Ed settled beside her, pointing to her workbag as he snapped the reins. "Taking work home?"

"I usually do." She refused to look at him.

"Don't forget to put *all* the ads in the paper."

Insufferable. As if her professionalism would allow her

to do otherwise. What did he take her for? Whatever his angle was, he'd not get the satisfaction of another word out of her.

She gripped the far edge of the seat, angling her body away from his as much as possible. As she did, he eased the wagon onto the small town's main street. They passed buildings lining both sides of the street until Ed turned the wagon onto a side street. A row of small houses ran the length of the road.

Ed pulled up on the reins in front of a white clapboard house. "Wait here."

"Why are we stopping?"

"I'll only be a minute." He jumped from the wagon without offering any real answer, then walked around to the back.

"Some of us want to get home before nightfall," she called out after him.

He ignored her.

She shouldn't care, but her innate curiosity got the better of her, and she stretched her neck to discover what mystery had halted their trip home.

From under the tarp, he pulled out a cradle. A beautiful, handcrafted cradle. His arms wrapped around the wood in a careful gesture, then he began the walk to the door. Rebekah followed his movements with renewed interest. She had a hundred questions, starting with, What was Ed McGraw doing with a cradle?

Ed didn't dare glance back, even if every hair on his neck

prickled from Rebekah's certain scrutiny. He'd never give her the satisfaction of knowing she flustered him.

Careful not to scuff the wood finish against the door, Ed settled the cradle at his feet, then rapped on the door. At least Rebekah appeared to be staying put in the wagon. All he needed right now was her nosy reporter questions interrupting his delivery. He'd handle her questions on the rest of the drive home.

The door opened a little at first, then swung wide.

"Ed, you finished it!" Jeb Nelson, a young man not much older than Ed himself, squatted beside the piece, rubbing his hand along the wood. His fingers followed the intricate carving before he turned his face up to offer an approving smile. "It's beautiful. Far more ornate than I imagined. My wife will love it. What do I owe you?"

"Same price we agreed on before." Ed shifted a little. Jeb was a friend. Ed had known him since they'd played tag in the churchyard. And besides, everyone in town knew Jeb hadn't worked in a week.

"But you added all that fancy work." His friend lifted his eyes from the cradle, rising from his squat as he did.

Jeb's wife, Clarissa, joined them at the door. "Ed! Oh, it's beautiful."

Pride straightened his shoulders as he directed his words to his old friend. "I quoted you a price. I'm sticking to it."

"Ed, you don't have to do that."

"I stand by the price I quoted you. That's all."

"If you insist." Jeb patted Ed's shoulder, his gratitude shining on his face. "I know another family that would love to have so fine a piece. I'd be happy to send them your way."

Ed reached out to offer the man his hand. He wanted this. His work had value. But promising to care for Rebekah along with the list of chores waiting for him back home made it near impossible. "Many thanks. Things are busy at the ranch right now, but I'll let you know."

"Would you like to stay for coffee? Feel free to invite your friend." Clarissa nodded to the wagon, then squinted. "Is that Rebekah?"

"Rebekah Edwards?" Jeb released Ed from his handclasp to stare at the wagon, then back at him.

Ed's palms began to sweat as he threw a glance over his shoulder at the wagon. Did everyone in town know about their dislike for each other? Rebekah perched on the edge of her seat, surely listening. "I promised her uncle I'd take her home while he's away."

Jeb shared a side glance with Clarissa. "I thought the two of you didn't get along. Remember, she named everyone that sang at the last young people's social in that newspaper article. Everyone but you."

"It's fine." But it wasn't fine. And the sooner he got her home, the better. "Guess I need to get going. Chores are waiting."

Clarissa rubbed the dress that flowed over her protruding stomach as she arched her brows in a sympathetic sort of look. "Give Rebekah our best."

Ed nodded, shaking Jeb's hand again. Their continued praise for his work amongst themselves, even as he walked away, warmed a place inside him that he hadn't thought of for years. His work with the wood was all his own to give.

Not a chore or a piece of the McGraw homestead. A piece of himself.

He settled back on the seat with a terse nod to Rebekah before he clicked the reins.

"Beautiful cradle. You really made it?" Her voice held a note of incredulousness, and he bristled. Didn't she think he had the talent?

"I did."

"How are the Nelsons?" Rebekah smoothed her skirt.

"Clarissa sends her best," he said grudgingly.

The wagon jolted as they left the town behind and angled onto the road leading home.

"That was kind of you not to charge them for the extras."

He shouldn't be annoyed that she'd listened, but he felt hot under the collar. That was his business.

He caught the sideways glance Rebekah sent him as if she'd expected a response. "How do you ever find time to work on furniture?"

"I make time." Ed worked the reins, keeping his gaze on the road as an awkward silence filled the space between them.

Rebekah cleared her throat. "How did you get started?"

"Am I being interviewed for the paper?"

She let out a soft snort before turning up her little nose, all speckled with freckles.

Rebekah let it go, and he maintained the silence as they rolled along the trail.

If only he had a way to speed this trip along. Dealing with Rebekah and her questions left the skin under his shirt with a burning itch like he had a bad case of poison ivy, all blistered and festering.

She'd been a thorn in his side since she'd come to live with her aunt while in school. Tattling to his ma that he'd made all the other boys laugh at her. He'd gotten a fine lickin' over that one. Now she sat trying to scribble away on a piece of paper, shielding it from his view when the wagon swayed him toward her. As if he cared what Rebekah wrote, then or now. He let himself drift into his thoughts as they traveled the familiar path home.

At the last turn on the road home, his shoulders lost some of the tension he'd worn for too long that day. He directed the horses past the trees by the road into the well-worn path to the porch of the Boutwells' one-story house, only to have all the tension return the instant he spied Heath Quade sitting atop his steed.

The sight of Quade waiting sent all of Ed's plans for a fast exit packing. What did that dirty snake want? Ed would never leave Rebekah alone with Quade, especially not after his promise to Vess.

"You expectin' company?" Prickles inched up Ed's neck, and he kept his voice low as the wagon approached the house. He scanned the area for any of Quade's hired men. His foot shifted to rest against the rifle on the floorboard.

"No." Rebekah stuffed papers in her satchel but glanced up.

"Fine day, isn't it?" Quade called out, aiming his remark at Rebekah as he shot a look between them, his eyes narrowed.

"What are you doing here?" Ed pulled up on the reins.

Quade tipped his hat. "I was in the area and wanted to check on Rebekah."

"As you can see, I'm quite well." Rebekah put her hand on the buckboard as if to exit from the wagon, but if she did, Quade might beg an invitation inside. What excuse would Ed have to stay then? He eased off the brake just enough for the wagon's slight roll to halt her quick exit without being too obvious.

She wobbled and gripped the back of the seat, sending a searing glance at Ed.

"No need to worry about Rebekah. I'll be around helping with the chores." He settled a hard look on Quade. "Vess asked me to look after things."

Rebekah huffed.

Quade kept his focus on her. "Vess never did give me a final answer about selling the place. Rather left things open-ended. You could sign the papers for him."

"My uncle will return soon."

The stiffening of her shoulders released a bit of protectiveness inside Ed.

"This can be a hard country for a little lady all alone at night." Quade shifted in his saddle, eyeing the fields behind the barn. "When the wolves howl."

Quade's veiled threat had Ed thinking about Kaitlyn's face, pale and frightened, when they'd found her tussling with her brother Michael, who'd had a gun. Michael had kidnapped her in the moments that Quade's cowhands had caused a scuffle—the perfect distraction.

Some instinct in Ed had his mouth moving before he'd thought the words through. "Rebekah isn't alone. She's got a whole pack of McGraws watching over her day and night."

Quade's eyes left Rebekah's face to glare at Ed. "That so?"

Ed heard Rebekah's intake of air, felt her bristle at his words. He put out a hand, hoping to keep her quiet.

"That's so," Ed said. He held Quade's stare for a moment that stretched long.

But the tension was broken when Quade reined his horse forward. He looked right at Rebekah, ignoring Ed completely. "Mind you be careful out here all on your own."

Rebekah opened her mouth as if to retort, but Quade spurred his horse and was gone before she could respond.

She turned on Ed with fire in her eyes. "Why did you do that?"

She was spitting mad, and her show of temper sparked his own. Couldn't she be grateful for once? "Why'd I stand up for you against a dangerous criminal?"

"He's not a dangerous criminal. He's a rancher."

If Kaitlyn hadn't asked the McGraws not to spread word of what Michael had done, Ed would have more than enough to tell of Heath Quade's entanglement in it all. The details perched on his lips, about to spill. But he couldn't. Not even to put Rebekah in her place.

She turned in a huff, gripped the side of the bench, and lowered herself to the ground. Ed jumped from his side of the wagon, hurrying to help her, but she spun around as she landed, nearly losing her footing. Her eyes flashed before she twisted back around to grab up the work she'd brought home. Her hands trembled. From finding Quade here? Or from her frustration with him? Maybe both.

"I can handle Mr. Quade without your help." With a sidestep, she dodged around him in her flurry to get to the house.

One of the horses whinnied, stomping its hoof with impatience.

Ed lifted her satchel from the back of the wagon. "I made a promise to your uncle, and I intend to keep it."

"You may have promised to help with the livestock and take me to and from town, but no one asked you to speak for me. Even with Mr. Heath Quade." Rebekah snatched her satchel from his hand. One fiery curl snapped from its pin to float down her back as she ascended the stairs to the porch.

"You know what he did to Drew."

She spun to face him.

"What does Drew say he did?" The blaze in her blue eyes took him back to the schoolroom. Everything he wasn't supposed to say stuck in his throat.

"Don't you have the good sense to let me help you deal with Quade?" He flung the words out there, half expecting another retort.

Rebekah's face went red, then drained of color. She stomped across the porch to let herself in. The door slammed behind her.

Ed worked his jaw as he averted his gaze from the closed door. He was here. Why not let off steam by tending to the confounded animals? Not to mention checking to be sure Quade hadn't left a man here. Or conveniently unlatched a gate. He stopped to grab the rifle from the wagon.

Once in the barn, he hurried to complete the barest necessities while he poked around for any trace of Quade's meddling. Ed would be back to finish things in the morning. For now, he needed to toss in some feed, check all the latches and outbuildings for intruders, then get home.

Finished in the barn, he made one last circle of the outbuildings, then rounded the house. The front door creaked.

"What are you doing?"

Why did every word from her sound like a demand?

He spoke through gritted teeth. "Checking everything before I go."

"Go home." She cocked her head in an *I said so* attitude.

He cocked his head right back at her as he stepped up onto the porch. "I'll leave as soon as I finish making sure you're safe. I made a promise, remember?"

"Drew. My uncle. They think Quade's a danger, so you're out here peeking around every corner." She made a motion with her hands to encompass the ranch. "It's all about what they tell you to do." She took one step closer. "Do you even have an original thought in your head?"

Anger stirred inside him. Nose to nose with her, he tried to grasp for a witty reply, but nothing came. He turned. In three long strides, he reached the wagon. No original thought in his head? He climbed back on his wagon perch and flicked the reins. Only doing what others told him?

Almost to the drive for Drew's place, he had it. The perfect reply to little Miss Rebekah Edwards's words. He had half a mind to turn the wagon around so he could face her with them. But a nagging voice inside him wondered if she'd been right.

Three

W HAT WAS IT LIKE? DECIDING TO come west in answer to Drew's ad." Rebekah stirred the wooden spoon around the pot as the mixture of mashed up raspberries and sugar began to boil. She was working in Aunt Opal's kitchen alongside Kaitlyn the day after Ed had dropped her at home to find Heath Quade waiting.

A long night of wrestling with the placement of mail-order bride ads, one in particular, had left her full of questions this morning. Who better to ask than Kaitlyn? Living on neighboring farms had brought them together, and it hadn't taken long for them to become friends.

"I wasn't looking for a husband. I needed a way to escape my circumstances. But God knew better than I did." Kaitlyn's head tilted to the side, and her eyes became unfocused, like she was lost in a memory. She shook herself out of it. "You're getting a nice rolling boil. It won't be long now."

"But what about meeting Drew? Was it love at first

sight?" Rebekah's real question bounced off the back of her mind. How would Isaac react if she dared to answer his ad?

"I did like him. But there were rough edges to file down." Kaitlyn darted a glance at her stepdaughter Tillie, who was happily playing with a doll in the corner of the room. The other two children had begged to stay with Drew and his brothers as they worked on repairs to the corral, or so Kaitlyn had told Rebekah.

"It must have been a big adjustment to marry into the McGraw family." Rebekah continued to stir the bubbling mixture of fruit and sugar. Four bachelors and three ornery kids couldn't have been easy to manage. After all, once Drew's first wife had passed, there hadn't been a woman's influence near the place until Kaitlyn had come. And since all the brothers had kept busy working the land and trying to prove everything up, well, things had been hard for them.

A gentle laugh escaped her friend. "It was. At first."

"Once you were married though . . ." Rebekah felt her neck heat at the questions she wanted to ask about love and marriage.

As Kaitlyn's brows rose, Rebekah stuffed her questions away. She hadn't decided whether she'd even respond to Isaac's ad. They hadn't spoken in months. The fact he almost never came to town added to the mystery. She didn't even know where he fit in his own family anymore, much less the community, since he'd left his job with the marshals.

Her brain muddled. "What I mean is, married life has been wonderful, hasn't it? Everything worked out fine?"

"Wonderful, yes. Trying at times too. All roses have thorns."

Wonderful . . .

A love like Drew and Kaitlyn's existed for her. Had to. As a young girl back east, before her father had died, she'd sit on a chair next to his desk while he read his dime novels aloud to her as he wrote them. The heroic cowboy had always won his lady's hand. Always. How Rebekah had longed for a romance like the ones she'd found between the pages of his novels. A valiant hero who couldn't live without her.

From her first sight of Isaac McGraw when she'd moved to Wyoming at eleven, he'd filled that role in her daydreams. But it seemed as if Isaac wasn't going to come courting her—or any other lady in Calvin, for that matter. Not if he planned to get a mail-order bride. How could she catch his attention before he did if he never left the McGraw homestead?

"Ed mentioned Quade was here when he dropped you off yesterday. Are you all right?"

"Why wouldn't I be?"

Kaitlyn's face tightened in concern. "He's a dangerous man—"

"Nothing to worry about, I'm sure." Her words sounded more sure than she was. She'd heard all the same rumors as everyone else in these parts.

"Can I help?" Tillie had left her doll behind to wander over to the stove. She pulled at Kaitlyn's apron.

"Of course. Hold the papers for us until it's time," Kaitlyn said.

Rebekah drummed her fingers as she stirred. Her friend's concern made it harder to brush off Quade's visit. Or Ed's concern. But she didn't want to think about Quade or Ed right now. She wanted answers about Isaac. And having Tillie interrupt only distracted Kaitlyn.

Kaitlyn turned to explain to Tillie what she needed to do.

"Let's test the jam." Kaitlyn stepped closer with Tillie at her heels.

Rebekah spooned a bit of the jam above the pot and tilted the spoon. The jam trailed in a thick stream. "I think it's ready."

Rebekah reached for the ladle, filled it with jam, then placed it inside the jar that Kaitlyn set beside the large pot. Tillie shifted back and forth on her feet, growing impatient. With careful motions, Rebekah scooped and filled.

The whole time she worked, the ads she'd brought home with her pushed to the front of her mind, especially one in particular. Did she dare to answer Isaac's ad? "You and Drew seem very happy."

"We are." Kaitlyn paused after placing another empty jar beside the pot. "Why haven't you married yet? Have you thought about it?"

Thought about it? She'd written a story about getting married to her hero at twelve. When asked to read it aloud to the class, all she'd gotten were heartless snickers and a heap of humiliation. Now the mail-order ad for the man who'd filled her thoughts for so long sat amongst the others on the table in the front room.

"I have considered it. Like any other girl." She let her

answer fade as she filled the last jar. "Tillie, hand us the papers. One by one."

"Like this." Kaitlyn bent to help Tillie separate the papers before focusing back on Rebekah. "If there's no one around here that suits you, you could always run an ad yourself."

"I suppose." Rebekah angled a glance at Kaitlyn in expectation. Did she know of Isaac's ad? "Or I could answer one."

Kaitlyn studied her for a moment, as if contemplating. "Now that I think about it, most mail-order brides move to be with their husbands. I know you'd never want to leave the paper."

But Rebekah knew exactly where she'd be if she wrote an answer to Isaac's ad. It wasn't like when she'd written to her aunt after her father had died. That letter had taken her from her home in the East to the wide-open spaces of Wyoming. A letter to Isaac might be the means to help her stay.

"This jam will set in no time." Rebekah wiped a damp cloth across the rim of the jar before reaching out to Tillie for a paper to seal it with. "Tillie?"

The little girl fumbled, dropping the paper to the ground, then bending to retrieve it.

Rebekah reached for the stack. "Here. Maybe it's better if you let me do it."

Tillie stuck out her lower lip in a pout. "But I want to help."

"There now, Tillie, hold this one for me." Kaitlyn offered a soft smile at Rebekah, then slid half the papers into her own hands, slowly doling them out to Tillie.

Finished placing the papers, Rebekah wrapped her hand in a dish towel before gripping the pot full of melted paraffin. She carefully poured it over the papers settled in the jars. The wax would harden to seal the jam.

"Together, we've done a fine job. Your aunt will be proud to find all these preserves when she returns." Kaitlyn beamed at Rebekah while giving Tillie a little side hug. "I'm pleased you're showing such an interest in domestic skills these days."

Rebekah nodded, slipping the heavy canning pot into the sudsy water they'd prepared earlier. The scalding water had cooled to a tepid temperature but was still warm enough to scour the pots. She'd helped Aunt Opal with canning before, but never with enthusiasm for anything other than tasting the sweet jam at the end. A glimpse of the ads all arranged on the front-room table reminded her why she wanted to improve her domestic skills. If Isaac wanted a wife who could cook, she'd not disappoint him.

"Can I help some more?"

From the corner of her eye, Rebekah spied Tillie reaching up for a towel to help dry.

"Take this damp rag to wipe the counters." Kaitlyn had settled into the role of mother for Drew's children without a fuss.

When Rebekah felt Kaitlyn's gaze shifted to her, she feigned being invested in scrubbing the canning pot to a shine.

"I imagine you're missing your aunt and uncle."

"Things are different with them gone. Their absence makes the night so quiet that all the noises are louder."

The old gate out by the barn had blown in the wind last night, keeping her awake. Being awake left her time to think about her options. Too much time.

Finished with the dishwashing, Rebekah helped Kaitlyn dry the pots and utensils as Tillie occupied herself pushing the washcloth over the counters.

Kaitlyn focused on the table full of ads in the other room as she dried a wooden spoon. "I think you might want to know—"

A sudden crash from behind, followed by Tillie's sharp cry, halted whatever Kaitlyn had been about to say. The swiping washrag must have caught a jar of the jelly and flung it off the countertop. It hadn't broken the glass, simply spattered jam across a startled Tillie and onto the floor. Large tears slipped down her cheeks as the girl froze in place.

"There, there. We'll have this cleaned in no time." Kaitlyn's gentle words soothed the crying Tillie as Rebekah helped clean the mess of jam from the floor. As Tillie's tears slowed, Kaitlyn caught Rebekah's gaze. "Let me help you with this mess."

At Kaitlyn's words, Tillie stifled her crying, moving tentatively with her stepmother. Rebekah continued her scrubbing, determined to get the jam off the floor without getting it on her clothes. She moved in a careful pattern. Kaitlyn kneeled close by, motioning for Tillie to follow her lead. After a few swipes of working in tandem, Tillie tried to wring out her "helper" rag, leaving more water on the floor than jam.

Where did Kaitlyn get her patience? "This way, Tillie."

Rebekah lowered her rag softly, then ran it in a circular motion.

Splat. Tillie's landed with a plop, then zigzagged as she worked. "This way?"

Rebekah bit back a retort as Kaitlyn moved in to guide Tillie only to have a splotch of jam fly her way. She swallowed hard. "I know you'll want to scrub those stains out of Tillie's dress sooner rather than later. Raspberries don't come out easily. And you two are tired. I'll finish up here."

"Are you sure?" Kaitlyn paused to study her, then reached over to gently gather up Tillie's rag with her own. A blessed yawn from Tillie only proved Rebekah's point.

"I am."

Kaitlyn rose, Tillie close by her side, and added the rags they'd been using to Rebekah's stack by the washbasin. "I've enjoyed our time together this afternoon. We need to visit more often."

"So have I." She wrapped her friend in an embrace, then pulled away before Tillie could grasp her with a hand still smudged with jam.

As Kaitlyn looped her hand in Tillie's, tenderness filled her eyes. "You're welcome to join us for meals anytime. No need to stay here all alone."

What if Isaac were to show up? What would Rebekah say if he did? Things were muddled in her head. Besides, if she went, she'd have to stay a bit, even if Isaac didn't show up. Which wouldn't get her work done. Even worse, she might have to endure Ed's presence all evening.

"Thank you, but I have work to finish before my next trip to town." Rebekah reached for Tillie's other hand, careful of her sticky fingers, while walking with them onto the small porch. Another embrace, and Kaitlyn offered one last wave before they turned to hurry away.

The woman was a saint, so patient with the girl.

Back inside, Rebekah wrung out another rag for one last wipe over the floorboards. From many years' experience, she knew that if she wanted something done correctly, it was up to her to take care of it. Just like this floor.

When she was finished cleaning up, she snatched a biscuit left over from their lunch and spread fresh jam over it. Snack in hand, she made her way to the ads on the front-room table, each one a lonely person's plea for the one who would fulfill them. Her eyes lighted on Isaac's ad. He needed someone. Why not her?

Rebekah sank into a chair at the table, then pulled out pen and paper from her workbag. If she wanted a real chance at marrying Isaac McGraw, this was it. She'd already tried everything else. She'd worn her prettiest dress when she'd expected him at church, made a point of bumping into him on the boardwalk when he'd been between jobs with the marshals, had even agreed to go caroling once—to no avail. But she was a wordsmith. This she could do. She'd woo him with her letters. Pen gripped in her hand, she paused.

She took another bite of biscuit. What about the other women who'd write? Other letters would come to the box at the newspaper office, no doubt.

No matter. She'd decide what to do about that when another letter came across her desk.

She popped the last bite of the biscuit into her mouth,

then licked the jam from her fingers. She'd write her letter, then drop the reply in the box at the office as soon as enough time had passed for a nearby town's mail to have arrived.

If her plan worked, she'd be Mrs. McGraw before next spring.

It'd been over a week since Ed had made that promise to Vess Boutwell, and it wasn't getting any easier to keep. The wagon's wheels rumbled against the rough road as it swayed on his way back from another trip to Calvin to retrieve Rebekah from the newspaper office. The constant rolling and lurching left Ed bumping against his quieter-than-usual companion. Not that he was complaining. He had more than enough on his mind without Rebekah adding a constant stream of chatter as the miles stretched along.

Jeb Nelson had met him in town with another order for a cradle. Even if Jeb hadn't been insistent about Ed taking the job for his friend, Ed still would have agreed to the order. Nothing in him wanted to refuse a chance to create with wood beneath his hands. But whether he had time remained to be seen. He hadn't counted on a response to Isaac's ad so soon. He'd hoped to have a little more time before he had to take care of the whole mail-order bride thing. Maybe Drew would write the woman back, and Ed would be free of that chore. Or Drew might insist Ed do that too. Should he even bring the letter up to Drew? Should he let Jeb know he didn't really have time for the cradle?

Another jostle of the wagon bumped Ed's shoulder

against Rebekah. She all but jumped in her attempt to scoot away.

"You all right? You been jumpy as a cat the entire ride."

It wasn't like he wanted to be here either. He'd rather be in his workshop, but Drew had claimed to be too busy today to see to Rebekah's trip from town.

"I feel as if my insides have been wrung across a washboard." She reached out to grip the side of the wagon as it lilted again. "I've been rocking back and forth for hours without a word of conversation. What has you so silent?"

She blamed him? He ground his teeth. She'd been quiet too.

"Work." And he didn't want to talk about it. Drew had decided the barn and chicken coop needed deep cleaning now that the weather had warmed. Ed had been knee-deep in dirty hay all yesterday while Drew and David had painted the outside of the barn. Nothing in him wanted to make conversation, but he couldn't stand any more of her nerves. "Everything okay at the farm? Quade leaving you alone?"

"Not that again." Rebekah huffed, then reached down to gather up her workbag. She'd scooted as far to the edge of the seat as possible without falling off. "No need to pull into the drive. You can drop me here at the road."

What had he said? *Jumpy as a cat* might have been an understatement. Ed pulled up on the reins as she leaned over the bench to retrieve her satchel—which resulted in her almost falling headfirst into the back of the wagon.

She spun to face him, eyes flashing.

He shrugged, widening his eyes innocently. "You asked me to let you out here."

"I didn't say throw me onto the side of the road." Rebekah sounded as mad as a wet hen.

Ed had to bite down to keep from laughing. Served her right after the parting comment she'd thrown at him the other day. "I had to stop the horses. How was I to know you would turn around and lean over like that?"

No reply was hurled his way. Only a fiery glare as she eased down from the side of the wagon. Her hand flew to her head to right her hat, then she offered him a forced sort of smile. "You're still the same boy from the classroom. You haven't matured a bit since your thirteen-year-old self."

Even if his brain—so easily muddled by her—had a reply, it'd do him no good. She sped toward her home with one hand on her hat and the other clutching her luggage. Next time he took her to town, maybe he'd take one of the children along. That would give them both someone more pleasant to talk to.

Ed clucked at the horses. Never mind Rebekah. He had more important things to think about. Like whether to finally talk to Drew about his proposed furniture business. Or at the least, ask him for more time away from the never-ending list of McGraw chores, starting with Isaac's ad. The letter demanding an answer all but burned a hole in Ed's pocket as he rounded the drive in front of Drew's place.

A faint hue of orange still clung to the darkening western sky as Ed unhitched the horses from the wagon.

"Good. You're back." From the terseness in Drew's tone,

there'd likely be a request for one task or another. What would Drew do if Ed dared to say no?

"Never reckoned how much time running Rebekah back and forth would take when I promised Vess. I don't suppose David could take her into town?" Ed hung the last of the tack on the wall after leading the horses to their stalls. He shot Drew a glance over his shoulder, gauging his reaction. It was a long shot, but he'd take it.

"He's a bit too young for that responsibility. Besides, you were the one that promised." Drew eyed him as he gathered up tools and placed them in the back of the wagon Ed had parked in the barn. "I noticed a stretch of fence between us and the Boutwell's is wobbling. Damage may even go farther along their property line. We'd best go repair it in the morning."

Ed stared as Drew continued loading the supplies for the fencing project as if the case was closed. They already had a portion of fence to fix elsewhere. He lifted his arm to run his fingers through his hair. The paper in his pocket crinkled. Might as well out with it.

"Got a response to Isaac's ad." Ed stepped closer to help hoist a roll of barbed wire into the wagon.

"You read it?" Drew stepped back to wipe his forehead with a kerchief.

"Skimmed it. It sounded nice." The flowery words might be too nice for Isaac, but who knew what his brother really wanted? Ed picked the letter out of his pocket. "Want to see it?"

"Nope. Answer it. We need him back." Turning on his heels, Drew moved to the other end of the barn and began rummaging through the tools. "Kaitlyn left a plate on the table for you some time ago. Better go eat it. We need to get an early start in the morning if we plan to replace that section of rotten fence."

Ed slipped the letter back in his pocket as he trudged to the house. If Drew wanted this done, Ed didn't have much choice. But his brother had a point. Maybe it'd bring Isaac around.

Once inside the house, the soft sounds of Kaitlyn reading upstairs told him the children were getting their nightly story. Rather than risk disturbing them, he wrapped the plate of food in a kitchen towel and slipped back out into the night air. A chorus of crickets greeted him.

"You leaving?" Drew approached from the direction of the barn.

"Didn't want to wreak havoc on Kaitlyn getting the children to bed."

Drew nodded. "See you bright and early."

Always bright and early. Ed trudged the well-worn path to his small cabin, chafing under the constant demands. Drew loved this land, and the never-ending chore list didn't seem to bother him at all. Not that Ed didn't love the land too, the legacy it represented. He just wanted . . . more.

He swung open the cabin door. The moonlight offered enough illumination for him to set down his plate and light a lamp. Once seated, he slipped the letter from his pocket. His fingers worked to pull the letter out, then he shook it open. He couldn't help glancing at it, sitting next to his plate, as he ate the cold supper.

If his answer succeeded in getting another reply, he could

pass the rest of this off to Isaac to finish wooing her. A marriage meant having Isaac back near the family. Back here to help. A glimmer of hope sparked. If things went according to plan, Isaac's mail-order bride should arrive before winter set in.

Four

THE BELL ABOVE THE OFFICE DOOR chimed.

"Give me one minute, Billy." Rebekah didn't look up as she worked the twine to tie a bundle of newspapers together. She hadn't counted on having to prep the papers for distribution by herself before the delivery boy, Billy, arrived. But Mr. Sullivan's rush to see his daughter, who'd been ill, had seen him racing off to catch the one o'clock train. "I just have to tie off this last stack."

A man cleared his throat, causing her to jump. Definitely not Billy. The twine fell from her fingers, leaving the papers to slide into a heap on the floor.

"Sorry to startle you." Mr. Jameson's figure blocked one whole section of the front window. The local rancher wore a big Stetson that reached nearly to the ceiling. "I have an envelope for Mr. Sullivan. Is he here?"

The man scanned the front office. Rebekah stepped from

behind her desk, dodging the misshapen stack of fallen papers. Her green sprigged calico skirt rustled as she moved.

"He has gone out of town for a few days. I'll be happy to deliver it to him when he returns." She held out a hand, tilting her head as she smiled.

Mr. Jameson eyed her. Didn't he trust her? Rebekah had babysat the man's daughters when they were little, after all. "Be sure it's kept in a safe place."

"And what is so mysteriously important?" Rebekah teased. She clasped the envelope with both hands as the man handed it over.

"List of candidates for president of the Cattlemen's Association." He tipped his hat and winked. "Don't want them getting out before next week."

"Don't you worry. This newspaper has a spotless reputation." At least, it would keep that spotless reputation as long as she got the rest of the papers ready on time.

Mr. Jameson turned to go, the bell jangling as the door closed behind him a few seconds later.

Rebekah studied the envelope in her hand. This week, when she'd taken care of the matrimonial ads, they'd all fit into the paper without a problem. Not a good sign. Not if they wanted more papers to sell. If only they'd been able to print this list of the candidates for president of the Cattlemen's Association this week. Even with the list, if Mr. Sullivan didn't get back soon, they might not have time to work anything up to print next week.

Rebekah gripped the envelope in her hands as she stepped toward her desk, then stuffed it in a pocket of her skirt before picking up the fallen papers. This could be her big break. She flopped the last of the folded papers on the stack, then ran the twine beneath the lot of them and pulled the cord up to tie it. If she reported on the men running in the election, things might pick up around here. What if this was her chance to make a difference with her reporting?

With both hands, she hoisted the stack of newspapers onto the front counter for when the delivery boy came by. Then she patted the pocket where she'd stuffed the list of people running in the election. One little peek at the list would give her enough information to get a story or two. A story that would sell more papers . . .

Her conscience pinged. Mr. Jameson had insisted it go to Mr. Sullivan.

She turned and made her way to Mr. Sullivan's desk, her steps echoing off the floorboards, then took the envelope from her pocket. The folded paper pulled at her with a magnetic sort of draw. What good did it do for her to sit around working up more matrimonial ads when the story of the year rested inside that envelope? Did she dare?

Her hand trembled slightly as she fingered the seal.

On the other side of the window, a wagon kicked up dust as it careened past the newspaper office, nearly hitting the hitching post out front. Shouts rose amidst the dust. Rebekah left the envelope unopened on Mr. Sullivan's desk in her rush to the window. Voices—worried voices—came from the direction of the doctor's office, where a crowd was already gathering. Rebekah pushed against the front door, her heart pounding against her ribs. The jangling bell rang in her ears as she sped down the rough boardwalk toward what must be the makings of a story.

She excused herself as she hurried past a group of women near one of the shops.

"Rebekah?" Merritt, a good friend and cousin to the McGraws, called out to her hesitantly. "Where are you going?"

In her rush, Rebekah waved her off. She needed to get this story. She'd have time enough later to catch up with Merritt.

"Get the marshal," a man from the group hollered at a bystander.

Marshal Danna O'Grady was already crossing the street at a jog. The men carrying the wounded man shifted to let the marshal get close. Rebekah shouldered her way amongst the sweaty cowhands. Her nose wrinkled at the smell.

Who lay on that makeshift stretcher? Someone mentioned "the boss." The boss of the ranch? Which ranch did they belong to? If only she could identify the man, she'd have a place to start investigating.

The marshal motioned for everyone to step back, then leaned in over the wounded man.

From here, Rebekah could only hear the cadence of their voices. She held her bent arms in front of her, pushing against the men crowding in only to take a sharp elbow in her side. She lost her breath. Kept going. It didn't matter how she shifted, she failed to make out more than a few words.

An attack along the side of the road. A bandit with . . .

"Bring him in. Quickly." The doctor held open the door

to his office as the men hoisted the injured man inside. The marshal leaned close to whisper to the doctor, who nodded his head with a grim set to his jaw. "I'll let you know."

"Marshal." The crowd began to break up around Rebekah, smothering her voice and carrying her backward as she struggled to gain her footing. "Excuse me. Press here."

A few of the rough cowboys eyed her with disinterest, but their hesitation gave her enough of a break to squeeze closer once again. She was almost in line with the marshal when another cowhand stepped in her way.

"Marshal." Sweat from pushing against the now dissipating crowd left sprigs of Rebekah's hair clinging to her forehead and neck.

Danna barely glanced up. "I need the ranch hands to come to my office." Marshal O'Grady motioned for the men to follow her.

Rebekah increased her pace, ignoring the side glances of the ranch hands she'd fallen in with as she pushed forward to walk in step with Marshal O'Grady. "For the record, who was that? Does the doctor expect a recovery?"

Marshal O'Grady didn't slow. "I'm in the middle of an investigation."

Her sharp words only took Rebekah aback for a moment.

"But where did it happen? Someone in the crowd mentioned a bandit?"

Marshal O'Grady stopped outside her office. She motioned for the ranch hands to continue inside, then turned to face Rebekah. Her eyes were sunken. Likely, the recent trouble in the area had been keeping her busier than usual.

"I'll pass along pertinent information to the newspaper when I have it."

"But—"

The marshal's frown brooked no further argument. As she stepped into her office, Rebekah reached for the door to follow, but the marshal pulled it closed.

Rebekah did a slow pivot to face the direction of the doctor's office. A man loitering nearby, no doubt hoping to have a story of his own to tell, eyed her with disdain before ambling away. She balled her fists at her side. Getting a story was hard enough. Proving herself as a young woman with the ability to write and tell a good story was even harder.

But she'd do it.

Mr. Sullivan may have told her to leave the candidates to him, but he hadn't specified anything about other news impacting the town. She pushed back the way she'd come. The dirt from the rumbling wagon and clomping boots had settled to leave a film across the boardwalk. The taste of grit filled Rebekah's mouth as she sauntered back to the newspaper office, listening for any other viable clues as she did. All she needed was a hint of something to go on.

She pulled on the door to the newspaper office. Maybe if she sketched the brand from the horses, she could find the name of the ranch. In quick steps, she swerved around the stacks of clutter in the office to her desk. As her fingers fell to her pencil, Rebekah nearly knocked a stack of freshly delivered mail from her desk. It must've come while she'd been gone for those few minutes. There, on the top envelope, were her initials. Just as she'd signed them on her letter to Isaac. She froze.

He'd written back.

She clutched the envelope to her chest. Everything around her blurred as she sank into her chair. She worked to steady herself, taking in long breaths and slowly exhaling. Her fingers refused to stop trembling as she slid open the envelope and pulled the letter from inside. Her eyes drank in the words as her fingers flew to her lips.

> *The cheerfulness of your letter put me in mind of a ray of sunshine. Something every man needs in their life. Especially when the winters are long . . .*
>
> *. . . I'm very interested in hearing more about you . . .*

Tough Marshal Isaac McGraw had written this. To her. It was everything she'd always dreamed of.

Even if he didn't know it was her, exactly. He'd written this letter, and she was reading it. If only she had someone to share the wonderful news with. No day had been better in all her history of days.

Only after she'd secured the letter in her satchel did she return to sort through the other envelopes. Three other letters for Box 256. For Isaac.

Rebekah placed all the other correspondence in the appropriate boxes except for those.

What should she do?

Tapping them against her desk, she worked her lip as

she stared at the feminine writing. A faint scent of rose oil wafted from one. These were other women's answers to Isaac's ad. It was her responsibility to place them in his box. Mr. Sullivan had left the mail-order ads and correspondence in Rebekah's hands.

It was the right thing to do.

But still, she hesitated.

Ed would arrive soon. He always checked for mail coming to the McGraws. Her hand trembled as she began to slide the letters into the box.

A wagon rattled past the window, then slowed.

Ed.

She jerked the letters back. Next time. She could put the letters in the box next time she was in town. A little delay wasn't a deception. Her hurried steps retreated toward her desk.

He'd step inside the office any minute.

Her shin clanked against the bottom drawer of her desk, still open from earlier. She bent to drop the letters in the drawer with shaking hands, shooting a glance out the window as she stood back up. With her foot, she slammed the bottom drawer shut.

She had to hurry.

She didn't want a chance to think. Didn't want to give the guilt clogging her chest time to settle. If she locked up and met Ed outside, he wouldn't have time to retrieve mail anyway. She lifted her skirt as she hurried up the stairs, then gathered her things and came back down, breathing quickly, to settle them at the front door. Then she grabbed up the satchel she'd left beneath her desk. One jerk on the door had the bell ringing as loud as her jangling nerves. She flipped the lock, pulling the door shut behind her. Her heart pounded in her ears as she scanned the boardwalk.

Ed was tying off the wagon just down the street from the newspaper office.

She'd made it.

Ed lifted the hoof of the sorrel mare. She'd favored this leg after he'd turned onto the main street.

There was the problem. A pebble had lodged in her hoof.

"Don't worry. I know it's uncomfortable, ol' girl—I'll get it out of there." Ed worked to soothe the mare. No doubt the pebble in her hoof irritated as much as, well, having Rebekah sitting next to him on the box seat and wanting to battle with words all the way home.

He pulled out his pocketknife to scrape the loose debris from the hoof. As soon as he picked up Rebekah, he'd be ready to turn around for the trip home. If he were lucky, he might get to his cabin while he still had enough daylight to work on the other cradle.

He straightened after sorting out the horse's hoof.

"Ed. Over here."

He spun to find Jeb Nelson waving him over to the new shop next door to the newspaper. Ed glanced back at the newspaper office window before tying off the wagon. He could see Rebekah gathering up her things. She could wait another minute or two. Last time he'd had to wait on her.

He strode down the boardwalk to the shop next door, where Jeb extended a hand.

"Good to see you again. This is Mrs. Caroline Wilson." Jeb shifted his gaze to the woman beside him. "This is Ed McGraw. He's the one I told you about. He built the cradle."

Mrs. Wilson fixed a kind smile on Ed. She had to be about his age. "I've heard wonderful things about your carpentry skills. And when I visited Clarissa, I saw the cradle. Your craftsmanship really impressed me."

"Thank you." Ed shifted under the praise, even as it bolstered a hidden part of himself. If only his brothers could hear her, maybe then they'd understand that his carpentry was viable.

"I'm opening up a new bakery here." The woman turned to usher them into the storefront. "The plan is to open in another month, but I'm going to need some display cases. The cost to ship them in is a bit much. Besides, I'm wanting quality. I was hoping you'd be willing to make one for me. We could do it on a contract basis. If I like it, I'll need two more."

She wanted quality. He could give her that. Display cases in a prominent shop in town meant a validation of his business. But it also meant a huge time commitment. Ed raised his hat to comb his hand through his hair. The long list of chores at home ran through his brain. "How soon would you be wanting it?"

"Can you get me the first one in two weeks? Or less?" Mrs. Wilson walked around the open area of the empty shop. "If things go well with the bakery, I'm wanting to fill this space with tables and chairs for folks to eat at. One display case may turn into a good-sized order. What do you say?"

Jeb grinned from behind Mrs. Wilson. All Ed's dreams of breaking into furniture building full-time were staring him in the face. He pushed back his mental to-do list for the homestead.

If he sealed the deal with this display case, he'd have all the orders he needed to convince Drew this was viable.

"It's a deal." Ed held out his hand to shake on it. "Let me take a few measurements."

Once he finished hashing out the specifics, Ed tucked the notes he'd made into his pocket. He said his goodbyes, then headed back down the boardwalk. Only then did he remember Rebekah.

She sat atop the wagon with her hands folded in her lap. He was sure to hear about how long he'd taken.

He hurried his steps. As he neared the wagon, he shot a glance up at her. Rebekah was smiling to herself with a notebook on her lap, her focus trained on something in the distance, as if thinking. Not a word about how late he was. He shrugged it off as he moved to untie the horses from the hitching post.

Reins in hand, he hoisted himself onto the wagon seat. "You ready?"

"Mmmm." Rebekah now held a notebook in her hand, scribbling away without paying him a whit of attention. Hardly the confrontation he'd expected. Was today his lucky day?

The tossing of the wagon along the street jostled him closer to her, sending a tingle along his arm. He shifted to put distance between them as she swiveled the writing away from him. What was she writing that was so confounded secret?

Ed looked back to the street in time to dodge a wagon in front of the doctor's office. He craned his neck. There'd been a group of cowhands milling around there when he'd pulled into town. As he shifted his focus back to the road, Rebekah twisted to peek back at the same wagon. Then she turned to settle herself, scribbling more notes.

"You seem awful interested in that wagon." Ed hitched his thumb back toward the doctor's as they rode past the edge of town.

"Mm-hmm." She kept writing.

"What happened?" Much as he hated to admit it, her indifference gnawed at him.

"A bunch of cowboys brought a man to the doctor." Her blue eyes flashed at him now. "Marshal O'Grady was there."

"Figure you got yourself a real story, eh?" It all made sense now.

"Did you recognize any of the men we just drove by, the ones in front of the doctor's office?"

Was it him, or had she just lit up like a kerosene lamp as she'd asked the question? "I recognized a wagon with horses from the Billings ranch. Saw some ranch hands milling around. If a man got hurt, I'm not sure that's newsworthy." Ed rubbed his shirt sleeve across his forehead. The June sun beat mercilessly today.

"What would you know about whether it's newsworthy?" After a huff, she went back to scribbling. Just like in school.

Even way back then, she'd sat at her desk writing, oblivious to everything going on around her. One day she'd been scribbling away, curls falling across her desk as she'd tried to hide her paper. His mouth grew a bit dry from the remembrance. If only that schoolroom story hadn't started all the trouble between them.

After a long while, Rebekah looked up from her scribbling. The wagon seat rattled as she shifted to face him.

"If you must know, the rancher was attacked along the road, according to the crowd. By a bandit. Maybe even the same one who burned down the cabin or robbed the stagecoach. And that *is* a story people want to read." She jabbed the pencil in his direction before returning to her notepad.

"Sullivan letting you report on it?" So that's what all the smug grins were about. As if Rebekah needed to get involved with outing criminals. "Why isn't he covering it?"

Rebekah shifted herself to sit up a little taller, tilting her chin. "Because it's my job."

"I thought your job was handling matrimonial ads and such." He could imagine her poking her nose where it didn't belong. Rebekah wasn't the kind of person who gave up. Their schoolroom grudge was testament enough to that.

"What do you know about my job?" Her tone grew indignant.

"What kind of injuries?" he pressed.

"I couldn't see," she said, still sounding miffed. "They carried him into the doc's office."

"If this bandit caused injuries enough that the rancher needed a doctor, you'd better let Mr. Sullivan handle it." Maybe he could get her to see how dangerous this might be.

"You, Ed McGraw, are not my keeper." Her blue eyes flashed at him before she tilted that chin of hers again.

"I may not be your keeper, but I made a promise to your uncle." Even now, the words tasted like ash in his mouth.

"We both know you didn't want to."

He pulled the reins up short as they rounded the road. For once, he had the perfect reply, but the words were lost as he stopped in front of the ambling cattle in the road. "You leave the gate open?"

"Of course I didn't leave the gate open." Her words were laced with scorn. "Maybe the fence was knocked down."

Ed scooted as if to light from the wagon when he spotted the break in the fence, near the road. From where he sat, the fence appeared to be leaning over, almost as if the fenceposts had been pushed over on each side. Maybe a cow could have done it, but . . .

"Drew and I went over this fence last week. We checked every inch of it." Ed leaned forward. He lowered his hand to reach for his rifle, even as he scanned the area for any sign of another rider.

"What are you looking at?" Rebekah leaned into his line of sight with her brows all pinched together.

He scanned the fields. They were empty except for the cattle.

"Any sign of a troublemaker." There was nothing obvious. He lowered the rifle, focusing back on Rebekah. "Seems I remember a certain person's comments on a woman being alone out here."

A shadow of contemplation skittered across her features, then left.

"Don't be ridiculous." She scooted to lower herself off the wagon seat. "It's cattle. They get out of fences, you put them back in."

Little good it would do to argue with the likes of Rebekah. He jumped from the wagon and rounded it to face her. "We need to circle around to the sides of the cattle and drive them back in. You go right. I'll go left."

Rebekah tilted her head, one curl draping over her shoulder as she did. "It's muddier there. I'll go left."

The woman would argue with a stump.

She gathered up her skirt and marched off to the left. Ed tightened his jaw. Best to get this done and get her delivered home. But as they pushed to get the cattle back in the fence, the animals weren't having it. No matter how hard he and Rebekah worked, one ornery heifer refused to cooperate.

"Let's get the others corralled in here, then I'll go after that heifer." Ed waved his hands above his head, chasing the cattle they'd rounded up farther into the fenced-off field.

Once he had them settled away from the opening, he spun to tell Rebekah to watch the break in the fence while he rounded up the last cow, but she was nowhere to be found. He'd nearly made it back to the road without sight of Rebekah when he spotted the heifer coming from behind the wagon. The cow was heading straight for him.

He stepped out of the way as the cow lumbered past him into the field. Rebekah came from the side, grinning with triumph despite the mud she'd been fussing about splattered across her dress. She herded the cow through the break in the fence, acting as if she had single-handedly saved the day.

"I thought I told you to stand back by the fence." He didn't want to admit how much her hard work impressed him. She could be the most stubborn and infuriating woman.

Ed leaned over to secure the fence, looping the loose wire in place until he could get the tools he'd need to make a more permanent fix. Rebekah leaned close against the post where she'd been helping him with the wire.

A loose tendril of hair clung to the mud splashed across her face. Her fair skin glowed from the exertion of having chased the cattle. Stubborn, infuriating . . . and beautiful. He swallowed hard. What if things had been different back in school? What if he hadn't laughed at her story and riled up the class to do the same?

"Are you going to stand here all day?" Rebekah pushed off the fence to start for the wagon. "I'd like to get home before dark."

Her words snapped Ed out of his thoughts. He tried not to show how shaken he was as he climbed atop the wagon, where Rebekah had already situated herself. Once in the seat, he drove the last bit to the Boutwell farm. He kept his focus forward. Blessedly, Rebekah didn't speak for the small distance until she alighted from the wagon in front of the farmhouse.

"Good evening." Her voice trailed off as she hurried up the steps, leaving muddy footprints behind.

Ed turned the wagon toward home. He didn't need any more errant thoughts jumbling his brain. He sent one last look over his shoulder to see her let herself safely into the house. He was tired and hungry. That was all.

$\mathcal{F}ive$

YOU RIDING OUT TO CHECK YOUR uncle's herd?"

Rebekah whirled with her hand to her chest, sucking in air. Her uncle's horse, Mabel, tossed her head. Brushing her hand along Mabel's forelocks helped still the clanging of her own pulse. No one was supposed to be here this early. But there sat Ed atop his horse, leaning against his saddle horn with one arm as he pushed his hat back with his other. She'd thought he'd be tied up at his place after picking her up in town yesterday.

He knew good and well she wasn't going out to check the herd. She shot him her best glare.

Rebekah stepped toward the corral fence, not wanting to answer him. Grasping the colorful saddle blanket as she turned back to the horse gave her a reason to keep her focus on Mabel. She spread the blanket, smoothing it over Mabel's back before turning to answer him. Nothing in her wanted to give him the truth, although she half suspected he knew. Why else would he be here this morning before he'd even had enough time to do the McGraw chores?

"I'm riding to the doctor's office to interview the injured rancher. Then I'm going to stop by the marshal's office for a statement." Rebekah caught sight of Ed's scowl as she moved to where the saddle sat atop the corral fence.

"You really think that's a wise idea?" When she didn't reply, his eyes scanned the field and then the property only to land on the woodpile next to the barn where she'd left the axe stuck in a chunk of wood. She'd been working out her frustrations on the wood.

His eyebrow quirked.

Rebekah heaved the saddle, but the cinch toppled off from where she'd temporarily placed it on the saddle horn, so she set it down to reposition it. "I have an obligation to the citizens of Calvin and the surrounding areas to print the stories of interest. Others could be in danger." She heaved again, this time landing the saddle on the horse without incident. "And to cover the stories properly, I need all the facts."

Her fingers worked to fasten the cinch, even as she darted her best *I dare you to stop me* stare at Ed. He dismounted, moving slowly in her direction as if he intended to do just that.

"You're latching that wrong." Ed pointed a finger at her saddle.

Rebekah jutted her chin. "Ed McGraw, I think I know how to put on a—"

But he was right. Heat flared at her neck as she hurried

her trembling fingers to correct her mistake. He'd not get a thank-you out of her for his meddling. He wasn't even supposed to be here. She managed a peek at Ed, who twisted his lips up like he wasn't even expecting her thanks. Yanking the cinch up tight, she finished fastening it, then straightened her shoulders.

"Why don't you go away? Go home." She waved a hand toward the road. "You're always complaining about too many chores to do."

She reached to unhook the stirrup from the saddle horn, letting it hang. But before she had the chance to hoist herself into the saddle, Ed stood at the front of Mabel, holding the bridle.

He let out a long sigh. "I'm going with you."

"No, you are not." Rebekah slid her foot into the stirrup, then swung into the saddle.

"Yes, I am." Ed flew toward his horse, mounting it in one leap like a well-trained horseman in pursuit of a dangerous criminal in one of those dime novels she loved.

But she was no dangerous criminal in need of pursuit. Rebekah swung her mount in the opposite direction only to be blocked by Ed's quick moves on Lightning. His boot nudged past hers as he moved as one with his horse. She used to think his horse's name ridiculous. Apparently, she'd never been around when Ed used it for cutting cattle. But she refused to be treated like cattle either.

She made another quick move on Mabel only to hear the shuffling of horse hooves and the breathing of their mounts. Lightning blocked Mabel's path to the road on the side, leaving Ed sitting so close atop his horse that the shadow of his broad shoulders fell across her.

"I don't need a nanny. I'm not a child."

"You're acting like one." His knee nudged into hers.

In her frustration, Rebekah let loose a deep, guttural growl.

Ed broke into a grin. Infuriating man.

Then he grew serious again. "I don't want to be the one to tell your uncle you got yourself killed chasing after a story."

"I'm not going to get myself killed." She'd not tell him there'd been a muddy footprint yesterday a little way down from the break in the fence line. Or that she hadn't slept for worrying about what it meant. "Fine."

"Fine, what?"

"Fine, you can come with me."

"Thought you'd never ask." He reined his horse around to follow her.

It fell into an easy trot behind hers.

"If you follow me around, I'll look like I'm not capable of doing my job." How dare he make her appear fragile and helpless? No one would take her seriously as a reporter if she were hiding behind Ed McGraw. She turned back to let loose the most intense stare-down she was capable of. "I'll never forget this, Ed McGraw."

"Just add it to the grudge you've held against me for the last fifteen years. It's not like I expect your forgiveness now." Ed's mumblings wrapped around her as she turned her attention back to the road.

"It's not like you ever asked for it. Even after completely

humiliating me," Rebekah snapped. She urged her horse forward.

That moment as a twelve-year-old, when she'd stood in front of the class to read her story aloud, washed over her. She'd never imagined the teacher would ask her to read her story to the class that day.

Rebekah had pushed up from her desk, her hands slick as she'd clutched the papers with her story scrawled in her own hand. The one with the dashing young hero. She could only hope she'd wrapped him in enough embellishment that no one would recognize their classmate, Isaac Mc-Graw.

Her voice faltered as she read aloud, praying no one would notice the similarities. But Ed chuckled.

His body shook as a full-blown cackle escaped while Rebekah tried to read on. And then the whole class erupted into a rippling mass of laughter. Rebekah wanted to hide, to run from the room and never return.

"Ed McGraw." The teacher rapped the desk with her ruler to silence the class. "What do you find so amusing?"

"The words. Like the hero is so great." Ed's words had been barely audible for his choking laughter. "It's just Isaac. Everybody knows that."

Her horse blew, the sound jolting her out of the memory. School had never been the same after that. But what did Ed care? He'd never so much as breathed a hint of an apology. What right *would* he have to expect her forgiveness?

I'll never forget this, Ed McGraw.

Ed's stomach knotted. Was Rebekah really still that hurt about what had happened so long ago? She'd gone unusually quiet, but it hadn't stopped her from insisting they go see the doctor, the injured man, and the marshal. A whole day lost trying to keep her out of trouble.

Ed had to give it to her—she'd been determined in her interviews, never backing off. If only the clues they'd garnered were actually valuable. He'd been mulling them over the whole ride back.

"A man with a straw-colored hat." His saddle creaked as he shifted to avoid an overhanging branch. He thought better when he talked things out. Especially when he was dead tired after riding up to the little cabin last night to talk to Isaac about the letters only to find the cabin empty. Isaac must have been camping close to where he was riding herd on the cattle, especially with the threat of wolves.

Never mind Rebekah's annoyed glance in his direction. She should remember from when he used to work his sums in class. He'd always worked them out loud, even if he had to mumble to keep from getting in trouble with the teacher.

"Face covered by a bandanna." Ed hadn't heard the marshal mention anything particular about the bandanna. The horse's hooves clomped along the dirt road. Sure would be handy to have Isaac around right now. He had more experience with hunting down criminals. Not to mention how nice it'd be to pass the letter-writing business off to him. Maybe then Ed could focus on making his own dreams a reality.

Rebekah leaned farther to one side of Mabel, as if scanning the ground.

"Coulda been young or old." Ed slowed Lightning to keep in step with Rebekah. Yep, it'd be nice to have his marshal of a brother around right now, but when Isaac didn't want to be found, there was nothing to be done about it.

She leaned to the other side now, craning her neck all around, head down.

"Rode a brown horse." He pulled up on the reins as he grasped to work it out. There'd been nothing specific. No motive he could see. "The bandit could have been anyone. Seems like he just beat up the man for what cash he had on him. Does that even make sense? For so little?"

"Mmmm." Sunlight played with the curls around Rebekah's profile, almost creating a sort of halo as she appeared to scour the ground.

"You aren't really expecting to find any clues here, are you?" Ed nudged Lightning forward again. "The marshal said for you to stay out of it. I agree. Leave the investigating to law enforcement. It's their job."

"This is my job too. As a reporter." She lifted her gaze, and her lashes caught the sun like her hair did. For one vulnerable moment, he didn't want her in the middle of a criminal investigation for no other reason than he wanted to protect her. Without even a thought of the promise he'd made to Vess.

Her shoulders slumped. "There's nothing here."

"That's what I told you."

Half a glare met him, then she began to turn her horse in the direction of home. He only had to slacken the reins for Lightning to catch up to Mabel. He didn't want to admit how much fun he'd had rounding up her horse this morning.

"Why is this so important to you, anyway?"

"I told you. It's my job."

"What does this have to do with mail-order bride ads? You're hiding something, aren't you?"

She shot him another one of her glares. Another reason not to be distracted by the sunlight playing tricks with her hair. If he thought about it, she'd been acting squirrelly all day. When they'd stopped by the newspaper office, she'd shuffled through letters, fidgeting around the office. Only after he'd stepped outside to check on the horses had she finished up, rushing out with a skip in her step. At least she'd emerged with another letter addressed to Isaac.

Curious thing, only having one response, but maybe the mail-order ad business was slower these days than Rebekah let on. He'd have to write back when he got done following her all over town. After that, well, maybe he'd finally have a chance to start on that display case.

Rebekah side-eyed him. "Mr. Sullivan has the list of men running for president of the Cattlemen's Association."

It didn't answer why she'd been acting strange, but he'd take the bait. "And?"

"I saw it."

"Isn't it confidential or something?"

"Heath Quade is one of them. So is Mr. Billings, the injured rancher." Her nose tilted upward in that triumphant tilt of hers.

"Quade? How can he run? He caused that dustup. He

put Kaitlyn in danger." Lightning nickered at Ed's heated tone.

"Maybe not everyone remembers it like your family does."

"You want a story? Come interview Kaitlyn. Then you'll have the truth to print about that snake." His last words were even more heated as he turned Lightning toward the homestead.

"Fine. I will." Rebekah's wide eyes made it evident he'd gotten his point across. At least enough for her to let him lead for a change.

Ed tightened his jaw as he rounded the drive that led to the McGraw homestead. He hated making their business everyone else's, but he had an obligation to let people know what Quade was like. As far as Ed was concerned, the man should be in jail, not running for president of the Cattlemen's Association. And if he had to put off working on the display case for another day to prove it, so be it.

An eerie level of quiet met them as they entered the homestead. Lightning balked and let out a nicker as if to ask what was going on. There had to be a logical explanation, but the hairs on Ed's arm rose all the same. When he passed the well, a bucket sat on its side as if it had been dropped there.

"Where is everyone?" Rebekah's voice had a softer tone than usual. "Tillie usually runs outside to greet me."

At the sight of a slumped figure by the outhouse, Ed nudged Lightning forward. Rebekah kept pace on Mabel. A surge of adrenaline raced through him as he got closer, and he worked his jaw. Drew lay face down in the dirt. A groan rose from his motionless body as Ed quickly dismounted. In two strides, he was there, his knees hitting the dirt.

"Drew." He lifted his brother half into his arms, pulling him across his knees and rolling him over. Drew's face emerged clammy and pale. Another groan was his only reply, filling Ed with dread. Drew's eyes fluttered, but he appeared unconscious. The stench of vomit hit Ed square in the face. At movement close by, he shifted to see Rebekah waiting, fists clenched, not five feet away. He locked eyes with her. "Run to the house. Fetch Kaitlyn." He was worried. Why hadn't Kaitlyn noticed?

She blinked as if the words hadn't settled in her brain yet. Then she pivoted toward the house, dust rising and filtering over on the light breeze to cling to his sweat.

"C'mon, Drew, answer me." He tapped the side of Drew's cheek, desperate to get a response.

Rebekah knocked on the door of the main house, the sound filling the silent yard, but no one came. A clawing began in the pit of Ed's stomach as he watched her let herself inside.

"You okay?" Still nothing but a groan for an answer. Ed shifted on his knees until he could lift Drew's shoulders and inch his way down to loop his arms under his brother's. Then he half stood and began dragging his brother toward Lightning.

He had to get him inside. Had to get him help.

The door of the house swung wide to show Rebekah alone. Where was everyone?

His breath came in gasps as he struggled to move his brother. His mind couldn't grasp what had happened here.

Rebekah raced down the porch steps. Her face matched the white lace collar of her blouse. She didn't slow her approach until she skidded to a halt next to him, her shoulder bumping his as she leaned down to help him drag Drew. Ragged breaths escaped as she fought to catch her breath.

"Where's Kaitlyn?" Ed's throat grew ragged and dry from more than the heat.

Rebekah shook her head as she gasped for air. "Everyone is in bad shape. Real bad shape."

"Is anyone awake?" Ed shifted to a better position to lift Drew onto the horse's back, and Rebekah sidestepped to give him room. She nodded her head, opening her mouth to answer, when Drew's hand reached up to grasp Ed's arm, heat pulsing from his skin. But his hand quickly fell away again. Ed watched his brother's eyes flutter for a moment as if he were fighting to regain consciousness, then shifted his focus past Rebekah to the house. "Nick? The kids? They're sick too?"

"All of them. What do we do?"

Six

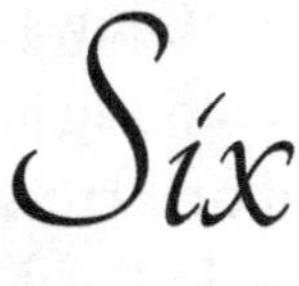

L ET'S GET YOU PROPPED UP IN YOUR chair." Ed shared a concerned glance with Rebekah, then they heaved together to lift Kaitlyn to a more comfortable position in her padded chair.

When they'd brought Drew inside, the full force of the illness had overwhelmed Ed. Everywhere, his family lay moaning, barely moving at all. He hadn't even known where to begin until Rebekah had started into nurse mode. She'd settled the men in David's room, placing pallets on the floor where necessary to create a makeshift sick room. Ed followed her lead, still reeling from the shock.

"Can you tell me what you made everyone for lunch?" Rebekah kneeled in front of the ashen Kaitlyn, running a cool cloth over her forehead as she worked to discover the source of the illness that had everyone down.

The shake of Kaitlyn's head was barely perceptible. "Jo…in…the barn."

Jo? He'd assumed she was in the back bedroom, where Rebekah had carried Tillie to rest, or maybe in the outhouse. Why had she been in the barn?

Rebekah rustled to her feet, then out the front door before Ed could force his muscles to move. She was as tenacious in caring for the McGraws as she'd been in getting a story. He swiped the cold rag across Kaitlyn's forehead once more, then rested it on her neck before moving to the other room to check on Tillie, who'd cried out for help. This was more than one man could handle alone. And why was everyone this ill? Why wasn't he? Had to be something that had happened since last night when he'd ridden out to find Isaac. He'd returned this morning and stopped at the main house only long enough to try to talk Nick or Drew into spending the day watching after Rebekah, but they'd both begged off.

A rattle at the door, then it clanged open. Rebekah entered with Jo leaning heavily against her. Ed left Tillie, calm for the moment, to help get Jo settled.

"She went to the barn to try to ride out for help." Rebekah panted out the words. "When she got there, the horses were sick too."

Ed stilled. "The horses? It has to be—"

"The well."

They pumped water into the trough from the well, used buckets to carry drinking water inside.

Rebekah grabbed his arm as he turned to head out to the corral. "I already covered the trough and opened the gate to the pasture where the creek is."

"Right. They'll go there to get water." He ran a hand

through his hair, then paced to the door. At least they had an answer. But how?

Rebekah finished settling Jo, then moved to where he stood at the open door. "Want me to unsaddle Lightning and Mabel? Put them in the pasture too?"

Right now, this moment, was the first time he'd been thankful for her.

Ed scanned the sick family members behind them. How had this happened? "I'll do it. I need to go see if I can figure out what happened to the well. You going to be all right in here if I do?"

Her head bobbed, a crinkle across her brow. "You think we're doing the right things? I've never seen a sickness like this before."

"We're doing good. You are, at least." He'd never seen her vulnerable like this. "It'll be all right. Everyone will pull through."

They have to.

Ed held her gaze, then moved through the open door onto the porch. The sun filled the sky as if all was right in the world, but something very wrong had happened here.

He rushed through caring for the horses before moving to the well.

A quick check of the well revealed a dead animal floating at the bottom. Something big.

He stood, shaking. Someone had to have done this on purpose.

Ed always double-checked to be sure the well was covered. So did Drew.

Anyone with a lick of sense knew that a dead animal in

the well was akin to poisoning it. Who would do such a thing?

He had a guess. But his family needed him at this moment. There'd be time for answers and consequences later.

Ed winced at the tinge of pain in his stomach as he hauled a bucket in to the stove. At least being gone from the ranch had left him in better shape than the others. As he trudged across the living room floor, he spied Rebekah moving from Tillie to Kaitlyn.

He was still shaking with anger as he said, "It's the well all right. We'll have to boil the water from the creek until we can dig a new one."

Her eyes went wide and fearful.

He passed Rebekah on his way back out to the creek to bring up another bucketful. She was wiping down Kaitlyn's face and neck with a cool cloth, trying to get the fever down. The sight of everyone so weak knotted his stomach.

When he came back inside, he found Rebekah in front of the stove, fine hairs curling around her face from the heat. She'd already lit a fire. He reached over her to set the pot in place, then stepped back. "Guess we can use milk to quench their thirst for now. If they can keep it down."

"I'll help you get everyone a round of fresh cool cloths, then I'll ride over to fetch Aunt Opal's canning pot too. If it's the well, we're going to have to boil a lot of water. I'll want to wash up the bed sheets and their soiled clothes for them as soon as possible. Not to mention the water I'll need for cooking as they recover enough to begin eating."

Leave it to Rebekah. To think he'd always thought her bossy. But tonight, he was thankful for her smarts. The two of them worked in tandem, placing clean cloths on feverish foreheads. As soon as they finished, Rebekah hurried off to get the other pot. While she was gone, Ed spent his time hauling the children out to the privy in his arms or helping the adults make the walk out there.

Rebekah whisked in the front door, out of breath, and set a couple of large pots in the kitchen, then kneeled where Ed sat next to Kaitlyn. "I'll take over. You look tired."

He gulped down the unbidden tears of weariness and worry. "Thank you for staying to help."

She smiled tentatively, worry shining from her eyes. Ed wanted to rest for one moment in their shared concern, but David let out a moan.

Ed ran David out to the privy again. He had half a mind to fork out a mound of hay for everyone to lie on out there so they wouldn't have to go so far, but the day had grown too hot. When he came back inside, Rebekah had stripped off soiled bedsheets and dipped out a pitcher of the water to cool after it'd boiled.

"Lean on me. There." Rebekah had an arm around Kaitlyn's waist, helping her out the door. As they passed Ed, Rebekah lifted her brows in a worried expression.

How long could this last? Everyone had grown so weak from loss of fluids.

The endless rounds of damp cloths, drinks of milk, and runs to the privy were interspersed with the scrubbing of laundry on the washboard out back. The stench was lessening as Rebekah took it on herself to clean out the soiled clothes and sheets. Ed kept pushing fresh water to anyone who was awake, making the rounds and worrying over his family.

As he hurried out the front door with Nick leaning heavily on his side, he spied Rebekah scrubbing up the floor where Drew hadn't been able to make it outside.

Ed rubbed the palm of his hand across his stomach as he leaned against the privy. At least he'd been spared the worst by running all over town taking care of Rebekah these last few days. He had to give it to Rebekah. She could have just gone home. But she'd stuck with him. Jumped in to help with all the tasks, pleasant or unpleasant. Mostly unpleasant. When she'd even gone so far as to start washing, he'd thought she was worrying too much about cleanliness—until he noticed how much better the place smelled. He guessed folks would recover faster if they breathed fresh air instead of stench.

After Ed settled Nick back in the sickroom with Drew and David, he returned to the living room to hear Tillie's quiet "I want my mama" and the soft sobs that followed.

"I have an idea." Rebekah bent over Kaitlyn, changing out the cloth on her head. When she turned toward Tillie, Ed couldn't help noticing the weariness in her eyes. "How would you like for me to rock you while I sing a little song?"

Tillie's face brightened amidst the paleness of her skin. She scooted away from her stepmother to where Rebekah took a seat in the rocker. Probably the first time Rebekah had even sat down since they'd arrived back here. She reached down to help Tillie up into her lap, placing a cooling cloth on the back of her neck in the process. A gentle hum left Rebekah's throat. Jo sighed with weariness as she walked over to sit at Rebekah's feet. Even David perked up, listening.

A sweet melody left Rebekah's lips to float around the room. It filled every crevice with its soothing softness. Ed spied a mess on the floor and set to mopping it up as he listened. He remembered her singing the song back in school. Remembered his young schoolboy infatuation with the fiery-haired Rebekah. Remembered her kindness to the littler children and her sweet, sweet voice.

Out the window behind her swayed the laundry she'd hung on the line. The gentle breeze lifted it as if in time to her singing as the sunlight faded. She'd worked as hard as he had today to care for those dearest to him, without even having to be asked. This must be what having a partner felt like. Someone to share your burdens. Someone to lighten your load. Someone who understood you in a way no one else did.

To think he'd hurt her so long ago without even giving it a thought. Rebekah more than deserved that long-overdue apology from him. She deserved his friendship.

"Uncle Ed." The now familiar cry escaped from David as he hurried for the door.

Ed rose to follow. For a moment, his eyes met Rebekah's. His apology would have to wait a little longer.

Darkness had settled over the homestead hours ago, but only in the past hour had the endless trips outside slowed. Rebekah moved to stand by the kitchen window as the chorus of crickets chirped on. She tucked a stray curl behind her ear, weariness threatening to overtake her. The children's fevers had broken, but Rebekah was worried for Kaitlyn. If her fever kept on, that couldn't be good.

Ed must be as exhausted as she felt, maybe even more so. Yet he'd gone over to see about the animals at her aunt and uncle's place after most of the sick had drifted off to sleep.

The aroma from the coffeepot she'd placed on the stove earlier told her it was ready. Reaching up on her tiptoes, she pulled down two coffee cups. The front door closed with a creak, and soft footsteps approached in that easy cadence she knew so well. Only this time, they stirred a sense of comfort in her instead of bristles.

"All the animals were fine at your uncle's place. I checked on ours too. All good." Ed spoke in low tones. He threw a glance over his shoulder to where the family slumbered. "Think I should go for the doctor?"

"Everyone has been calm this past hour. For the most part." There had been that last trip with Tillie. But Ed appeared so weary that she'd hate for him to ride out without a chance to rest. "At least they can sleep."

His blue eyes fastened on her as he moved to wash his hands. "It's the fever I'm worried about."

Rebekah poured the coffee in silence. Nothing in her dared voice her own concerns. Ed needed good news. "You've done all you can for now. Perhaps the fever will break in the night."

He didn't answer as she moved from the kitchen out to the table. As she sat, she placed one cup opposite her before taking a sip of her own coffee. A rustling sound escaped the kitchen. Maybe Ed had finally decided to get a bite to eat.

In a matter of minutes, he emerged with a plate of cheese sandwiches. He blinked as if startled to see her still there, waiting at the table.

Where did he think she might've gone? It was a sign of his exhaustion and worry that she'd surprised him.

"I figured you might've taken one of the girls' empty beds upstairs. Want a sandwich?" He scooted the plate across the table at her as he sank into a chair. Only then did his eyes shift from cup to cup, realizing she'd made him coffee. The corner of his mouth lifted as if in surprise that she'd thought of him.

She took the offered sandwich as he sipped the coffee, then she pushed the plate back his way. The softness of the bread blended with the cheese to satisfy the hunger she hadn't stopped to recognize before. They'd worked in tandem all afternoon. Most of the night too. Mixed with the pleasant food was pleasant company. Odd how agreeable his company had become in so short a time. The irritation that had stung so badly this morning had faded as they'd worked together.

"This sandwich is perfect." She watched him smile a weary smile as she took another bite. This comfort in someone's presence. This knowing how to work together. It was what her imagination conjured up for her every time she wrote a letter to Isaac. Every time she read his responses.

"I've been meaning to tell you something." Ed shifted in his seat. Was he uncomfortable? He scanned those sleeping in the living area as if to be sure they were all still deep in their slumber. With the cup at his lips, he took another sip, then leveled his eyes on her. "About that incident in school."

"Do we really need to talk about it?" That day intruded on the peace of this moment, threatening to evaporate the camaraderie between them and making it the last thing she wanted to discuss.

Ed stared into his coffee cup, fidgeting it back and forth before raising his gaze again. The faint light of the lamp softened his features. "I shouldn't have done what I did. I wasn't at my best back then."

"Not that day, at least." Before she could go on, he held up a hand.

"I always felt like I was in Isaac's shadow. When you started reading your story, all I saw was Isaac being made out to be a hero again." His jaw worked in a different sort of way. Not like when being forced to do a task he didn't want to do. More like trying to hold on to a piece of himself to keep it from escaping for her to see. "I laughed to hide my hurt. It was never meant to hurt you. And I'm sorry for it."

Her stomach dropped as she registered the fear in his face as he glanced at his family again. Here was the evidence that he was only human. He'd made a mistake.

As they sat together in the night's quiet, all those years of promising herself she'd never forgive Ed McGraw faded away as so much foolishness. The mistake of a hurting boy clashed against the tenderness of the man sitting across from her now.

"You were just a kid." She'd made her own mistakes, hadn't she? Played her own part in this ongoing spat?

"Still. It wasn't right." He ducked his head. And somewhere in the back of her mind, she imagined him carrying her letters in his saddlebag after picking them up in town to unwittingly deliver them to his brother who rode the herd. Imagined him bringing Isaac's letters back in return. Always doing whatever his family needed.

This Ed she'd seen today was so unlike the image she'd carried for so long. This man had ridden around with her all day as she'd pursued her story, then returned home to a sick family and put off sleep to care for them. This man had chosen to offer a truce. How could she not freely give him the forgiveness he asked for?

Rebekah straightened up in her chair and reached her hand out over the table. "Friends?"

A slight smile tilted up one side of his mouth. He swiped his hand across his britches to dust off crumbs from his sandwich, then lifted it to wrap around hers. A feeling beyond warmth, almost a tingle, jolted from his hand to hers. "Friends." Her stomach tumbled even further.

Ed withdrew his hand slower than she'd expected, leaving her to contemplate this strange new sensation.

With his eyes averted, he cleared his throat. "You best try to get some rest. I'll ride for the doctor in the morning."

Seven

I've enclosed a pressed flower from a field near where I live. It is a favorite of mine . . .

. . . There are many things I dream of. Dreams are wonderful things that give us hope. And no man can live without hope. One dream I hold very dear involves you . . .

THE DELICATE SCRAWL OF THE HANDwriting stared up at Ed, pulling him in to read the words one more time. He brushed the sawdust from his hand before picking up the softly scented paper. A pressed columbine fluttered to the ground. As he bent to grab it, the unfinished display case beckoned. He ran his fingers over the soft petals before placing the flower back on the bench. How well he knew the power of dreams. Only now, he'd added dreams of her, the woman intended for his brother.

After three days filled with running Rebekah to town, chasing down elusive clues for her story, and caring for a sick family, he finally had a moment to make progress on the display case. But he'd spent more of this early hour pondering Isaac's latest letter.

He smoothed out the paper. This letter may have been intended for his brother, but in the moments Ed wrote to her, the letters belonged to him. As if she saw him, with all his hopes and dreams. Surely the woman on the other end felt it too. That connection with the real man behind the letters. So why did Ed also feel a pang of guilt? Guilt at writing under a pretense.

A light rap sounded on the door as it swung open, letting in the fresh morning light. Drew stepped inside, his face still as pasty-colored as the dough their mother used to leave out to rise.

"Morning. Wondered if you have a minute." Drew's eyes skimmed the sight of the half-finished display case.

Maybe he wouldn't ask about it, but if he did, Ed might as well give him the speech he'd been rehearsing for the day when he would confront his brothers about a furniture business. A day he'd planned for the future, but why not today?

"Sure. C'mon in. How are you feeling?" Ed reached around to grab a stool for Drew, unsure if his brother had the strength to balance himself there for long.

"That another letter?" Drew pointed at the paper on the bench before settling himself on the stool.

"Same girl. Not so sure she'll make a good fit for Isaac though." How could she? He didn't want to discuss this with Drew. Didn't want to face the fact that she was intended for Isaac. Not when the letters sank into his heart like they did.

"Hand it here. I'll take a look."

Ed swallowed hard. "Not necessary. I'm taking care of it. You're looking a little under the weather still." He hurried to push the letter into the drawer of the bench before taking up a piece of wood for his display case. "Should you be up and around?"

Ed slid the plane over the wood intended for the side panel of the cabinet. The soft scraping worked to soothe his tension. Let his brother ask about the furniture. It'd be easier to explain than how he felt when he read the words in that letter. He lifted the plane to run his hands over the smooth wood.

"Keeping a homestead running doesn't afford any time off. You know that." Drew rubbed the back of his neck. Ed bristled. No doubt his comment meant to hint about the furniture.

Ed knew good and well that Drew was right. But no man could live without dreams. Without hope. He took another swipe over the wood. This was Ed's dream.

Drew coughed, the action making him look a little green. "Doctor confirmed a poisoned well was why we all ended up sick. Said he'd let the marshal know and confirmed we can't use the well again."

"Quade?"

"Do you know someone else who would do something

like that?" His brother followed the movements of Ed's hands with his eyes. "But we have no proof. No one saw who tossed that dead deer in the well."

"Same old problem. You got any ideas?" Quade was skilled at keeping his nose clean. One of these days, the McGraws would catch Quade crossing the line. The man had wanted their land for the water rights for so long that the feud stretched back to their pa. Pa had spent a night in jail after the argument had led to drawn guns years ago. Quade just wouldn't let it go. It had been too much to hope that the quiet they'd been having would last.

"Maybe you ought to tell Kaitlyn not to let the kids bring the dogs in at night," Ed said.

Drew gave him a blank stare, then nodded. "We'll have to dig a new well. Hauling water from the creek to boil takes too long. And it's already shaping up to be a dry summer."

Ed stepped away from the piece. He'd been thinking on the well situation himself. "I suggest we hire help for that. It's a big job, and everyone is still a bit down from the poisoning."

"Except our neighbors are all busy with their own chores. Trying to keep their farms running while Quade puts pressure on folks to sell. Not to mention the rumors of a rancher being attacked and the other farm that had that blaze." Drew hung his head. "Not sure who to trust. Don't know who might be on Quade's payroll."

An expectant silence filled the air between them.

"Which brings me to the point." Drew rubbed the back of his neck again, looking for all the world as if he didn't want to say what he was about to say. "Isaac's still riding herd on the cattle, trying to eliminate the wolf threat. Can you dig the new well?"

Ed stood not a foot from his half-finished display case. The one due to the bakery in less than two weeks. All the extra duties, watching over Rebekah, and now this. Drew hadn't even said a word about the case, not even a question. Just another request for Ed. He scrubbed a hand over his face. No way would he be able to finish in time for the bakery's opening.

His eyes leveled on Drew, but his brother had shifted to focus out the window. To the ranch. Which needed fresh water. His family needed a new well.

"We need Isaac." The words slipped out in desperation for another pair of hands. As they did, his gaze landed on the pressed flower. If they brought Isaac back from his hiding place, the letters would go to him. Isaac would have the privilege of writing to Ree. *Why?* Everything in Ed wanted to shout the question. Why did Isaac get everything he wanted? Just like when they were kids.

"I'd go for him, but Kaitlyn needs me here until Merritt can come stay for a few days. And Nick hasn't recovered enough yet." Drew stood, placing his hat back on his head.

There weren't any other available men to hire. Even so, Ed opened his mouth, ready to tell his brother everything about the furniture, the letters, his own dreams.

"We don't have time to waste. We need the well. Everyone's counting on you." Drew headed to the door, a sure sign he expected Ed up there digging at the first available moment.

Ed bit back his arguments. His family needed him. He

watched through the open door as the golden hues of the sunrise all but engulfed his brother's retreating figure, then he picked up the tarp in the corner, flipped it open, and spread it over the top of the cabinet.

With a sharp jerk, he scooped up his coffee cup from earlier. The liquid had grown cold, but he downed it anyway. It wasn't half as good as the cup he'd shared with Rebekah the other night. Ed shook his head. What was she doing in the middle of his thoughts? One cup of coffee was, well, one cup of coffee. He'd apologized. They'd shaken on it. Their long-standing feud over and done. So why had that handshake given him so much grief in a different sort of way? He could still feel the rapid beat of his heart like that night.

Ed left his empty cup on the bench and hurried to put on his boots. There were chores to be done. A well to be dug. He didn't have time to dwell on things he had no business thinking about. Like Ree's letters that he wanted all to himself, when she'd been writing to Isaac. Or Rebekah's handshake.

He hurried out the door, across the field, and into the barn. The shovel leaned against the side wall. He snatched it up and began shoveling the stalls even as he warred inside himself. He dug in over and over, scooping twice as fast, hoping to buy himself time he didn't have. But all he managed to do was sling manure all over himself.

He halted, bracing his arm on the top of the shovel. If Rebekah were here, she'd raise her eyebrow before slowly letting out a clear, crystal laugh. Ed shook his head. She just had to get under his skin. A slow grin pulled at the corners of his mouth. Then he turned and dug the shovel back in.

Each scraping shovelful chanted *You don't have time. You don't have time.*

Not for his furniture. Not for the girl in the letters. Not for Rebekah, now his friend.

"Nice work on that story, Rebekah." The praise from Reverend Carson as he backed out of the newspaper office filled her with hope.

Rebekah waved goodbye before leaning over the layout for the ads, ready to start on the typesetting. She reached for her apron, tying it up to keep the ink from staining her clothes. Mr. Sullivan brushed past her as he shifted back to his desk. Maybe this would be as good a time as any to ask about the story on the candidates.

"That's the third compliment I've heard."

Rebekah eyed Mr. Sullivan. He didn't even look up. "How was your daughter?"

"Oh, everything's fine. The treatments seem to be working." But he'd left town to rush to her side. Things must not have been as bad as he'd thought. Or he didn't wish to share details.

"What did you think of my story?"

"Good enough." His words were distracted as he ran his fingers down a ledger at his desk, then picked up a stack of invoices.

Rebekah smoothed the front of her apron. "Do you think it was good enough to give me a chance to write the bios for the candidates? The ones for the Cattlemen's Association."

Mr. Sullivan continued shifting through the invoices and adding figures to his ledger as if he hadn't heard her. Maybe he hadn't. No doubt his daughter's fight with consumption weighed on him. Rebekah had even heard him mention helping her and her husband with the cost.

She glanced at the work she was supposed to be doing. This was her chance.

The clop of her boot heels echoed off the wood flooring as she neared. He remained focused on the unruly stack. Rebekah settled her fingers on the desk edge, then leaned forward slightly. She kept her eyes trained on him, licking her lip.

"Since you liked the story about the bandit, I would love the opportunity to write the bio stories on the candidates."

Mr. Sullivan tapped his pencil against the desk as he lifted his face. "You can interview the candidates."

Her heart felt about to explode.

"If they agree." His eyes were calculating. He pointed the pencil at her for emphasis, bursting her bubble. "I plan to write up an article on each one too. I'll decide which one is better and publish that."

She took a deep breath, then let it out. It wasn't all she wanted, but at least it was a start. "I promise you, these interviews will be the best articles I've ever written."

"Hmmm." He closed the ledger and pushed back from his desk. "You ready to set the type?"

"Of course." She spun to go gather up the ads from her desk. The elation she'd imagined feeling at the chance for the story had been tempered by his gruffness. What had him so riled? Maybe the expenses for his daughter's care were more than he'd imagined. She dared not ask.

Careful not to disturb her layout, she transported it to the table they always used when setting the type. Mr. Sullivan tied a leather apron around his waist as he came to stand beside her. They worked in tandem, placing the letters in the composing sticks. As they worked, the stain on Rebekah's fingers grew darker from sliding the letters. The bell over the door jangled as Mr. Lee delivered their mail.

"Morning, Mr. Lee." Mr. Sullivan greeted him, walking toward the bundle of mail he'd left on Rebekah's desk.

"Morning, Mr. Sullivan. Got you another bundle of them letters." The man winked at Rebekah. He knew they were her specialty.

She grinned and waved as he let himself back out. Mr. Sullivan picked up the stack, shuffling through the letters. A sensation as active as romping foxes started in her stomach. Those letters were her job. Mr. Sullivan didn't intend to distribute them, did he?

"Where is your letter opener?" He'd pulled a particular letter out of the stack and left the rest for her.

But as her stomach quieted, he reached for her bottom drawer. Her hand flew to her lips as she sucked in a gasp, undoubtedly smearing her face with ink. There was no way to stop him from seeing the stack of letters all neatly bundled together in the drawer.

Rebekah froze in place, pulse racing, as he pulled the bundle out.

"What is this? Why are all these letters addressed to Box

256 in here?" His eyes moved to rest on her, confusion in his crinkled face. "Why aren't these delivered?"

"I've been busy." Her voice faltered as she spoke, betraying her.

"What?" The left side of his lip lifted in incredulity.

Rebekah intertwined her fingers in an effort to calm herself, fishing for an explanation. Any explanation besides the whole truth of the matter. "One day, I was in a hurry. The letters were in my hand. I hadn't decided what to do with them—"

"What to do with them? You put them in the box. What have you done?" The volume of the question grew with each word. She'd seen him angry before, but it had never been directed at her. Her stomach knotted.

"I didn't mean to withhold the letters." The words tumbled out in a flurry. She wiped her fingers across the apron and rushed to her desk as if there were a way to undo this nightmare. The fire in Mr. Sullivan's eyes halted her before she'd made it halfway. Inhaling deeply, she tried to calm the hurried beating of her heart.

"Do you understand the trouble this could cause?" He fanned the letters as he pulled them from the drawer. "If anyone found out we withheld mail?"

"I . . . I . . . I can explain." Her mind grasped for an explanation, even as she pushed out the words.

"I don't need an explanation. I need it fixed." He slammed the drawer closed. "I'm disappointed in you, Rebekah. This is an important part of the paper. Was I wrong to trust you with it?"

"No one knows about this." Heat rose in her face. Her

plan had seemed so simple and innocent. Nothing like this was supposed to happen. She risked losing her access to the mail-order letters and ads. What if he took back the chance to write the articles too?

"Is that the box for the McGraw ad? They're the last bunch I need poking around here causing trouble. Especially now that Quade's—" Mr. Sullivan slapped the mail on the desk, his words trailing off as he brushed past her to his own desk, the letter he'd been searching for earlier in his hand.

Her mouth opened, then closed. The McGraw ad. Ed's face popped into her mind. She pushed the thought of him away. It wasn't his ad.

"I'm so sorry, Mr. Sullivan. I'll fix this—"

"You think you want all these stories for the paper, but you can't put responses to the matrimonial ads in the right place? What are you trying to do, play matchmaker?" He swung the letter opener he'd found in a grand gesture, then set back to opening his mail. "This isn't a ridiculous dime novel like your father wrote. This is real life, and you can't mess with people's lives like this."

Rebekah gripped the desk to steady herself. Her father's novels weren't ridiculous. Those novels were more than just stories. They were her connection to him. A connection that filled her with dreams of what she could be. Filled her with dreams of a hero to love her like no other. And she'd have her hero in real life, even if she had to write him herself.

When Mr. Sullivan didn't look up again, she moved with slow steps back to the composing sticks. Her heartbeat sounded in her ears as she fought to push back the tears from the sting of it all. With trembling hands, she worked to set the type. She'd figure out how to handle the letters later.

Mr. Sullivan barely spoke the rest of the day as they finished up the printing. The doctor had already agreed to take her home this week when he'd been out to check on the McGraws' progress during the illness. Especially with Ed needed at the homestead to help as they recovered. At first, she'd imagined herself elated to be riding with anyone other than Ed, but she found herself missing their conversation.

As the doctor pulled into her drive, Rebekah failed to think of an excuse to accompany him over to the McGraw place. Once on the porch, she waved, then let herself inside.

She put on a kettle of water for tea. The letters were heavy in her pocket. Her fingers interlaced with the ribbon on her hat as she worked to untie it. As she did, her feet carried her to the familiar shelves in the corner. They held the books her father had written before he'd passed. So many that they tumbled over one another in a jumble. The shelves simply didn't have enough room to hold them all in the organized fashion she'd prefer, but they were all there. She picked up her favorite, running her hand along the worn cover. It took her back to the days she'd sat on her father's lap as he read to her. The kettle whistled, pulling her from her reverie.

After she'd steeped a cup, she lingered at the table with Isaac's letters. There'd been three so far. She ran her hand along the top page. Rebekah blinked at the tears trying to escape. These letters filled the place in her heart that her father had once filled. A man wrapping her in words, telling her how valued she really was. And yet, after all her careful planning, Mr. Sullivan wanted her to give over all the other responses. There hadn't even been time in the letters to properly discuss marriage. She couldn't give up. Not yet.

She'd find a way to fix this. She'd find a way to keep Isaac for herself. Picking up the letters, she hugged them close to her.

At least Mr. Sullivan hadn't changed his mind about the coverage of the candidates.

Back in the kitchen, she set Isaac's letters on the counter before placing a bit of cheese on the last slice of bread she had. She leaned her back against the counter as she tore off a bite, then eyed it with a crinkle of her nose. When Ed had made one, she hadn't imagined a person needed any special talent for it. But this sandwich didn't taste the same. Or did she miss his company? The man she hadn't been able to stand only a few weeks ago had now turned into a friend.

Her eyes fell back on the letters. Ed had given her the gift of a chance with Isaac when he'd placed that ad. All she needed was a little more time.

Eight

THE VERY NEXT DAY, REBEKAH EASED up on Mabel's reins, giving her horse leave to catch up with Ed's as they rode toward the Quade ranch. But Lightning sidestepped in a way that prevented her from riding close to him. Ahead of her, Ed's shoulders loomed broader than she remembered. She reined Mabel around to the other side, attempting to sidle up on the left, but Ed reined Lightning back until he was nudging Mabel aside. This Ed was different. Less scowls and more smiles. He'd taken her offer of friendship seriously.

Rebekah leaned to the side as a branch brushed close. A chuckle escaped Ed.

This was intentional. "Mabel and I aren't cattle that need to be cut from a herd, Ed McGraw. I'm on a mission to get an interview, remember."

Yesterday evening, when Ed had come by to tend the livestock, she'd rushed out of the house to meet him. She'd been missing her aunt and uncle dearly. With all the other McGraws still recovering, it had been a relief to see him. When she'd let slip about her plan to ride out to interview Heath Quade, Ed had insisted on coming. Sure as the sunrise, he'd shown up early this morning to ride out with her.

Ed flashed a serious look at her over his shoulder.

"I don't see why an interview is necessary. Why can't you just write that Quade's a crook and be done with it? Save a lot of time that way."

"You know why." This earned another wry glance from him as he slowed Lightning enough to ride side by side with her.

"Has journalism always been so important to you? Always been your dream?" He shifted his focus to the road, then back to her, genuine curiosity written all over his face. Curiosity without an ounce of snark in it.

"I want to run the paper one day. I even have a plan to own it." She'd never told anyone her dream before for fear of censure. But Ed didn't laugh. There wasn't even a twitch of his mouth.

"You like the facts or the writing?"

"The writing, mostly." She angled herself, shifting Mabel's reins slightly, to avoid a low-hanging branch on her side of the road. The movement left her so close to Ed that her thigh brushed against his. He shifted away on the horse's next step, but not before she saw the way his hand fisted and then flexed on release.

"What inspired your love for writing?"

Never had she imagined him with so many questions

bottled up inside. He'd always been short on words in her presence. This was all so new. So nice.

"I used to watch my father write novels." Thinking about Papa brought an old pang of sorrow, one that somehow eased under Ed's gentle gaze.

"It made you want to write too?" He bobbed his head as if contemplating this new revelation. "Why go into newspaper reporting? Why not write a novel yourself?"

She paused as silence filled the space. They'd called a truce, shaken on being friends. Did she dare to trust him with the truth?

"I've tried." Rebekah scanned the trees and the curve in the road ahead that led up to the Quade house—anything but look at Ed.

"And?"

Why did it matter to him? He'd never thought much of her stories in school.

"A rejection notice came in a nice envelope." Rebekah straightened in the saddle. Her story hadn't been good enough.

The thud of the horses' hooves on the dirt road filled the space between them as they started up the drive toward the Quade home accompanied by a low, gentle laugh from Ed. Not the laugh from the schoolroom. A different one, more like the Ed she'd begun to know this morning.

"That's their loss. They didn't know what they were talking about. You were always at the top of the class. Your stories were good then." He glanced at her with a knowing look. "And I've read your story in the paper. I say you're a top-notch writer. You got this interview, didn't you?"

A grin passed across his features as they approached the porch. She didn't know what to do with his compliment. Good thing the house was in sight. She'd do better to focus on the interview.

As they approached the house, Rebekah could see movement inside through the wide glass windows. Mr. Quade's daughter, Isabella, exited the house to stand with her hands folded in front of her. The last Rebekah had heard, Heath Quade's two other daughters, born out of a second marriage, were in the East somewhere at a finishing school. All but Isabella, the eldest. Isabella wore a dress that was both expensive and practical. Her dark hair was pulled back in a bun with loose tendrils around her face highlighting her high cheekbones. Isabella had only grown more poised, even prettier, since their school days.

Rebekah dismounted as Ed tied off the horses to the hitching post.

"Good morning." Isabella's smile didn't quite reach the depths of her eyes.

"Hello, Isabella," Rebekah said.

"Morning." Ed's voice held none of the harshness she'd expected. For all his dislike of Heath Quade, it obviously didn't extend to Isabella.

Isabella returned his greeting with a nod, then motioned to the house. "Father said you were coming."

"Thank you, Isabella." Rebekah followed her through the entryway. She couldn't help an awareness of Ed's presence close behind her.

The home was built from large stones, with strong beams supporting the ceiling. They passed a large space they must use for the family room. Lavish items filled the room. Pieces that might be found in an East Coast parlor, likely shipped out on the train. It must have cost a large sum. But Heath Quade had been running cattle in these parts for a while, and rumor had it his second wife had brought a lot of wealth to the marriage.

Isabella led them down a hall and then ushered them into the parlor. Rebekah paused near the door when she caught sight of a man emerging from what appeared to be the kitchen in the back. When she angled to study him, he pulled his hat low, as if not wanting to be seen. The motion gave her a quick glimpse of a dark mark where the base of his thumb met his wrist—a tattoo.

"I ran into Clarissa Nelson the other day in town. She tells me you made them the loveliest cradle." Isabella's light voice snapped Rebekah's focus back to the parlor. She'd hesitated in the doorway, and Ed and Isabella were already inside the well-appointed room.

Ed lingered not far from Isabella, his face practically glowing at the praise for his workmanship. "I did make them a cradle. Not sure if it's the loveliest."

"She mentioned you might be starting a business." Isabella was offering Ed a seat on the horsehair sofa.

Ed declined the offered seat with a shake of his head. "I've toyed with the idea. Calving go all right for your herds?"

Ed making friendly conversation caused Rebekah to blink. Was his smile a mite…flirtatious? It made Rebekah's stomach do a funny twist.

The two of them standing there were both so attractive,

so athletic. One might think they'd be well matched. If the McGraws weren't at such odds with Quade.

And if it weren't Ed.

Rebekah walked into the room, drawing Ed's warm gaze. He motioned for her to take the seat he'd been offered. She took it and tried not to feel the awkward moment of silence her entrance seemed to have caused.

"That's a pretty dress, Rebekah," Isabella offered.

Rebekah caught the flicker of Ed's gaze. She ducked her head and opened the notebook she'd brought with her, turning her concentration to the list of questions she intended to ask Mr. Quade.

A gentle laugh escaped Isabella, Ed smiling along at something he'd said. Rebekah smiled to cover for not having paid attention. Now that she and Ed were friends, things were different than before. He'd even ridden along with her today without mentioning the promise to Uncle Vess. But did *different* mean her stomach cinching up like a too-tight belt when she watched Ed answer Isabella? She pressed her fingers to her temple. None of this made any sense.

"I'll tell Nick you were asking about him. It's been a long time since we all used to race horses after school." Ed had fallen into reminiscing with Isabella.

"My apologies. I haven't offered either of you anything to drink." Isabella clasped her hands, the gentle smile back on her face. "Would you like coffee?"

"Yes, thank you." Rebekah's voice blended with Ed's. She shot him a look out of habit, but half regretted it when he raised those brows at her.

The moment Isabella turned from the room, Ed paced the floor once, then stopped close to the sofa—so close his boot touched Rebekah's. The clanging of cups on saucers echoed from the kitchen. Ed seemed to concentrate on the doorway, as if making sure no one entered.

When he leaned down close, his breath fell hot on her ear. "Don't forget to see if Heath Quade has an alibi for the day of that bandit attack. I'd like to see what he says."

Ed had never been this close to her before. If she turned her head . . . well . . . the warmth of him so close unnerved her in a strange new way.

He stepped away and Rebekah flipped the page of her notebook. Aimlessly, she began sketching. Anything to redirect her mind and calm her nerves before Mr. Quade entered the room. A replica of the tattoo on the man's hand took shape unexpectedly as she worked to distract herself.

Ed cleared his throat behind her. She turned back the page, sitting up straighter.

Isabella returned with the coffee. As she handed them each a cup, Heath Quade stepped into the room.

Ed's eyes locked on Heath Quade's as the man's lips drew into a tight line. No doubt the others in the room could feel the palpable tension at Quade finding a McGraw in his parlor.

Rebekah cleared her throat. "Thank you for agreeing to this interview."

If she wanted to take the lead, he'd let her. Ed leaned against the wall by the window, watching Rebekah's reflection in the glass. Probably best if he kept sipping instead of talking. Except his next sip revealed how close the bottom of the cup was, and Isabella had already exited the room with no sign of returning soon.

"What made you want to run for president of the Cattlemen's Association?" Rebekah perched, prim and proper, on the edge of the settee, her pencil at the ready over that notebook of hers.

"I want nothing more than to give back to my community. Serving as president of the Cattlemen's Association is the best way I can imagine doing that." Quade moved to the large leather chair in the room, not far from Rebekah, as he spoke.

Resisting the urge to add his own thoughts on Quade's supposed desperation to give back to his community, Ed let his cup clank a little heavily on the fancy saucer. Rebekah scribbled away. He caught a swift flash of Quade's subtle but hostile glance in his direction before Quade's focus returned to Rebekah.

"What is your opinion of the current president?"

Quade drummed his fingers against the arm of the chair before droning a lengthy explanation of his views on the current president along with a bit of his own background and ranch.

Ed pushed back a snort. Too bad Quade had left out the part about trying to steal the land out from under the McGraws. All for a batch of water rights.

"Were you there when they brought the injured man into Calvin? The one who'd been attacked by a bandit? I know the man is a cattle rancher. Do you think there might have been any foul play related to his cattle business? Any comment on that?"

Good for Rebekah. Pinning him down to where he was that day under the guise of an interview question.

"I wasn't there. My ranch hands and I were busy working on a fence in the south pasture. But I did hear the terrible news, although I don't believe it relates to cattle rustling. And I'm sure Marshal O'Grady is doing a fine job of finding the man responsible." Quade shook his head in sympathy as if genuinely moved by the situation. He then offered a smug smile before pulling out a toothpick.

"Of course." Rebekah tapped the notepad with her pencil. "You've mentioned a lot about your history here and your family, but I don't recall you mentioning your first wife. There have been rumors of a mystery surrounding her death. Any comment on that?"

The man shifted a little in his chair, his brows rising. "The loss of my first wife is a painful subject. I'm sure you'll excuse me if I don't wish to talk about it. Frankly, I wouldn't expect a seasoned reporter to even ask such a thing. But I understand Mr. Sullivan probably didn't have anyone of that caliber to send."

Rebekah smoothed her hand over her skirt as her head tilted to one side. She wore that smile plastered on her face, the one where her lips turned up but no teeth showed. The one that usually came right before she let loose with a comeback. But she simply glanced Quade's way, then down to her notebook.

"Several members of the community are concerned at the amount of land you are amassing and what connections you may have had at the land office. Specifically with Ernie Duff."

"I—I don't believe Mr. Duff works for the land office anymore." Quade rolled the toothpick in his fingers a little faster.

"They are asking why, when you have such a nice spread already, you are buying so much land. Some even question if you are building more of an empire for yourself. They wonder if you will only help the larger ranches or, if elected, represent even the little ranchers. Like the ones you are buying up."

Quade shifted in his oversized chair. "Land is a legacy. I don't feel I'm amassing more land for the land itself. It's more of an investment in my roots here, for myself and my heirs. A true testimony I plan to stick around to invest in the people of this community."

Heath Quade had turned that around, but only the ones who hadn't been on the receiving end of his bullying ways would believe it.

Time for Ed to get his questions answered.

"I don't suppose you heard about the well being poisoned out at our homestead?" Ed turned from watching the reflections in the window.

"Poisoned?" Quade shook his head slowly. "I may have heard a rumor."

"Mind if I question your men about their whereabouts the night before last? I'd like to see if any of them saw anything." Ed circled around to place the empty cup and saucer on the coffee table in front of the settee, never taking his eyes off the man's face.

"No one but the marshal questions anyone on my ranch. If you can convince her that there's a good reason to interrupt their work, I'm happy to let Marshal O'Grady talk to them."

"What about you? Where were you that night?" Ed's jaw tightened as his fists balled.

"Ed." Rebekah's call came out quick and sharp as she rose from the settee.

Mr. Quade stood to his feet from the large chair.

Isabella entered the room, her face pale as if she'd been listening outside the door. She shot a glance at her father. "We'd be happy to help you in any way possible."

How had the man managed to raise such a proper daughter while hissing through the grass himself?

"I just remembered a prior appointment." Quade brushed past them on his way to the door. "We'll have to finish another time."

Something in the way Quade hurried out told Ed there wouldn't be another time. Rebekah must have caught it too. She fidgeted with her notebook, then shot Ed the raised-eyebrow look.

Isabella nodded, looking chagrined. "Thank you for coming to interview my father. I'll show you out."

Ed followed behind Isabella and Rebekah to the front door. Stepping outside, he tipped his hat at Isabella as she closed the door behind them, then turned to help Rebekah into the saddle.

"Sorry I cut your interview short." He hated ruining her interview when she'd been so set on it, but Quade needed to be confronted.

"Your apologies appear to be quite frequent." Rebekah leveled him with a stare before she leaned over to stuff her notebook in the saddlebag. But this wasn't the place for squabbling over a shortened interview.

"I am sorry," he repeated quietly.

Her expression softened.

Ed walked around to his horse, grabbed up Lightning's reins, and swung into the saddle. With a nod to Rebekah, he followed her out of the Quade ranch. If anyone wanted to make trouble, he wanted to be closest to where he figured the trouble would come from. With Quade, that would be from the rear.

Once he got Rebekah back home, he dismounted to help her unsaddle Mabel. A good excuse to make sure the barn was clear. Then he'd check the house. Being around Quade earlier had his hackles up.

"Are you planning to stay? I can handle this on my own." Rebekah cocked her head to one side, her sharp tone making a rare appearance again. The interview must have ruffled her feathers. Not that he'd hold that against her.

He did a quick check of the stalls, then returned to heft the saddle to its place while she finished giving Mabel a brush down. Satisfied the barn held no danger, he stopped near where Rebekah stood.

"I'm going to go check the house." He patted Mabel, then nodded to Rebekah.

"You really don't trust Mr. Quade, do you?" With the brush still in her hand, she lifted her satchel to hand it to him. "Take this to the house for me, will you? I've got a few nuggets in there I plan to put to good use in my article."

A soft chuckle escaped him as he ambled to the house with her satchel in tow. Leave it to Rebekah to have a plan.

Once inside, he left the door open for extra light. He swept through the rooms, but nothing appeared out of the ordinary. As he passed through the main room, an overloaded bookcase all but begged for relief. When he got his furniture business going, he'd offer to make the Boutwells another one at cost. He ran his finger over the shelves. Books were stacked on top of each other. Several were written by a man named Edwards. Rebekah's father?

A dime novel stared back at him. One with a hero atop a horse, guns blazing, complete with a marshal badge. Like Isaac. Something in him sank. He'd mended fences with Rebekah. They were friends, or at least talking civil most of the time. Shouldn't bother him she still wanted Isaac over him, should it?

He hadn't realized until this moment that, in all their time together, he'd been falling for Rebekah. But what about the woman in the letters? She acted mighty interested in marrying Isaac. If that worked out, Rebekah might take the revelation pretty hard after all these years. But maybe not so much if the woman really fell for Ed instead. But what did he want? All of it filled his gut with a sickening feeling. Maybe they'd been playing with too many lives, too many people's feelings, while trying to fix Isaac up. Things weren't supposed to be like this.

Ed started for the door when he remembered the satchel across his shoulder. He pulled it down and slung it over a chair back. As he did, Rebekah's notebook spilled out open onto the ground. He bent to scoop it up, then stilled.

There, on the page of her open notebook, a familiar looping handwriting beckoned. Ed stilled with his finger on the page. His hand went cold. He knew the delicate slant of those letters. Knew it by heart. His fingers ran along the words from her interview, *Wyoming Cattlemen's Association*, as his pulse pounded in his ears.

Every letter to Isaac started with "Dear Wyoming Rancher," a funny sort of endearment the woman had decided on, making it so much easier for Ed to let himself sink into the letters. He tried to swallow against the sudden dryness in his mouth. There it was, the same fanciful rendering of *Wyoming*.

All this time, he'd been writing to Rebekah—for Isaac. And all this time, he'd been falling in love with Rebekah through her letters. His mind whirled in a confusion of letters, loopy writing, and a fearsome tug on his heart.

From the open door, he caught movement from the direction of the barn. With a flurried grasp, he flopped the notebook closed and replaced it in the satchel, then hurried out the door.

Rebekah approached the house, lifting a hand to wave as he swung a leg up over his saddle. He tipped his hat to her, then spun Lightning to take off for the McGraw homestead before she said a word.

He didn't even glance back. Didn't want to. Couldn't. He was too afraid to admit to himself why this revelation hurt so much.

Nine

E D SLAMMED THE METAL TIP OF THE shovel into the ground at the bottom of the ten-foot hole only to have it clank against a rock in the soil. The vibration jarred his arm clear to his shoulder.

He finally got a chance at making his dreams of building furniture for a living come true, then slam. Everything was halted by a poisoned well.

He clanged the shovel to the side of the rock.

He finally found someone who understood him, only to be hit with the realization it was Rebekah.

Clang. The shovel rang out as it hit the granite one more time.

He stopped to lean against the handle of the shovel, sweat trickling down his face and his back, soaking his shirt. He'd been working on this off and on whenever he had a chance the last few days. Today he'd planned to finish it. For at least part of the day, David had been available to hand the buckets of dirt up to him as he dug deeper, but it hadn't been enough.

A rumbling protest rose from his stomach. If he'd thought it'd take until evening to get this far, Ed would have stopped for lunch instead of just eating a leftover biscuit he'd stashed from breakfast. Not like the family noticed he'd skipped it anyway. Proof he was no better off than he'd ever been.

He tugged at the gloves to slip them off, giving his hands a chance to cool. The blisters screamed at him as frustration settled in his chest. If he'd hit water today, there'd be no need to be digging again tomorrow. The deepening red of the horizon told him he'd be back in the morning after slipping over to tend to the Boutwell livestock. A task he planned to accomplish before there'd be any chance of seeing Rebekah up and about. How did he face her after she'd written those letters? Worse yet, how did he tell her who she was really writing to?

He leaned his head against his hands atop the shovel handle. For all intents and purposes, he might as well be invisible down here in this hole, trying to figure out what to do. His brothers all had their own issues. Isaac seemed so lost in his grief that riding with the herd was all that suited him until he decided to open up to the family. Nick wasn't up to digging but had ridden out with Drew earlier to see about the animals at the Boutwells' for him.

Nick's dog Patch let out a bark. Ed stepped onto the ladder and climbed up to peer out of the hole, watching Patch rise from beneath the shade tree to amble his way. Ed reached out a hand, but the dog picked up his pace, tail wagging, to trot right past the hole Ed stood in. One look over the edge toward the house showed Kaitlyn headed his direction with a bundle of some sort in her hands. Jo and Tillie trotted behind her, then veered off toward the clothesline with a basket between them.

Placing both his hands along the side of the hole, he pulled himself up, kicking off the end of the ladder with his feet to hoist himself over the edge. A dirty, sweaty mess of exhaustion. Exhaustion that seeped past his weary muscles all the way to his heart.

He landed at Kaitlyn's feet, then rolled over to a sitting position.

"I figured you needed a hot meal. The family hasn't seen much of you lately."

They all knew where he was. Not that he'd felt sociable.

"I have to do this job." He brushed his hands across the only clean spot on his shirt before turning to peek at the plate she'd uncovered.

"Ham, biscuit, corn on the cob." Bending close, she handed him a damp cloth to clean his hands with, a reminder of her prim and proper ways. "And a glass of lemonade."

Finished wiping his hands, he reached for the glass and downed it, then he set the glass upright in the grass and dug into the plate. Patch let out a whine as he flopped close by.

"Want to see me now that I've got food, eh?" Ed tossed the dog a piece of ham, then shoveled another forkful for himself.

Silence fell.

"Are you all right?" Kaitlyn stood where she could keep

an eye on Jo and Tillie as they worked to take clothes off the line.

"The well." There wasn't time between bites to offer more explanation.

Ed kept chewing, not wanting to answer.

Kaitlyn sat on the ground near him. "I doubt Drew meant for you to push this hard. If he knew you were so worn out, he'd find another way."

Drew would find another way. One that might see him staying up into the night to do it himself. But Ed just nodded, shoving in another bite of ham and licking the salty juice from his fingers.

"Unless something else is bothering you."

Ed stopped chewing. "Nothing else."

He thought of the unfinished work on the display case for the bakery. Between helping the family recover and now digging the well, his chances of completing it were slipping away.

He couldn't even think about Rebekah.

"Did you and Rebekah have a fight? I thought you were getting along." Kaitlyn ran her hand along Patch's back as he sidled up to her.

The food turned to sawdust in his mouth as he imagined Rebekah sitting at her table, penning one of those letters. To Isaac.

He should have known she'd want to answer Isaac's ad.

"Ed?"

"Naw." His voice sounded harsh to his own ears. "Nothing happened."

"I don't believe you."

If Kaitlyn hadn't become a friend during the past months, he would've told her off. But he needed a friend right now.

"It's Rebekah."

"Rebekah?"

"The woman answering Isaac's ad is Rebekah."

"I don't understand. You'd better start from the beginning."

He hadn't exactly been forthcoming about how many letters had been exchanged. Kaitlyn's brows rose higher and higher as his story unfolded.

"You fancy Rebekah?" She couldn't keep the note of incredulity from her voice.

Ed ducked his head, pushing together the scraps on his plate.

She touched his arm. "If you and Rebekah are getting along better, isn't that a good—oh."

Kaitlyn seemed to have realized the crux of the problem. Rebekah was the woman meant for Isaac. And the woman who'd always wanted Isaac.

Ed stood and offered his scraps to Patch.

Kaitlyn joined him, shielding her eyes with her hand as she glanced at the girls again. Tillie had let a shirt fall in the grass, and Jo was scolding her.

She shifted her clear eyes back on him. "I'd say it's perfect."

"How? I was supposed to find a wife for Isaac. He's the one she's always wanted."

"People change."

Memories from their school days rushed back at him. All those times Rebekah had walked out of her way on the way home from school, just so she could chance talking to Isaac. Her hurried steps, trying to keep up with Isaac's long, most certainly annoyed, strides. Always hoping for a word from him. Others may not have noticed it, but Ed always had.

"Has she asked for a meeting? Didn't you say before that the woman signed with only her first name?" Kaitlyn's questions drew him out of his woolgathering. "If she hasn't revealed herself but she knows, or thinks rather, that it's Isaac, then she must not be sure."

Rebekah'd been perturbed when Ed had placed that ad. But now that he'd put the pieces together, he realized that every time she'd received one of the letters, she'd lit up.

"Why are you giving up so easy?" Kaitlyn reached out to take his empty plate. "You're tall, strong, handsome."

Heat rose up his neck.

"You own your own property. Have a house on it." Kaitlyn pushed on. "You're loyal as the day is long."

"I'm not Isaac."

"Ma, I need help." Tillie cried out where she stood with a too-big laundry basket in front of her.

"I'm coming." The return cry rang in Ed's ears before Kaitlyn turned her gaze back on him, her hand on his arm. "You don't need to be Isaac. Be yourself. You're deserving of love."

Ed shook his head as Kaitlyn moved toward the clothesline, wrapping an encouraging arm around Tillie in her approach. She didn't know Rebekah like he did.

Kaitlyn and the girls waved as they moved toward the house.

Ed looked at the hole. Then the setting sun.

He didn't want to dig anymore. He might as well call it a night.

He began the walk home. Was it really his best chance to win Rebekah? He'd given up in school when she was twelve, writing about Isaac. Now she thought she was writing *to* Isaac.

Patch followed along beside him, head down, almost as if he were mirroring Ed's mood. When Ed reached his place, he shooed a hand at Patch.

"Go on home now."

With a push, he opened the door to his cabin. A hint of light remained. Enough to light his lamp. He carried it to the workbench. The cabinet was close to completion, but his deadline loomed even closer. As he lifted an arm to sand the wood, his muscles screamed. If Isaac were back here, he'd have another pair of arms for all this endless work. But if Ed wooed Rebekah, the entire plan for Isaac would blow up in his face. If he didn't woo her, she might end up with Isaac. What if that made her happy? What if it didn't? Her handshake of friendship that night at the homestead flashed through his thoughts. How she'd grinned at his teasing on the way to Quade's house, even opening up about her dreams.

His arm dropped to his side. There wasn't a place in him to pull from to work on the display case tonight, and he had another day of backbreaking work waiting on him tomorrow.

What if he asked Rebekah to go courting? He imagined her expression if he tried to tell her face-to-face. Would she be happy to have him court her? He wasn't Isaac. Isaac had always been all charm, while Ed was . . . Ed. Kaitlyn's advice echoed in his mind. But what if Rebekah turned him down? He'd be losing to Isaac all over again. Only worse.

A flash of a barn dance from when he was fifteen wove its way into his crowded thoughts. He'd been wanting to ask the pretty, dark-haired cousin of Jeb to dance but couldn't work up the courage. That was when his buddies had brought him a cup of something sure to give him a bolster. More like a horrid stomachache. One that'd left him running for the back of the barn to heave the contents of his stomach while Isaac twirled the pretty girl onto the dance floor. Ed had passed Rebekah on the way out, her brows lifted high at his stumbling rush. Not to mention the humiliation of his brother's scolding all the way home for drinking what he'd later discovered to be moonshine.

When he'd confessed to Pa why he'd done it, Pa had told him to quit trying to be someone he wasn't. God had made him Ed, and that was all that mattered. In time, the right girl would see him as her hero. Just as he was.

He let the sandpaper fall to the floor beside the display case, his eyes going to the most recent letter sitting on top.

Kaitlyn had told him to court Rebekah. But he didn't have enough courage to ask her outright.

A letter had started it all. He'd write another one. Maybe his words on paper could change her mind.

He grabbed up a paper he'd been reserving for writing up invoices and began his letter. Writing furiously, he poured his heart out on paper. It wasn't long before he had a letter he was satisfied with. One with all his declarations of feelings for her. After reading it one more time, he picked up the pen to sign his name. And stopped.

He stared at the page. If he signed this, there was no going back. If he won Rebekah, how would he explain all this to Drew? Surely Kaitlyn would soften his brother, who didn't know about Ed's conundrum.

He'd spilled out his feelings on the page. If Rebekah knew him like he'd begun to know her, she'd guess it was him. It seemed so obvious. He stared at the paper, his shaking fingers clutching the pencil. Did Rebekah want him? Ed McGraw?

He was afraid to find out. He left the signature blank and folded the paper to stuff it in the envelope, then put the direction on the outside as he'd done at least half a dozen times before. This time, his anticipation for a reply swirled in his gut with a fear he'd never faced before.

He wouldn't sleep tonight, that was for certain.

Rebekah touched her fingertips to her lips as she reread the lines once more.

> *Every time I find your letter in the box, my heart aches with joy at the thought of reading it . . .*

This letter mined the depths of romance unlike any before it, almost as if Isaac knew it was her. As if he were truly falling in love with her.

I long to hear what you have to tell me . . .

This was what she'd always wanted. From the very moment she'd first laid eyes on Isaac McGraw.

I can hardly concentrate until I can find a place all alone to read your words . . .

So why did Ed's face keep invading the space in her head as she read the letter? His comments about what he'd really thought about her in school. The fact he liked her writing. His hand at her hip as he'd boosted her into the saddle at Quade's place. The protective way he'd checked the barn and house.

Rebekah ran her fingers from her lips up her cheek to her temple. Nothing made sense now that she and Ed were friends. Life had been easier when they hadn't had a nice thing to say to one another. Hadn't it?

"What is that? Is that another mail-order bride letter?" Mr. Sullivan's sharp baritone over her shoulder sent a jolt through Rebekah.

"It's personal," she murmured as she slipped the letter back in its envelope. Her cheeks flushed. If only she'd waited until later to read her letter.

She spun, locking gazes with Mr. Sullivan. "This letter is addressed to me."

Neither one broke the stare. Even as her insides trembled, the words still warmed her. Nothing in her wanted to let him read it to prove the letter belonged to her.

Sullivan broke the stare. "Did you deliver the letters to Isaac?"

She pushed the envelope into the pocket of her skirt. "I said I would."

His eyebrows hitched. But she found she couldn't even be sorry for the misleading words, not while her heart sang. She'd won Isaac's heart.

"My article is ready." Rebekah reached for the papers with her article scrawled across it and held it out to Mr. Sullivan, only too ready to divert the conversation. "The one covering my interview with Mr. Quade."

"I'll read it later." He walked to his desk, tossing her article to the side.

"It's the facts. An exclusive interview." Desperation clung to her words as she watched him from across the room. Wasn't he even going to read it?

"Not sure we'll have space for it." Mr. Sullivan mumbled the words as he focused on the ledger on his desk. It wasn't his usual day to pore over the books. He only paid bills and tallied the ledger every other week. Why busy himself with it now?

She stepped in that direction, ready with an argument to plead the case for her article. "Has the circulation for the paper improved this month?"

Mr. Sullivan slid his arm over the page. He eyed her as if he knew where she was going with this. "We can talk about your article later."

"It's just that our readership seems very interested in the candidates—"

The ledger slammed closed, echoing through the office.

Was he hiding something in those pages? "I only need you for one thing: the matrimonial ads. If you can't do that right, then maybe you shouldn't be employed here."

All her words stuck in her throat. Her fingers brushed the pocket where she'd slipped Isaac's letter. She swallowed hard, thinking of all the other letters she'd hidden. She'd not done her job properly. Not all of it.

Mr. Sullivan's eyes narrowed. "I want a yes or no answer. Did you deliver the letters to Isaac? And make a formal apology?"

Rebekah couldn't stop the trembling of her fingers. "I will."

He shook his head, his face reddening. "You . . . I . . ."

She had to stop him before he fired her on the spot. "I'll do it first thing tomorrow."

"See that you do. I can't have the paper's reputation suffering over this." He locked the journal in a drawer, then marched to the front door. Every footstep jarred her worn nerves.

"Deliver those letters or you're fired." As the door slammed behind him, the bell rattled in time to the shaking of her hands.

Rebekah fingered Isaac's letter in her pocket. More work waited for her on her desk, but it could wait. She'd already worked on the next edition of the paper until it was almost dark. Mr. Sullivan would be back first thing in the morning to help her set the type for this week's edition.

She crossed the newspaper office to the stairwell in the back, then clutched the railing tightly as she climbed to her little cot upstairs. After pulling the bundle of letters from their hiding place in her satchel, she placed Isaac's letter on her pillow and set the rest of the bundle on the cot.

The soft fabric of the quilt atop the cot crumpled when she sat and leaned over to unlace her boots. Who would have imagined letters causing so much trouble? They'd always fixed everything for her. A letter had gotten her here so long ago when her mother had decided to remarry. Aunt Opal and Uncle Vess had come to get her when she'd written, bringing her to this wide-open territory from the crowded city back east.

She tugged to pull off one boot, then the other. She had no regrets about writing that letter. It'd brought her new opportunities and so much joy. Coming here had meant working at the paper and meeting the McGraws. But if she lost her job, how could she afford to stay? All the years of working her way up from sweeping out the office to setting type and writing articles only to be on the verge of losing it all? What would her aunt and uncle do? Especially since her pay often helped cover the bill at the general store. It wasn't like she could depend on others to pull them through. Her aunt and uncle had strong views about charity. If it came to that, they'd likely sell the ranch that they loved so much.

Walking on her stocking feet, she moved to the window. A group of boxes waited, arranged to create a sort of seat for her. If she hadn't come west to be with her aunt and uncle, Rebekah didn't know what her fate might have been at the hands of her stepfather. He'd been impatient with her, even cruel at times. Her mother had tried to smooth things over, needing the financial security he offered. But the Boutwells had been there for Rebekah. She could never let them down.

Through the windowpanes, the stars shone above the fading sunset.

Her journal and a pen waited in the secret place between the box and the wall. With her hand, she reached in to pull them out. The journal fell open to a blank page. Did she dare try to write another letter?

Dear Wyoming Rancher,

She put a line through the words. Crossed them out more fiercely as emotion poured through her. That wouldn't do at all. She tore out the page, took a deep breath, and then began on a new sheet.

Dear Isaac,

Her chest heaved under the weight of what she had to write.

I can keep the secret from you no longer. I am writing this letter to tell you an awful truth in hopes that you will find it in your heart to forgive me.

With each stroke of the pen, Mr. Sullivan's words echoed through her mind. She had to deliver the letters to Isaac. She couldn't imagine how he'd respond. She hadn't spoken to him in . . . months. What if she couldn't find a way to make things right?

Her mind whirled. If she revealed her deception to Isaac, Ed would find out too.

She could imagine the disdain in his eyes. Easily. Would their friendship end when he found out she had been writing to his brother and scheming to marry him?

Their friendship would have to change if she and Isaac took the next step in their relationship. That was only natural.

So why did her stomach knot when she imagined Ed finding out?

. . . I am ashamed to tell you that I held back the other letters that came in response to your matrimonial ad. My reasons were selfish, as you can surely guess . . .

. . . my feelings for you have grown . . .

. . . I have attached the other correspondence . . .

. . . My job at the paper once felt secure, but with all that has happened lately, it no longer does . . .

. . . With so much uncertainty in my life, your letters have been my only constant. I would like to define our relationship. I need to know if . . .

Did she dare to write the word?

In her mind's eye, she saw Ed's sparkling eyes and quicksilver smile.

And then Isaac, standing at the back of the church like the last time she'd seen him. Brooding and enigmatic.

She couldn't imagine Isaac saying aloud the words he'd written in his letters.

But Isaac was the man she'd always dreamed of as her husband. Determined, she put her pen to paper again.

> *. . . you truly feel as I do. That we have developed a connection worth taking a chance on. If you do, I see no reason to put off our engagement any longer. With great anticipation, I await your reply.*

Rebekah signed the letter. Her breath caught as she fought the pounding inside her chest. She'd done it. She folded the paper, then rose and returned to the bed. Cupping her hand over the candle, she blew out the light with a shaky breath. She slipped off her blouse and skirt, then settled on the cot in her cotton underpinnings. The bundle of letters glared at her, even in the dusky light of the musty room. She slid the new letter under the twine holding the bundle together. Isaac's letter to her lay open, staring back at her. Sitting cross-legged on the little cot, she reached out to fold it up.

Her job, her future, and her love for her aunt and uncle and their farm all rested in her getting that bundle of letters to Isaac. All the feelings she'd ever had for Isaac McGraw laced her letter of explanation to him, now attached to the top. Marrying him seemed like the answer to all her troubles. So why did it feel like a betrayal of her friendship with

Ed? She swiped at an interfering tear. In a quick motion, she scooped all the letters up and shoved them in her satchel.

Pulling her knees close to her chest, she stared out at the night sky. Was it possible God would listen to her prayer for help after she'd jumped into this mess with both feet, directing things the way she wanted them to go? Aunt Opal always said God was there with the answers when we needed them. *We just have to trust, ask, and let go.*

Rebekah flopped back against the pillow. She'd never been too good at letting go. But if she'd ever needed an answer, it was now. With her eyes closed, she tried to imagine her future. But as hard as she tried, it wasn't Isaac's eyes staring back at her.

It was Ed's.

Ten

DELIVER THOSE LETTERS OR YOU'RE *fired.*

Rebekah hadn't been able to sleep and had left town before dawn. She'd convinced the doctor to let her ride with him in his wagon after overhearing the day before that he'd be going to check on Mr. Billings. He'd dropped her at the Boutwell place, where she'd waited until he was out of sight before saddling Mabel.

Mr. Sullivan's words rang in her ears as she rode Mabel up the lane leading to the McGraw place. The leather reins stuck to her clammy hands. The bundle of letters was tucked away in the saddlebag, along with the letter of apology she'd written to Isaac for having withheld them. Her stomach flipped in all directions at the thought of turning them over.

"Giddyup." She urged Mabel forward.

She took in the yard of the McGraw homestead as her

thoughts ran rampant. This could become her home. Her stomach twisted.

The children were running off in the direction of the creek, not even taking notice of her approach. Two figures on horseback rode in from the field, but they were too distant to make out much about them. She strained to make them out. Not Isaac. She'd know his posture anywhere.

Rebekah rode toward the lone McGraw working in the yard. Ed. Her heart pounded.

She pulled up on the reins to halt Mabel a few feet from where Ed pushed a wheelbarrow of dirt, sweat leaving his dusty shirt clinging to him.

He settled the wheelbarrow next to the old well. When he lifted his face, she caught a glimpse of his expression from beneath the brim of his worn hat. A sort of curiousness mixed with anticipation.

As she dismounted Mabel, she let the reins drop to the ground. Her legs felt unsteady from her nerves as she landed on the ground not ten feet from where he'd been shoveling dirt into the old well.

"Afternoon." He lifted his hand, brushing away the trickle from his forehead with the back of it.

With him standing there, the budding friendship between them having grown so precious to her, she couldn't even choke out a greeting. Ed's expression morphed in the silence. A sort of shadow falling over the eyes that had been so warm only minutes before.

Every part of her insides trembled at what she had to do. Asking Ed to give these letters to Isaac loomed ten times harder than rehearsing it in her head as she'd ridden out here. But the upright, impartial journalist she'd come to envision herself as had to do this. For her job. For her family. For herself. Her hand shook as she reached for the saddlebag, barely able to lift the flap. The letters must be delivered to Isaac. She had to tell him. Had to right this.

"You're filling in the well alone?" The letters slid easily from the saddlebag into her hand.

He sent her a sharp look, then went back to shoveling.

"How is everyone feeling?"

Ed's shovel raked through the dirt. A bird fluttered in the nearest tree. A light thump filled the air as the dirt hit the bottom of the hole. Lightning offered a nicker from the corral.

He kept his head down. "Better."

"Has Isaac come off the mountain yet?" The letters weighed heavily in her hand as a flutter raced in her chest.

A soft snort escaped from him as he dug the shovel in again. "No."

A little niggle of unease twisted inside her. How had Isaac's letters been delivered to town if he was always away from the main house? And from his family? She knew how important the summer grazing was for the cattle. Every rancher around did.

When she saw him next, she'd find out how he'd managed it.

"Can we talk? Can you stop working for a few minutes, please?" Why was Ed making this so much harder on her?

Ed dug the shovel into the dirt, leaving it standing there. He turned to face her. The intensity of his stare further unnerved her. His expression reminded her of the old Ed. How she longed to see the man she'd befriended.

"If I can't deliver these to Isaac, then . . . can I give them to you?" She thrust the bundle of ten letters toward Ed.

With one hand, he worked to pull off one of his gloves, then reached out to take the bundle. Questioning eyes met hers as he shifted.

"Those letters. They were addressed to the box you rented. Isaac's box." The words came out in stammers.

"All of these came today?" He knit his brows together in confusion.

She ran her hands across the front of her skirt, smoothing it even as she stood there, trying to force the words out of her mouth. "I held them back for reasons of my own. Selfish ones. I've explained it all in a letter to him. There on top."

Ed ducked his head. Why didn't he say anything? His jaw worked instead. He darted his eyes back to her again. "You've been writing to him?"

His mouth was set in a grim line, just like whenever he'd glanced at her back in their school days. He didn't look surprised. He must've guessed.

When Rebekah nodded, Ed went back to staring at his boots.

"I know you're not Isaac's keeper"—to her horror, she began to ramble—"but the last few times I've been out to the ranch, I haven't seen him. It's important that he gets those. Will you give them to Isaac? I'd consider it a favor to me."

His eyes lifted to scan the fields. A muscle in his jaw ticked. She'd proposed marriage to Isaac in the letter she'd written him—the letter that Ed was now holding in that bundle. The absurd thought intruded. How could she face this tension between them at a supper where the McGraw family gathered? She couldn't bear it now, much less in a hazy, imagined future.

She gathered her skirt in one hand. "Will you tell Isaac that I'm sorry?" Her words tumbled out in a rush.

His nostrils flared. "You should tell him yourself."

Her nose burned with the threat of tears. "I can't stay."

Silence threatened again, and she couldn't bear it. She spun on her heel to mount up Mabel. Rebekah gathered the reins in her hands and turned Mabel back toward the road. The catch in her heart meant tears any moment.

A glance back revealed Ed near the well, his shoulders slumped and head down. Why hadn't he been angry with her for the deception? She'd sensed he was holding himself back, as if there were walls between them. But no anger.

Her tears were no longer willing to be held back. She prodded Mabel forward at a quick canter.

Moisture dripped down her cheeks and fell, even as she tried to make sense of her emotions. Why was she crying? She'd proposed to Isaac. If he felt as passionate about her as he'd written in his letters, soon she'd have everything she'd dreamed of.

But Ed's reaction had shaken her.

The vision of him, standing near the well with his head down, pinged sharply in her chest. His old way of scolding her would have been more welcome than the distance he'd put between them. All the moments of that day together caring for the family flashed through her mind, along with the endless rides to town. He'd become a friend. Maybe her closest friend. And now she'd admitted to deceiving him and his family. Of course things couldn't stay the same.

She'd made her choice. Nothing left to do but wait to see what Isaac decided.

"It's time to settle this." Ed's thoughts spilled out. He stashed the letters Rebekah had written to Isaac in his saddlebag. In a fit of frustration, he'd hidden those other letters Rebekah had brought for Isaac in a drawer at Drew's house, at least until he figured out what to do with them.

Lightning nickered as Ed swung into the saddle, as impatient to get going as his rider. Giving Lightning his head, Ed clung to the reins. His horse must have sensed his mood. They rode hard toward the mountain area where Isaac hid out in that old unfinished cabin. Along the path leading to the shelter, he watched for signs of his brother's presence. Isaac didn't always stay put. In fact, he seldom did anymore, but Ed aimed to find him today.

The sun on his back should have warmed him, but he shuddered as he passed a clearing in the woods. A rabbit skin hung to dry. Apparently, Isaac had time for hunting while avoiding all the chores back home. Lightning bobbed his head, sidestepping as Ed clenched his jaw. He fought to slacken his tight grip on the reins as he rode in the direction of Isaac's cabin.

The roof was missing some shingles that still hadn't been replaced. Shadows from the trees cast a dismal gray over the place. The door stood open, revealing the emptiness inside. The rough wooden exterior needed more chinking to fill the holes where light came through the logs. Why did his brother choose to live here?

Isaac had been here all right, but when? Not too long ago, if he judged right from the smoldering firepit, even if Ed was no scout like his brother. If Isaac got it in his head not to be found, he'd cover his tracks. But this fire hadn't been stomped out.

As he approached, he thought he caught sight of a figure in the woods behind the structure. A twig snapped. This was no time for games.

"Isaac! Come out now!" he bellowed. If only the effort would release a bit of his tension, but it wound it tighter. A branch cracked behind him. He spun Lightning around.

A moment's silence filled the space—all but the call of a distant bird.

"What do you want?" The deep rumble of Isaac's answer came from beside the cabin. He hadn't been there a minute before. Water dripped from his hair, and his face shone from a scrubbing, as if he'd been down to the creek. His figure appeared gaunt, eyes empty.

Isaac moved easily. His calm demeanor added oil to the fire inside Ed. Isaac'd been holed up here while Ed had given all he had to help keep the homestead going. This was the man Rebekah wanted? The man Ed had given her hope of winning with all those letters he'd written her?

His letters.

Ed nudged Lightning forward with his legs, sending him moving with the speed of a cutting horse. Straight toward

Isaac only to swerve. Ed jumped off while the animal was still in motion and dropped next to his brother.

As he got close, he reared his arm back, swinging his punch at Isaac. The last time he'd swung at his brother had been long before he'd even left to become the great Marshal Isaac McGraw. Not usually one to be taken by surprise, Isaac almost missed ducking but moved out of the way at the last second.

"What was that for?" Isaac dodged another swing.

Ed swung again. This time he hit his mark. Isaac stumbled back, wiping at his lip. They circled each other, evenly matched. How was he managing to hold his own with this hero?

Sweat beaded on Ed's brow. He stumbled a little as he circled Isaac. Those moments with Rebekah, caring for the family, calling their truce, flooded over him. "You weren't there."

At Ed's words, a flash of surprise crossed Isaac's expression. It was enough for Ed to land a punch in his gut. Isaac grunted. Anger flashed in his eyes. Guess he wasn't dead inside after all.

"The whole family got sick." Ed sidestepped a jab from Isaac, his breaths coming fast now. "Someone poisoned the well. Tillie—and Jo—they could've died."

Ed landed another punch.

Isaac took a step back and held up one hand. "Stop."

But a vision of Rebekah's face, earnest and hurting—and wanting Isaac—slipped to the front of Ed's mind. His heart squeezed, and he lost his composure, flying at his brother.

"You're a selfish piece of cow dung. Never giving anyone else a second thought. So high and mighty."

Isaac landed a punch to Ed's jaw, knocking his head back.

Ed stared at his brother, wiped a trickle of blood from his mouth. Ground out, "We don't need you."

Isaac's gaze shuttered. He stepped back fully. "Is everyone all right?"

"No thanks to you. Rebekah helped." All the fight went out of him.

He just wanted this to be over.

He whistled for Lightning, who moved close.

Ed ran his hand along Lightning's side until he reached his saddlebags.

"I located the wolf pack." Isaac's muffled voice came from behind Ed. "Ran off the lot of 'em."

Ed ignored the rambling about wolves. His throbbing hand fumbled to pull out the bundle of letters. Pain pulsed through his jaw where Isaac's punch had connected, but it was faint in comparison to the pain in Ed's heart. At a swift pat to his hindquarter, Lightning lumbered back to the edge of the clearing, where he'd been eating before.

Ed swung around, still stiff from the fight. His step caught, and the letters flung to the ground at Isaac's feet.

"What's this?"

"Love letters," Ed spat. "To you."

Isaac didn't move. Just stood there with arms crossed, brows raised in question.

"Drew and Nick hatched a plan to get you a wife. We placed an ad. You've got an interested party." At Ed's quick movement of his arm, fire flamed in his ribs. He clutched his midsection as he lowered himself to sit on a stump by the fire.

"I don't want a wife!" Isaac's green eyes went icy. "The three of you had no right."

"Isaac McGraw doesn't want the prettiest girl in the whole town." Ed waved a hand in the air as his voice rose. "Did I mention this girl's got spunk? She's not afraid to get the story, no matter who it is. Even Quade. She rides well, rounds up cattle, thinks for herself. She'll adore the ground you walk on, always has."

He let his head hang, not from the pain of his brother's punch but from the pain of losing Rebekah. Who wouldn't want her? His hand itched to reach for the letters, still spread on the ground. Those letters explained the whole thing.

Isaac's eyes glittered. There was anger in the set of his jaw. "Who is it?" He swiped at his upper lip. "You said there was an interested party. Who?"

Isaac always knew where to land a punch.

"Rebekah Edwards." Ed's throat burned as he said her name.

His brother's eyes squinted in disdain.

Ed couldn't take it. He rose and grabbed the letters off the ground. Rounded on Isaac, who braced like Ed was going to throw another punch. "She's the best thing that'll ever happen to you." Ed shoved the letters against Isaac's chest.

"I don't need a wife." Isaac made as if to throw the letters into the fire.

Ed made a quick swipe for them. Caught them midair as Isaac watched. He always saw too much.

"You like her." He didn't ask a question. Ed didn't have to answer.

The fire crackled. Ed ached inside and out. But he'd done what he was supposed to do. He was finished with this.

For a moment, he considered handing the letters back to Isaac, but he couldn't bear it if Isaac threw Rebekah's letters in the fire. Ed took them with him as he headed for his horse.

"From the way you came up here all fired up, it sounds like *you* want a wife." Isaac's words chased him. "If Rebekah is so great, why don't you marry her?"

From the saddle, Ed couldn't look at his brother as he admitted, "Because she doesn't want me."

Eleven

REBEKAH MISSED ED. IT'D BEEN TWO days since she'd seen him.

If only he'd been along for the ride today.

The thought smacked into Rebekah's chest as quickly as the sweet-smelling honeysuckle vine at the end of the lane had smacked across her boot. Her ride to the home of the final candidate interview hadn't been the same without Ed teasing her for searching out clues or chiding her for trying to go alone. And she'd all but proposed to Isaac in her letter of apology.

What if Isaac had been there to promise Uncle Vess he'd look after her? What would these last few weeks have been like? No image appeared, no daydream. The grin tugging at her lips faltered. She didn't know if Isaac would have teased her or argued with her or if his eyes would have sparkled at her. She didn't really know Isaac McGraw at all. She knew Ed.

But she had no right to expect Ed to want to come with her today after what she'd done.

Earlier this week, Mr. Sullivan had been distant while they'd worked to put together the next issue. He was clearly still unhappy with her. So she'd come to get another interview in the hope that he'd see her determination and forgive her. Going it alone was the only way to get the story. Which left her riding Mabel up to the house of candidate number three. At least the 160-acre homestead was just off the main road between her home and Calvin.

A ranch hand, the one Mrs. Jones had introduced as Jimmy the last time she'd been here, sat on the porch with a rifle across his knee. He came to attention. "Who's there?"

"Rebekah Edwards." She lifted her arm to wave.

Jimmy offered a greeting as he lowered his rifle to rest beside the chair he occupied. Another man she didn't recognize leaned against the side of the house, tipping his hat at her before turning to wander to the back. She didn't recall them always being this vigilant at the Joneses' ranch.

Rebekah dismounted as the familiar figure of Margaret Jones stepped out the front door. The woman stood wiping her hands on her apron as Rebekah's footsteps echoed across the wooden boards of the porch.

Margaret worked to smooth her hair and dress, which looked as if she'd slept in it. Lines around her mouth made her look haggard. "Oh, Miss Edwards, I forgot you were coming today."

"What's going on?" Rebekah let her eyes roam to where Jimmy waited before landing back on Mrs. Jones.

Mrs. Jones's face paled a little. "The doctor was here only an hour ago."

Inside the house, it was quiet with the curtains drawn. Bandages were laid out on the table in a pile. A hound dog greeted her with a whine.

A clanging noise sounded outside by the barn. Margaret jumped, hand pressed to her heart. Rebekah's nerves began to jangle.

"Follow me." Margaret took her down a short hall to what appeared to be the main bedroom of the house. Frank Jones lay in bed, bandages wrapped around his forehead. Bruises swelled on his face and arms. "Rebekah Edwards is here."

Rebekah stilled in the doorway, her heart pounding. Who would do this to Frank? And why?

Frank pushed himself up in bed, wincing as he did. His wife bent over him, fussing as she worked to help him, only to have him brush her off.

Rebekah moved closer to the bed, her unease growing. "Is there anything I can do to help? I could bring over a meal."

Bruises ran up Frank's neck and over one side of his face. Watching him wince with each movement told her there were more injuries she couldn't see.

"Maybe it would be best if I come back another day." She took a step backward.

Margaret cast a quick glance between Frank and Rebekah. "Yes, this isn't a good time."

Frank shook his head. He lifted his hand. "No. Stay."

Rebekah lowered herself into the wooden chair beside

the bed, probably pulled in from the dining table. "What happened?"

Frank cleared his throat. "I was on the road yesterday evening."

He coughed. Margaret reached a glass of water over to him. He took a quick sip, then waved the glass away.

Margaret nodded to her notebook. "Do you want to write this down?"

Rebekah chided herself, flipping it open. Must be her unease over the whole situation.

"He was jumped. On the road back from town when it happened." Margaret's brows furrowed tight as she moved closer to the bed to fluff the pillow his bruised arm rested on. She leaned closer to him. "All of a sudden a man with a bandanna—wasn't it a bandanna?—came upon him with a gun."

"If you'd let me answer." His voice remained calm as she finished arranging the covers and pulled back. "The man came up from behind. Must have thought I had the payroll for my ranch hands on me. When I didn't have anything for him to take, he let me have it." Frank held up his injured arm as evidence.

"Is there anyone who holds a grudge against you?"

Frank and Margaret exchanged glances, shaking their heads.

"Mr. Billings was attacked by a bandit. Brought into town." Rebekah gripped the pencil tighter to steady her hand. "He was running for office too. He was on the list of candidates."

"Seems mighty coincidental that they were both running for the same position." Margaret shot her husband a worried look.

"I woke up with my eldest boy, Elmer, standing over me. Came after me when I didn't arrive back in time for supper." He motioned to his side table, and his wife reached over to pick up a knife and a piece of newspaper. "Found this next to me. Stuck in the ground."

"That must have been frightening." Rebekah's mind raced, trying to tie the pieces together. It appeared the candidates were being targeted. But why?

"Elmer didn't notice the paper until later."

Rebekah leaned over to grasp the article from the paper as Margaret handed it to her. The one Mr. Sullivan had run announcing who was running for president of the Cattlemen's Association. If someone was targeting all the candidates, was Quade next? But she'd already been to interview him. All Ed's warnings rushed back at her, even as she tried to push them away.

"You didn't come here to talk about a bandit. What questions do you want to know about my candidacy?" The words had a quiet determination, so out of place when the man couldn't even sit up.

Rebekah couldn't let this go. "Have you told the marshal?"

He stared at the bruises on his arm before continuing. "Not yet."

"Anything else you can tell me? Did you recognize who did this?"

"Like I told you, the man came at me from behind. I remember seeing a bandanna over his face. He did have a tattoo on his hand. Like this." Frank traced out a pattern on the blanket.

Her chest tightened. She handed him her paper. "Can you draw it here?"

"I'll try." As Frank sketched, Margaret worried her hands. After a few minutes, he handed the notebook back to her. "Think the marshal can use that?"

"It's something to go on." Her own words sounded as if she were listening to herself from afar. She'd seen the same tattoo on the man's hand at Mr. Quade's ranch. "I'll make sure to get it to her."

"If this is about you running"—Margaret shot Rebekah a worried look—"maybe you should drop out."

"I'll be fine, dear." Frank scanned the room, turning his attention back to Rebekah. "You didn't ride out here by yourself, did you?"

His concern touched her. "The McGraws have been looking out for me."

At least, they had been. One in particular. If only he were with her. "I'll send the marshal to you. And I'm certain the parson will organize some help for you."

His brow wrinkled. "What about the McGraws? I thought you said they were watching out for you."

Rebekah averted her gaze. She couldn't answer that right now. "I'll leave you to rest. Thank you for your time."

Margaret motioned for Rebekah to follow her to the door.

"Thank you." The older woman's hand clasped Rebekah's with a slight tremble. Her lips quavered as she spoke. "Good day, Miss Edwards."

Rebekah walked toward Mabel and mounted as the door closed behind her. The moment she'd held a drawing of that tattoo—for the second time—nerves had stolen over her. Ed's insistence that Quade was a snake rang through her memory. The cowboy with the tattoo had been on Quade's ranch. In his kitchen. Was he working for Quade?

Her mind whirled with questions.

If the bandit had attacked from behind, could the rancher be mistaken?

If the cowboy was the bandit, did Quade know?

Riding Mabel at a canter, she jumped at every shadow. Mr. Jones's story had to be written. The tattoo's detail had to be printed. But Mr. Sullivan was still sore over the letters. He might refuse to let her write this story.

A flock of sparrows took flight, and Mabel spooked. Rebekah barely kept her seat.

If Ed were here, she could talk to him. He'd know what to do. She slowed Mabel—no need to break her neck. She was suddenly aware of even the smallest noise in the distance.

The edge of town loomed near. She pulled back to slow Mabel as they entered the busy main street. Sweat ran between her shoulder blades from the heat, the effort of hard riding, and her nerves. Familiar faces tipped their hats or smiled in her direction. She should feel safe here. Laughter erupted from the saloon as she passed, sending her heart pounding.

She found the marshal's office empty. Heart still racing, she glanced down the boardwalk. Was it safe to go to the newspaper office?

Ed unloaded the display case into Mrs. Wilson's bakery.

"You're days late, but this is a beauty." Mrs. Wilson ran a hand along the sheaves of wheat Ed had carved into the trim.

Ed shifted a little, his throat growing dry. "I'm sorry it's late. I'd still like to start on the table and chair set we talked about."

"I'm not sure." Mrs. Wilson hesitated. Her eyes darted around the room. The counter filled the wall across from the large window, the space in between just waiting for several sets of table and chairs. "I can't hold off on serving customers because the furniture's late. Can you guarantee a delivery date this time?"

"I can't give you that. I'm still helping my brother run the ranch." Everything in him ached at having to say it. Isaac hadn't come off the mountain, and there was too much work to think of asking Drew for a break.

The woman rubbed her hand along the piece again. Stepping back, one of her children ran up to pull at her skirt.

"I'm very busy. I hope to be open by the end of July." She bit her lip, then bent to pick up the fussing toddler. Her mouth pulled in an apologetic sort of grin. "I'm not sure I can wait if you can't guarantee delivery. No matter how beautiful your craftsmanship."

He nodded, throat hot. He'd known what the consequences would likely be for not delivering on time. It couldn't be helped.

Ed walked back to his waiting wagon with the heaviness weighing hard on him. Back at the homestead, they needed to get ready to bring in the crops. Drew was trying to keep a vigilant watch on the land, rotating night duty with Ed and Nick. The extra work was wearing everyone down. Drew had been on edge this morning when Ed had pressed to come to town for the delivery.

He should be rushing home, but he lingered near the wagon. Couldn't help looking down the street toward the newspaper office. Rebekah's smile had grown to be a balm for him. He couldn't stop thinking about the last letter he'd written. The one she hadn't answered. Instead, she'd come looking for Isaac. The hurt from seeing her might break him.

A movement outside the marshal's office grabbed his attention.

Rebekah stood at the marshal's door, easing it shut as if in slow motion. When she turned, he caught her haggard expression. Her hair had come loose in more than one place, clinging to her neck as she ran a hand along the crinkles in her usually neat skirt. He watched her traipse down the street, though she didn't seem to see him. Saw her bite her lip. Saw her jump like she was frightened.

Something was wrong.

His feet carried him to her before he'd thought it through.

"What's the matter?" he asked.

"Ed." The relief in her voice created a thrum of protectiveness inside him.

"You all right?"

"I'm fine." She studied his face, then dropped her eyes to her hands.

He should take a step back, but he couldn't seem to make his feet move.

Her hand fisted in her skirt.

"Marshal O'Grady isn't there. Or her deputies." She acted indignant. Or scared?

Hadn't he passed the marshal on his way into town? His pulse upped a beat. "What do you need the marshal for?"

"You were right." Her mouth trembled, just slightly. "I went to interview the last candidate."

"Alone?" He bit down on his back teeth. If only she'd told him. He shifted his eyes to take in a passerby, then took her arm to stroll down the boardwalk toward the newspaper office.

"He'd been attacked." Her voice lowered as a woman passed by on their side of the boardwalk.

His pulse quickened. She'd put herself in danger. This was what he'd warned her about a hundred times.

"Exactly why you should have taken me." He leaned closer to his left side, where Rebekah walked, to speak the words through half-clenched teeth. All while smiling at the milliner as they passed her store. This couldn't happen again.

"I think I know who it is—the bandit." She gripped Ed's arm as she whispered out the words in a hurry. "The man had a tattoo. I saw him on Quade's ranch while we were there, doing the interview. Not his face, but I saw the tattoo. Did you see the man?"

"No." He'd known it all along. This was proof Quade was in on it.

"If I print the story with the description of the tattoo, then someone will surely come forward to identify this man."

"Did he see you?" When her brows crinkled in confusion, he went on. "The bandit. At Quade's place."

"I don't know. I don't think so."

Some of the tightness in his chest eased. Maybe things would be all right. Quade didn't know that she'd put together the identity of his hired man.

"Let me give you a ride home," he said.

She glanced at him, clearly confused by his suggestion. "I'm—it's my day in town." She gestured to the office. "Mr. Sullivan is counting on me to arrange the typeset and print the paper while he's gone. His daughter is still ill. I have to do all I can to help keep the paper afloat. A big story means paper sales. And I still need to speak to Marshal O'Grady. I'll have to write up a detailed description . . ."

"Rebekah, you can't." Desperation leaked out in his voice. She couldn't be serious. Quade had no mercy. He'd almost killed Jo. Tillie.

This time, when her gaze met his, he saw the determination. Maybe even a hint of excitement shining in the depths of her eyes. "The truth needs to be printed. I have to, Ed, you know that."

He didn't know anything. He pulled her close, not caring that they were out in public, clearly visible on the boardwalk. Instinct told him to pull her closer.

Her lips parted, and he took his chance. He leaned all the way in and his lips were there, on hers. His hand clutched her shoulder as he pressed in. She responded to his kiss, and he let his grip loosen. His hands moved down her arm, relishing the softness of her hands as he clasped them. She smelled of honeysuckle and roses. His mind became shrouded in a fog of Rebekah. He didn't want to pull back. How had he managed to be here to start with?

Breathing ragged, he pulled away far enough to get a look at her face. Her eyes were wide and searching. And then she lowered her eyes, her lashes hiding her from him.

I've explained everything in a letter to Isaac. Her words from the last time he'd seen her blasted him, making his face flame.

"Maybe we shouldn't have done that." He stepped back, releasing her hands. At his sides, his hands flexed. He wanted to reach for her again, search her face for an answer. If he'd ever wanted her to argue with him, this was it.

Rebekah never wavered. She always knew what she wanted.

One hand came up to brush her cheek. Her brows flickered low. "Ed, I—"

Disappointment settled deep inside him. "I'll come in to fetch you tomorrow."

When she raised her chin, lips parted to protest, he shook his head tightly. "I have to keep my promise to your uncle."

He turned away, walking toward the wagon without really seeing any of his surroundings. And she didn't call him back.

Twelve

THE BELL ON THE DOOR JANGLED. REbekah started, hand flying to her chest.

She'd been jumpier than usual. After going to see the marshal four days ago to report the man with the tattoo on his hand, she'd been warned by the marshal against printing any information in the newspaper, but not forbidden. With Mr. Sullivan out of town to visit his daughter, it'd seemed the perfect opportunity for Rebekah to print the news. News that might up the readership and save the paper. And hadn't Mr. Sullivan taught her that the truth must be told?

Even now, the marshal and her deputies were busy searching for the criminal. The one who'd eluded them at every turn.

She closed her eyes tight, exhaled, then opened them as she spun to face the door.

"Everybody all right?" Mr. Lee handed over a stack of mail, a questioning expression on his face.

Rebekah offered a reassuring smile that all was well, even as sweat slicked her hands.

Mr. Lee tipped his hat, backing up to the door to let himself out.

Shuffling through the stack, she separated the items and ambled back to place all the bills on Mr. Sullivan's desk. Too many bills. Mixed in amongst the other mail were a few letters for mail-order bride ads. None for Isaac. None for her.

She hadn't slept a wink last night, thinking about what had happened.

Ed had kissed her.

She shouldn't be thinking of it. Not after her proposal to Isaac in the last letter she'd sent.

But when she'd been in Ed's arms, she hadn't thought of Isaac once.

She'd not had another letter since writing her apology to him. She didn't know what to do. The busywork wasn't enough to distract her mind. She tapped the envelopes against the desk before moving to place them in the appropriate boxes.

Finished, she wandered back to her desk. Rebekah eased her chair back and began opening her desk drawers one by one, taking everything out of them, wiping them out, then replacing the items in a tidier manner. This place needed a good dose of organization. Mr. Sullivan had been gone so often lately. When he was here, he acted out of sorts. His usually organized desk was a mess. She'd caught the Late Notice stamp on more than one invoice.

At least he'd return to find her area in order. When she fumbled the bottom drawer open, all the memories of those hidden letters flashed back. If she hadn't hidden them, Mr. Sullivan wouldn't be so angry.

She shook the image of his frustration away. In its place, the replay of Ed's encouragement flashed through her. He believed in her writing. Warmth crept up from her neck to flush her face. She placed both hands on her cheeks to cool them.

There had to be another way to occupy her time and push back her nerves. Slamming the drawer shut, she raised her head at the very moment Ed strode past the big window of the newspaper office. She stood, smoothing her skirt, her hands trembling, but for an entirely different reason.

Perhaps he had an errand in town taking him past her office. Once he reached the end of the window, he paced back to the door, moving his lips while mumbling to himself.

What was he doing? Why was he in town earlier than usual to take her home? He looked as conflicted as she felt.

He came back again, heading toward his destination—to see her?—with shoulders straight and determined.

The bell of the door to the newspaper office jangled, and her heart began to pound. One hand flew to tuck a loose strand of hair back in place.

Ed stepped inside. His hand tapped his hat, but he didn't remove it, as if deciding whether to stay. His clear blue eyes locked with hers. A hint of a shadow darkened his cheekbone beneath one of his eyes.

"Morning, Rebekah." His lips lifted in a sheepish sort of grin. One that made her heart leap in her chest. She wanted to see that smile all the time.

He removed his hat, then replaced it. His fingers trailed over the twine on the nearest stack of papers. She'd never seen him so unsettled.

"Morning." That kiss from the other day clouded her thoughts and made her nerves worse.

"Do you have time for a walk?" The words rushed out of him faster than she'd ever heard him speak. Surely he hadn't come to town early just to walk with her.

"I do." She pushed the chair back as she stood, smoothing her skirt. She couldn't bear to stay in the empty office a moment longer. A walk with Ed was the best distraction she could think of. This recent development in her own feelings left her more curious than all the flip-flopping her heart had done earlier.

"Actually, I need to—" Ed fumbled his hat. He stepped back to open the door, holding it for her. "The weather is fairly mild for a summer day."

They'd taken a few steps down the boardwalk before she realized he was offering her his arm.

"It is a fine day." Rebekah looped her arm through his extended one. For a moment she found herself holding her breath, his arm warm under her fingers. His muscles were tense.

The clomping of his boots filled the awkward silence. "I, um, did you get the paper all ready to go out?"

"They're waiting for pickup." She'd expected him to bring

up the kiss. Hadn't he said they shouldn't have kissed? She didn't want to hear him say it again. "How's the family?"

When she tipped her head, she caught the way he worked his jaw.

"Any news from the marshal?" he asked.

She shook her head. He hadn't answered her question.

"What about your aunt and uncle?" he asked before she could press him on it.

She leaned into his arm. "Are you anxious to be rid of me?"

"No." His instant response warmed her. Until he added, "I wondered whether Vess had tried to make you see sense. After you wrote him about the bandit and the ranchers."

She glanced across the street, knowing it would mean he couldn't see her face directly.

Ed slowed and tugged her to where she faced him. His eyes searched her face. "You didn't tell them about the bandit. About what's been going on around here. And now you're putting yourself in danger."

It wasn't a question, so she simply hiked her chin and held his stare.

He didn't like it. She could see his thoughts in his expressive eyes, the tic at one side of his mouth. But he gathered her arm in his again and started walking.

The end of the boardwalk loomed ahead, but Ed made no sign of stopping. This time, a silence fell between them.

She hadn't meant to hurt his feelings. She cleared her throat. "I appreciate your protective manner."

"You do?" Now he was looking at her directly, and she couldn't make out the emotion passing through his eyes.

Her breath froze in her chest. Everything was unsettled between them.

"Has Isaac—" She broke off the question as she registered the minute tightening of Ed's eyes.

His lips settled in a determined line. He nodded, almost to himself. "We should talk about Isaac. He's not—I'm the one—"

A shot echoed from somewhere nearby. Dirt kicked up in front of the boardwalk, only feet from her shoes.

Realization crashed into him, and Ed jerked his head up, grabbing Rebekah's arm to pull her back on the boardwalk while keeping his body between her and the direction of the gunshot. His hands moved to her forearms, pulling her close to him as a woman screamed from somewhere behind them.

He had to get her to safety. Rebekah's head lifted as she tried to peer past him.

"Keep your head down." He hissed out the words.

His first thought was that a brawl at the saloon had gotten out of control. But it was early in the day. The street had emptied after the shot. He pulled Rebekah back toward the town, his elbow knocking against the side of the dry-goods store as he passed around the corner. A woman shoved her child through a shop door. Ed pushed Rebekah behind him, shielding her body with his as he made for the front of the store.

"Let me see." Her words were terse as she pushed her hand against his shoulder, struggling to see past him.

"Get back," he grunted.

"Can you see anything?" Before he could stop her, Rebekah peered around the corner again. He wrapped his arm around her waist and pulled her back as a shot rang out and splintered the shingle that'd been right by her face.

He'd been in plain view for much longer than she had. "Whoever is doing the shooting is aiming at you."

He must have said his thought aloud, because when their eyes met, hers were wide and terrified. Another shot rang out.

Ed pushed Rebekah against the wall. Face-to-face, they were close enough to kiss.

I'm the one who sent you those letters.

The words stuck in his throat. "C'mon. Let's head for the marshal's." He guided her forward, weaving into another one of the alleyways. An angled shot nicked the side of the buildings.

A man on a horse raced past what Ed could see of the street, his hat pulled down over his eyes and a bandanna covering the rest of his face. Seconds later, the marshal followed close behind on her horse, moving so fast she was a blur.

Heart still racing, Ed stood slow and easy, then motioned to Rebekah.

"You'll be safe at the marshal's office." He wrapped his arm around her shoulders in a protective stance as he led her back to the boardwalk.

He opened the door, letting her walk in first. Others from the town were peeking out from their shop doors as he stepped inside behind Rebekah. She turned slightly to face him. How he'd wanted to tell her about those letters.

"I'm so glad you were there." Her lip trembled, then she folded into his arms.

As she leaned closer into him, the shaking of her delicate frame unnerved him. This was not the time to tell her, just the time to hold her. Ed let his eyes close as he wished for all he'd ever wanted to become a reality.

He lost track of time as he held her, until a rattle at the doorknob startled Rebekah. She pushed away from him, swiping at her eyes as she did. A tear-dampened spot on the front of his shirt clung to him, reminding him how close they'd been. The door swung open, bringing a faint breeze along with a whiff of open spaces and horse sweat.

"I lost him at the canyon." Marshal O'Grady frowned. "I've sent my best tracker after him."

The marshal rounded her desk, glancing in concern at Rebekah before her sharp gaze met Ed's. "Several folks grabbed me and said he was aiming at you. Seemed to think someone upset with you saw you in town and took a shot."

Her pointed stare landed on Rebekah again.

Ed focused on Rebekah with concern. Her haunted eyes met his. The gunshots had shaken her like nothing else had. If only she'd listened to him before.

"I'll need statements from both of you." The marshal made her way around the desk, then settled herself in the chair. "Have a seat."

Ed pulled out a chair, directing the still-shaken Rebekah to sit. She wound her hands together on her lap, a slight tremble still noticeable. His mind worked as Rebekah recounted what had happened. It was a big risk to take a shot in town, where anyone could see. What had prompted the man to do it?

"I've heard rumors coming out of the Jones ranch," Danna said slowly. She played with a pencil on her desk. "And cowboys talk when they come to town to visit the saloon. That article you wrote has caused quite the ruckus."

Rebekah was so shaken that she didn't argue. She wasn't all right.

"We're putting a posse together to go after the shooter." The marshal rose as if dismissing them. "It will take some time."

"Rebekah can't stay alone at the Boutwell place. She'd make an easy target." Ed took a step in the marshal's direction.

"I agree." Marshal O'Grady shoved her hat back on.

Ed couldn't see Rebekah's face where she sat in the chair, but he felt the moment of hesitation before she said, "But I can stay above the newspaper office. Surely I'll be safe there."

The thought of someone taking a shot at her again when she was alone and vulnerable plagued him—an image of her, lifeless and cold, that he had to blink away. "Come stay with Drew and Kaitlyn. We take care of our own."

Ed threw a pleading glance in Marshal O'Grady's direction as Rebekah stood, shaking her head.

"You should listen to Ed," Danna said gently.

Rebekah wanted to accept. He could see it.

He pressed. "Kaitlyn will be upset if you don't come. If anything happened to you—" He watched her focus out the window, considering. "*I* don't want anything to happen to you."

"Would you come with me to the newspaper office? I have to gather my things before we leave town." Her fingers rubbed across her forehead as she let out a soft sigh. "With Mr. Sullivan at his daughter's again, I also need to lock up the office."

Ed slipped his hand under her arm. "Of course. You ready?"

The nod of her head was so slight that he wouldn't have noticed if he hadn't been so fixated on her—so grateful she'd heeded his warning this time and let him protect her without argument.

It wasn't until they were seated beside each other on the wagon bench, rifle across his knees, that he realized he might've made a mistake. He'd come to town to confess everything. The letters. His feelings. Now he was bringing her home. Closer to where Isaac was. At least his brother hadn't come down the mountain, even after their brawl.

He needed a chance to state his piece to Rebekah.

He broke from his vigilant scan of the road to glance her way. She was still shivering beside him, worrying her lip between her teeth.

Not yet.

Soon.

Thirteen

AS THE HOURS PASSED, REBEKAH'S MIND kept replaying and replaying what had happened in town. She filled two notebook pages with details but found it difficult to concentrate. Ed must've sensed her upset, because he'd mostly let her be.

Finally, she'd nodded off against Ed's shoulder.

And only moments ago, had woken discombobulated to realize they'd almost arrived at the McGraw homestead.

"You all right?" He reached out to place a hand over hers. Almost as quickly, he removed his hand as he turned to pull up on the reins.

His action reminded her of his awkwardness in town. That walk.

Rebekah let her eyes linger on his profile. His protection today went deeper than a promise to Uncle Vess. And that rattled her as much as the shooting had.

"Whoa . . ." Ed guided the horses to a stop beside the barn. His jaw worked.

As Ed shifted on the seat to get down, a familiar figure caught her eye.

Isaac.

Everything froze inside her, choking her.

His features were as chiseled as she remembered, his stubble rugged as he worked to unsaddle Bullet. He looked up with hooded eyes and hailed them with a single wave.

She waited for the familiar buzzing in her veins.

And felt nothing.

Nothing at all like the way her heart had raced when Ed had held her in his arms in town.

Ed didn't greet his brother. Suddenly, she was aware of his silent tension. Ed clambered down from the wagon.

Isaac almost looked . . . dismayed when his eyes flicked her way.

A sense of discomfort surged inside her. Isaac knew about her deception. She'd even proposed to him, but there was no warmth in his greeting.

Her breath caught wrong in her chest. She'd been staring.

Ed was waiting beside the wagon, but he wasn't looking at her. Just waiting, head down. When she reached out, he took her hand and slowly helped her out of the wagon.

"Hello." Ed offered the mumbled greeting to his brother without even turning in his direction.

Her greeting for Isaac was laced with determination. "Hello."

Ed started unloading the wagon, ignoring them both. A gnawing pit formed in her stomach.

That wasn't the Ed she'd come to know.

Of course. She'd told him she'd written to Isaac, answered his ad. Ed knew things were unresolved with Isaac.

It was time to fix that. Ed disappeared around the side of the barn, and Isaac kept brushing down Bullet, leaving her to stare at his back. She moved closer and then waited.

Isaac didn't look up. He brushed his horse as if no one in the world were near. As if she weren't standing there waiting for him to acknowledge her presence.

Maybe this was Isaac's answer to the question in her letter. She ran her fingers over her hair, hoping curls hadn't escaped unbidden, then smoothed out the front of her blouse and skirt.

"I haven't seen you around town. Are you okay?" She leaned around where he worked to move in closer.

"Why wouldn't I be?" His answer was cool. Lines pulled around his eyes, as if he were haunted by something. He hoisted the saddle from the corral fence, heading for the barn with it.

Rebekah watched him walk away. Ed still lingered out of sight. This was her chance to clear things up with Isaac. Her chance to tell him things had changed.

She lifted her skirt to follow Isaac. Her eyes took a moment to adjust to the light inside the barn. As she stepped behind where Isaac settled the saddle on a stand, he spun and pulled up before he ran into her. His shirt and pants appeared more worn, less like the polished Isaac she remembered. Even his signature holster and six-gun were missing.

"I thought you were out there with Ed." The disgruntled tone in his voice unsettled her.

Rebekah twisted her hands together. "You haven't been to church lately."

"No. I haven't." He skirted around her, walking back out of the barn, leaving her standing there. Alone.

Her cheeks heated. No heroine in her father's novels ever had to endure such treatment. Not from the hero. The memory of Ed standing in front of her to block the bullets, wrapping her in his arms, letting her cry on his chest as he held her, intruded on her musings.

Isaac returned, leading his horse. Everything she'd laid bare in those letters . . . through his silence, it couldn't be more obvious that he didn't feel the same way she had.

Hurt throbbed in her chest. And then she thought of Ed, outside.

Isaac shuffled past her and she followed. It had always been like this. Her following him.

"I think we need to talk through things," she blurted.

"There isn't anything to talk about." He cleaned his tack. He didn't even pause or look at her.

She looked at his face once more. Felt nothing. It made her next words come slightly easier.

"I mean the letters. Especially the last one." She waited, her heart hammering in her ears.

Ed's shadow darkened the door. He flicked a glance at her, expression unreadable.

And still her heart responded.

He led the horses inside.

"I put your stuff on the porch," he said as he brushed past her. He quickly loosed the horses into their stalls, then passed by her again, not looking back as he left the barn.

Her eyes followed Ed as new determination flowed through her. She marched up to Isaac.

He dropped his hand from where he hung the bridle on the barn wall to half turn in her direction. "Those letters." He kept his head ducked. "They never should have happened."

She thought of the beautiful, romantic words he'd penned. For one moment, she was torn. She wanted to know whether his feelings had changed when he'd learned of her deception. But it didn't matter.

This was her answer.

She left the barn. The flare of embarrassment lasted only as long as it took for her to glimpse Ed striding across the field toward a smaller building in the distance.

She hurried after him.

"Ed."

The breeze blew the words back at her as she hurried after him. Cows lowed from somewhere nearby.

Almost frantic, she cupped her hands around her mouth. "Ed!"

As he reached the small porch of what must be his house—she'd never been invited—she saw him go still. He must have registered she was following him.

He glanced over his shoulder, but he was still yards away, and she couldn't read his eyes. He went inside, and for a moment, her stomach dipped.

But he left the door ajar.

Stepping onto the porch, the rough scratching of sandpaper filtered through the doorway to meet her. She paused at the threshold to catch her breath. In the center of the main room, she spied Ed, muscles working in his arms as he shoved the sandpaper forward and back. He stood amongst the sawdust.

Awkwardness descended on her as he kept working without acknowledging her presence.

She took a moment to catch her breath. And look around.

Neatly stacked planks of wood lined the back wall of the cabin, with a cot along the wall to her right. The patchwork blanket covering the cot had been pulled up and smoothed over. To the left of the door, an oak cabinet ran along the wall. Not far from the cabinet sat a wood stove with a pan hanging on a peg above it. A basin sat beneath the window, where Ed kept his razor and a bar of soap.

This wasn't just Ed's workshop. This was his home.

Warmth spread through her. A warmth that had gone missing when she'd talked to Isaac. All those years, she'd been wrong. It wasn't Isaac she wanted.

All of it rushed forward inside her. The kiss. Ed protecting her.

She stepped into the room.

The sanding stopped as Ed straightened. When he finally met her gaze, his face wore a resigned expression.

And a bout of shyness hit her.

Was Rebekah about to let him down?

Ed watched her warily as she stood just inside the cabin. He'd seen the eagerness, the way she'd looked at Isaac when they'd pulled up in the wagon.

Ed had been prepared to spill it all. Because that kiss had made him hope.

Why hadn't she said anything yet? Her eyes darted to him and away as invisible tension stretched between them.

She moved to his worktable, not far from where he'd been sanding, and gently touched some of the unfinished pieces there.

It wasn't like Rebekah to hold back. He steeled himself for what she would say.

"I've been wanting to see your cabin since it was built."

He got distracted for a moment by the strands of hair that had come loose to tumble around her face and shoulders. Her words registered as her head turned.

"It's nice."

Her skirt swirled through the sawdust as she moved to his bench of tools, leaving a pattern across the floor. He was conscious of the mess, wishing he'd swept up. But she didn't seem to mind it. Her fingers ran over some of the chisels he used. She sent an admiring but quizzical look to him.

What had happened back there? Had Isaac had a change of heart? Ed couldn't seem to find his voice, too afraid to ask.

"You don't mind if I move these tools to look at them, do you?" Rebekah pointed to a pile of clamps.

"You can't hurt anything. Watch out for the blades." He stepped over to lean past her, moving them away from her delicate fingers. Just as quickly, he shifted back to settle himself back on his stool.

"What do you use this for?" She held up a chisel.

"It has a lot of uses." He was so twisted up inside that he

didn't know how to tell her about a chisel and when to use it any more than he knew how to tell her the truth about the letters and his feelings for her. His glance skittered to his bed in the corner, hoping the letters' hiding spot underneath the cot offered enough concealment. He'd stuffed all the ones she'd written there after his confrontation with Isaac.

Rebekah seemed oblivious to the tension vibrating through him. There was only a gentle curiosity in her voice when she asked, "How do you have time to work on pieces like this with all the ranch work?"

She walked to the other side of the cabin and pointed to the chair he'd been working on in hopes of getting the other job at the bakery.

"Your work is beautiful," she said softly. "The craftsmanship of that cradle was impeccable."

The admiration in her voice confused him. Maybe that was why he blurted, "I've sold more pieces since then. Would have sold even more if I could finish them faster."

"Would you ever open a shop in town?" Her eyes met his.

"I have responsibilities here." The words hurt to say.

Her expression softened, and he couldn't quite look away.

He tracked her movements as she crossed the floor to where he sat.

"You can put yourself first every now and again." Her voice was quiet and serious. "Wouldn't Drew understand if you asked for time?"

He'd never talked to Drew about his work. He'd just always done whatever his brothers asked.

He didn't have an answer for her, but she didn't seem to require one.

And he clearly wasn't getting any more work done tonight.

He double-checked the latch on the box of sharp tools. His eyes lifted to find Rebekah staring at his hands. She was close. His heartbeat pulsed in his ears.

"Why do you double-check everything?"

"What?" He blurted his surprise at the question.

"I've seen you do it before."

If he'd heard anything but gentle curiosity in her voice, he wouldn't have answered. He didn't want to be a story. But whatever was still between them, he wanted her to know.

"When I was a boy, Pa took Drew and Isaac with him for a chore. Funny, I don't remember what." He shook his head. "Nick was sick, so I had to stay home with Ma and Nick. They fell asleep. That's when I decided to go to the barn and look after the chores. In my head, everyone was going to be so proud of me. Ed the wonder boy. Taking care of the chores."

She moved closer to where he stood, reaching out to touch his hand. The warmth of her spread through him, urging him on. "What happened?"

"I forgot to close the stall door. The horses got out. I figured Pa'd be furious—they were part of our livelihood." He turned his eyes to her face. "I went after them."

"You caught them?" Her eyes widened. She was looking at him with a kind of hero worship he'd seen her direct at Isaac before.

His stomach twisted. But he forced the words out anyway, knowing he was about to erase that look from her face.

"I got lost." He fiddled with the sandpaper when it was too hard to look at her. "I was out in the woods all night. Isaac found me. Said he was tired of having to babysit me."

For a moment, Ed got lost in the memory. Felt the same mix of terror and relief he'd known back then. The same anger at himself, that he couldn't be better than Isaac.

"Anyone can get lost." Rebekah's words jolted him out of the memory.

He stared at her hand clasping his. His heart was pounding in his ears again. He didn't know what to think about this gesture of comfort. "If I'd double-checked the latch, I'd have been the hero for once."

"Not every hero walks around with a six-shooter on his hips. What about Joshua walking around Jericho? Wasn't he a hero when the walls fell?" Leave it to Rebekah to try to bolster him.

He cocked an eyebrow. "Right before they went in to fight?"

She gave him one of her looks, but with a hint of a grin. Now that she'd mentioned it, he'd heard of plenty of men who were known as heroes without a six-shooter on their hip, as she'd put it. Missionaries, preachers, statesmen. All because they'd done their best with what God had given them. They were worthy of being seen. Maybe he was too.

"Today, you were the hero. At least to me." She was looking at him like it was true.

His hope grew with her praise. He wanted nothing more

than to repeat the kiss he'd given her before. But first, he had to tell her.

The words were on his lips—

"Uncle Ed!" A shout accompanied Tillie and Jo spilling into the cabin. Instantly, he released Rebekah's hand and took a step back.

"Rebekah!" The delighted squeal came as the girls made a beeline for Rebekah.

"What have I told you about being careful in here?" He ruffled Jo's hair as she walked past him.

She ignored him. "I didn't know you were here, Miss Rebekah."

Both girls circled around Rebekah. Ed still wanted to talk.

"Don't you have chores?" he asked.

Jo rolled her eyes. "It's almost supper." Her face lit up. "Are you staying, Miss Rebekah?"

Tillie looked up from where she'd bent to draw something in the sawdust on the floor. "Oh, please say you're stayin.'"

"She's staying," Ed said quickly. Rebekah hadn't seemed so sure in the marshal's office, and he didn't want her getting any ideas about going back to the Boutwells' place.

Over the girls' heads, Rebekah held his gaze for a moment that stretched long. "I do need a place to stay. Your uncle protected me today when someone started shooting in town."

"He did?"

"Someone was shootin' at you?"

"Uncle Ed?"

"Why'd they shoot?"

The girls' exclamations tumbled over each other. They stared at Rebekah and Ed expectantly.

"Why don't you tell them?" Rebekah suggested.

He had to clear his throat. "I don't want to talk about it." He didn't want to remember the terror that had crashed into him when he'd thought he might not be fast enough, strong enough.

Rebekah's gaze softened as if she'd read his thoughts. He wouldn't mind it if she always looked at him like that.

And then Tillie tugged on her skirt, demanding, "What happened?"

The story spilled out of her, details he hadn't considered, like their reflections in the store windows as they'd darted past, the way the wind had ruffled their hair as they'd run through the alleys, even the scents behind each store. She even remembered the place they'd paused to take a breath. How close the side of the building had felt against her back as they'd paused in that alleyway.

"... and your Uncle Ed kept putting himself between me and those bullets flying at us."

The way she was looking at him . . . like he was Isaac.

You don't need to be Isaac. Be yourself. You're deserving of love.

Kaitlyn's words from weeks ago replayed in his mind.

"Pa doesn't have any stories like that." Jo scowled.

"Yes, he does." Tillie elbowed her sister, who shot her a glare. "Remember when—"

The girls began arguing even as Rebekah smiled at him faintly.

Luckily, the dinner bell rang out.

Jo and Tillie scrambled for the door.

He rubbed the back of his neck, all of it descending on him at once. He wanted Rebekah in his life. Wanted a family with her.

He was going to have to tell her everything.

"I need to talk to you."

But before he could say anything else, Tillie rushed back inside and grabbed Rebekah's hand. "C'mon! We gotta tell the others about Uncle Ed."

Rebekah sent an apologetic look over her shoulder. And then she was gone.

Fourteen

THE NEXT MORNING, FOR THE FIRST time in a long time, Ed overslept.

He was walking toward the main house, still stuffing the tail of his shirt into his trousers. No need to rush down. There'd be no breakfast waiting.

But he'd get to see Rebekah.

The whole family had stayed up talking after the kids had gone to bed. Everyone but Isaac. Ed couldn't deny the relief he'd felt that his brother hadn't come in for supper.

He'd sat at Rebekah's side as she'd retold the story of what'd happened in town for Kaitlyn and his brothers after the meal. Then Kaitlyn and Drew had rehearsed Quade's involvement in Kaitlyn's troubles. Nick and Drew had gone back and forth conjecturing about why Quade might be targeting the candidates. Other than the obvious.

Ed had stuck around far too late, hoping for a chance to talk to Rebekah about those letters. Which hadn't happened. But he'd enjoyed every minute spent near her. He'd have to find a time today. Maybe he'd ask Kaitlyn to help him find a moment alone with Rebekah.

He'd spied Isaac and Nick already riding out while David disappeared into the barn. Probably starting on the chores Ed hadn't been there to do.

The front door swung open as he reached for the latch.

Drew stepped into the morning light, not even flinching at their near collision. "You're late. See you at the barn."

Ed let his shoulders sink as he trudged to the table for whatever cold food he could scrounge up. He scrubbed a hand over his face only to find Rebekah setting a steaming plate at the place where he always sat at the table.

"I fought off the horde to save you a decent plate of hot food." A warm smile lit her face.

"You didn't have to."

"I know."

What did that mean? She'd wanted to?

He swallowed hard as he pulled out the chair and seated himself. He grabbed up the coffee mug in front of him. When he took a swig, he realized it was actually hot.

Rebekah didn't move from her spot. She was studying him.

"I should cook for myself." He shoveled in a bite. It wasn't the first time he'd had the thought. But maybe the first time he'd said it aloud. "There's rarely much left by the time I get here."

"You deserve more than the scraps, Ed McGraw."

He didn't quite know what to say to that. Only knew how it made him feel—like he could fly.

He was aware of Kaitlyn bustling around in the kitchen, only a step away, or he might've blurted out his feelings for Rebekah then and there.

"Did you sleep well?" He dug his fork into a steaming slice of ham.

Rebekah flitted a glance to where Tillie played in the other room, then shifted her gaze back to him as she settled into a chair kitty-corner to him. "I woke up several times." Her eyes dropped to her hands. "Even had a nightmare."

Her voice, so low and sheepish, tugged at him in a new way. "You'll be safe here."

"I know you'll protect me, Ed."

She was pensive, troubled. Her brow was drawn.

"Do you regret having written the article about the bandit?"

"Of course not. I won't let someone intimidate me into hiding the truth." Her tone held fiery determination even as she fiddled with the edge of the table.

"That's what I thought you'd say." He grinned, letting the smirk linger as he noted the smear of flour across her cheek.

She cocked an eyebrow. "What?"

"You have a . . . a . . ." Ed swiped at his cheek.

Rebekah rubbed the back of her hand across her cheek, but missed it. He leaned across the table, running his thumb across the lower part of her jaw.

"There." His eyes collided with hers. He didn't dare linger too close for long.

The moment was broken when Kaitlyn scurried in from the kitchen, then stopped short. "Is that all the dishes? Ed, I didn't know you were here."

"Almost finished." He shoved in another bite.

Tillie called out for her mother to help her with a word in a book. The front door creaked open. Ed noticed Drew pop his head and shoulders inside, though he couldn't make himself look away from Rebekah.

"Ed? You ready?"

Ed stood halfway out of his chair, swigged the last sip of coffee.

"I'll take care of your dishes." Rebekah's fingers closed over his as he gave her the cup. Sparks flickered up and down his arm.

"Thanks," he coughed out.

He headed for the door.

"I'll be sure to save you a plate for lunch," she called out.

He couldn't help looking over his shoulder, catching Kaitlyn's raised eyebrows and Rebekah's blush as she ducked into the kitchen.

Hope buzzed in his chest as he emerged onto the porch.

Drew was waiting nearby with both horses saddled and ready to ride out. He was staring at the new well. Drew looked up as Ed joined him.

"This is fine craftsmanship. Especially for a well covering." Drew eyed him as he tapped the top of the well.

Ed didn't want to discuss the well. He wanted to saddle up to ride out. Riding meant fresh air and plenty of time to think. Besides, the sooner they left, the sooner they'd get back. Back to Rebekah and her smiles.

"I couldn't just throw together a haphazard cover."

"No, you couldn't." Drew handed him the reins to Lightning, then swung into his own saddle. "But your older brother was trying to offer a compliment."

All Rebekah's words about his carpentry work flooded back to Ed's mind as he placed his foot in the stirrup and pushed up to land in the saddle. Her words rolled over with the image of her placing that steaming hot plate of food at his spot this morning. He tugged slightly on the reins to signal Lightning to follow Drew.

"I would like more time to work on my carpentry." There. He'd said it. Not so graceful as Rebekah would have wanted, but it was out.

"Haven't you already been working on stuff?" Drew asked absently. His gaze was on the field ahead. "A . . . bookshelf?"

"A cradle." Ed's words emerged sharp. "And then a display case for the new bakery."

Maybe it wasn't Drew's fault he didn't know what Ed was working on. He was busy with his family, his new wife.

"It's not enough," Ed said, voice more even this time.

Drew was slow to answer. "There's not much spare time around here."

"The ranch will always be a part of me. But I want more."

Drew frowned, but Ed rushed on. "Just think about the money I could bring in. For the family."

Drew eyed him. "I didn't know this meant so much to you. Why didn't you say something?"

Ed was still at war with that sense of duty. He didn't know how to explain it. He shifted the reins from one hand to the other as he wiped his sweating palms on his jeans. "I've felt selfish for wanting to ask time away from the chores. But now I'm asking."

With a half chuckle, half huff, Drew continued scanning the field as if watching for the herd. "All the work you do around here? You're about the least selfish person I know."

But that was the problem. His brother didn't know all of it. Didn't know how selfish Ed felt at the moment, wanting Rebekah for himself when they'd all set out to unknowingly pitch her together with Isaac through that crazy mail-order-bride plan.

"You wanting to leave the home place altogether?" Drew's focus landed on Ed now with scrutiny.

"We've all worked too hard to keep the homestead going for me to just up and leave. I can use the money I earn to help the family," he repeated.

Drew considered for a long moment. "Maybe you should keep your earnings. It's time for you to have something for yourself."

Could it really be so easy?

Drew's gaze cut to Ed. "Especially since you and Rebekah seem to be getting close."

"What?" He flushed. All of a sudden, he felt as if his collar was choking him. "Did Kaitlyn tell you?"

"You think someone had to tell me you were sweet on Rebekah?"

Drew had noticed?

"She's nice. A little independent, but she's sure got eyes for you."

Ed's heart pulsed at his brother's words.

"Why don't you make things official? Ask her to come courting."

"There are complications." Ed pushed Lightning faster, outpacing Drew's horse.

"You mean like the bruise on your cheek we've all been trying not to notice?" Drew came even with Ed again.

Ed felt a phantom blow where Isaac had hit him. "That, and more." He blew out a blustery breath. "She's always wanted Isaac."

"That's not what I saw last night," Drew said. "Since you were little, you've always tried to compete with Isaac. Have you tried being Ed?"

"What's that supposed to mean?"

"Be the steady beau who's always there. A shoulder to cry on,"

Ed snorted and Drew grinned at him. They both knew Rebekah wasn't some fainting lady from a dime novel.

Ed hesitated, then blurted, "And if that's not good enough?"

Rebekah had pined for Isaac for a long time. Did feelings like that just go away?

"Best advice I've got." Drew flicked the reins to speed up his horse, then called over his shoulder. "Strays up ahead."

Ed gave Lightning his head.

Rebekah had been waiting for him this morning. It meant something. Drew thought so too.

He knew what he needed to do. He just needed time to do it.

Later in the afternoon, Rebekah helped Kaitlyn prepare supper in the kitchen.

"Me 'n' Isaac. We brung celery and carrots." Tillie made the announcement as she dumped the carrots onto the counter. "I even washed them. He told me to bring them inside."

That sounded right. She'd seen Isaac in passing earlier this morning. He'd been headed to the barn and had clearly been surprised to see her. For once, she'd been able to read his expression.

And then he'd hightailed it to the barn without even a hello.

Thus, it wasn't a surprise that he hadn't come inside, not when he knew she was here.

"Brought." Rebekah corrected Tillie in unison with Kaitlyn. Rebekah fumbled through the drawers, finally finding a knife and chopping the vegetables.

Kaitlyn added spices to the pot of venison while Tillie skipped around the kitchen. The girl narrowly missed bumping Rebekah's elbow, which could've sent the knife she held slicing into the fingers of her other hand.

"Can you take these to Kaitlyn?" Rebekah handed Tillie a bowl of chopped carrots.

Rebekah let her eyes wander out the window. No sign of Ed. How like the day she stood by the window, waiting to see if Isaac would be the one to drive her aunt and uncle to town. Only this time, she was hoping to see Ed. Her feelings had changed so much in the course of a few short weeks.

A humming, spinning Tillie bumped into her. The knife

clunked to the countertop. Both of them daydreaming seemed a recipe for disaster.

"Can I help?" Tillie asked.

"Not right now." Rebekah skirted around her with the celery. She needed to focus.

"I can do it." Tillie hurried to place her hands under the bowl, walking with Rebekah as if carrying it herself. "Let me pour it."

"You might pour the pieces in too fast. I'll do it." Rebekah was aware of Kaitlyn watching from the stove. Tillie had Rebekah ready to snap with her constant chatter. How did her friend manage?

A pout spread on Tillie's face but faded as Kaitlyn offered to let her stir. The quick motion of Tillie's stirring splashed a bit of stew onto Rebekah's apron.

"Tillie, be careful."

Kaitlyn placed a hand on Tillie's shoulder, then bent to whisper in her ear. Tillie grinned and skipped into the front room before Kaitlyn turned to focus on Rebekah.

"She's only a little girl. She won't be doing everything exactly like you do."

"I want it done right." She probably deserved Kaitlyn's reprimand, but Rebekah's hand trembled as she stirred the stew. Her own distraction had caused her to lose her temper.

"Seems you want it done to suit you." Kaitlyn's brow quirked up even as kindness filled her eyes. "But you can't control everything. You'll end up miserable and it won't work. You need to give God control of your life."

Rebekah kept stirring. Was Kaitlyn right? That last letter

Rebekah had sent with the proposal to Isaac had only made things worse.

"I guess I've been trying to arrange things to suit myself for so long that it's hard not to." She watched the vegetables bob and swirl in the stew as she stirred. "It's how I got here. Writing a letter to Aunt Opal to come get me. My mother didn't know until Opal arrived to take me out west."

"Why did you want to go west?" Kaitlyn asked.

"Things were hard after my father died." Rebekah dropped her voice low, aware of Tillie's listening ears nearby. She hadn't talked about this in a long time. Hadn't thought about it either.

"My mother met someone. But I just wanted my father back."

A gentle hand landed on her arm. It helped soothe the emotions that threatened to choke Rebekah. Mama had had stars in her eyes from the first moment she'd met Claud Browning.

The face of her mother, worn and weary with trying to run things, flashed before her. Rebekah had wanted her mother happy. Wanted to see her smiling again. But not with Claud, the man who'd become her stepfather.

Kaitlyn listened, seeming to understand that Rebekah wouldn't be able to go on if she was interrupted.

"My stepfather didn't want me around. Wanted to send me to boarding school. And Mama didn't want to anger her new husband. So I fixed it. I wrote a letter to Aunt Opal. And I came here." Rebekah remembered those first days in Calvin. Missing her father and mother so much that it made her ache inside. She hadn't been sure she'd made the right choice. Not until later. Now, she loved the wide-open spaces of Wyoming and her home with the Boutwells—even if Rebekah hadn't seen her mother since, and even though they only corresponded by letter occasionally.

Kaitlyn touched Rebekah's shoulder. "I'm glad you did."

Rebekah lifted her eyes to the window again. She'd frozen in fear when the shooting had started yesterday. If Ed hadn't protected her, she might be dead. A shiver ran through her.

"Hoping to see Isaac?" Kaitlyn interrupted Rebekah's thoughts. "Or Ed?"

A flush of heat blasted her face. She hadn't meant for Kaitlyn to catch on.

"Ed couldn't keep his eyes off you last night."

Rebekah concentrated on wiping off the counters. It was easier than meeting Kaitlyn's knowing gaze.

"I know we once talked about you running an ad for yourself. Or answering one. What did you ever decide?"

This wasn't going away. She placed the washrag in the sink, then faced her friend. "I was writing letters to Isaac, in response to his ad."

Kaitlyn waited. If this news had surprised her, she certainly didn't show it. Had Ed told her? Or Isaac?

Embarrassment flared, but with Aunt Opal gone for the foreseeable future, Rebekah didn't have another woman to talk to. Maybe Kaitlyn could give her advice to help her out of this muddle.

She told Kaitlyn all of it. Answering Isaac's ad. Holding back the letters. Mr. Sullivan's anger.

"Now I don't know what to do." The words from her proposal letter to Isaac flashed through her mind.

I would like to define our relationship. I need to know if you truly feel as I do.

Isaac hadn't even wanted to talk to her. And Ed was there, with his steady warmth.

"For so long, I thought I hated Ed," she murmured. "But spending time with him . . . he's not who I thought."

Now everything was a muddle.

"I always thought I wanted a hero like my father wrote in his books." Rebekah looked straight at Kaitlyn. "Like what you've got with Drew."

Kaitlyn's eyes danced as she covered her mouth with one hand. "Drew isn't perfect. Is that what you heard when we talked? Oh, Rebekah, things were difficult when I came. Surely you remember all that happened? It wasn't easy. When I arrived, I had to convince Drew to let me stay. As a business arrangement." Kaitlyn's eyes peered into Rebekah's as she slid her hands down to hold her friend's hands. "We had to get to know each other. We had to make a choice to love."

Had Rebekah let her imagination run away with her in this too? Drew and Kaitlyn always appeared so perfect. Rebekah's pulse thudded in her ears. Were those roses without thorns existing only in her mind? All running through the filter of her books?

"But the love you read about in books is so, so—" Rebekah released her grip on Kaitlyn's hands to wring her own in the air. Why didn't she have the right word? She always prided herself on having the right word.

"Real love is a choice." Kaitlyn searched Rebekah's face as she spoke. Her words were gentle.

Rebekah had been in love with the idea of Isaac. The hero. Yet Ed had acted the hero on the boardwalk in town, shielding her from the shooter. But hadn't it also been heroic when he'd patiently explained his tool to Tillie? Helped David with his chores? Set aside his dreams for the sake of his family?

The knowledge sank into her, settling deep.

Fifteen

OURS LATER, REBEKAH CARRIED A stack of bowls to the table as Kaitlyn settled the pot of stew on a hot pad in the middle. Tillie darted around her to place spoons at each chair.

"Where are you going to sit?" Tillie glanced up at Rebekah from the other side of the table.

"We need to wait and see," Rebekah hedged.

Isaac had come inside with the other McGraw brothers, and everything she hadn't said to him was right there. He stood in the parlor, speaking in low tones with Drew and Nick, while Ed had come to her by the dining table. Until David had distracted Ed with a hand-drawn map laid out on a corner of the table.

"Everyone come and sit down," Kaitlyn called from the kitchen. A pot rattled.

Ed's eyes met Rebekah's as Isaac strode toward the dining table. Ed moved to stand beside her, one hand coming to rest on her lower back. From the corner of her eye, she saw the way his chin jutted out. In Isaac's direction.

Heat flamed Rebekah's cheeks.

There was a shuffle as the kids scrambled for the table.

Ed pushed in Rebekah's chair before taking his own next to her. Somehow, Isaac landed in the chair on her other side.

Rebekah caught the twitch in Isaac's cheek as he glanced past her at Ed, then back to the bowl in front of him. She shifted in her chair. Could things be any more awkward?

"Let's bow our heads," Drew said.

"Hold hands," Tillie instructed Rebekah enthusiastically.

Rebekah felt a moment of rising panic as everyone else bowed their heads.

Isaac's rough hand hesitated before gripping her left hand as Ed's fingers hovered close to her right. With a quick motion, she threaded her fingers between Ed's. A jolt of warmth and comfort flooded her at his touch. There'd been no feeling from Isaac's grip, only a knotting in her stomach of what she had to tell him.

"Dear Lord, we thank you . . ." Drew began the blessing in his matter-of-fact manner.

How had she found herself seated next to the man she no longer wanted after all those letters?

". . . and bless the hands that prepared it . . ."

And on the other side, the man she'd once despised, the one she'd once tried to avoid at every chance but now wanted to lean into. Her emotions tumbled wildly.

Her heartbeat drummed so loud in her ears that she almost didn't hear Drew's "Amen."

Isaac released her hand in one quick motion, jaw twitching. Ed let his hand stay linked with hers until he was forced to reach for a bowl that was passed his direction.

"Uncle Isaac. Did you catch the wolves yet?" Tillie blurted her question.

"Another scoop?" Kaitlyn's query didn't distract Isaac.

Who looked like he would rather do anything other than answer. He wouldn't be catching the wolves. He'd be getting rid of them.

"Not yet." Isaac took the bowl from Drew to set it in front of him. "Wolves are good at hiding."

"Did you know I taught Patch a new trick?" Tillie must have saved a hundred questions for her uncle while he'd been off hunting wolves or whatever he did up at that cabin.

Rebekah thanked Kaitlyn as she handed her a bowl of stew amidst all the giggles and voices around the table.

"I stopped off at your uncle's place today," Ed said, his head tipped closer and his words just for her. "Everything's fine."

She'd been trying not to think about what'd happened in town, how she didn't want to go home. How she was letting down Uncle Vess by not taking care of things at the house herself.

"You okay?"

"Not really." In fact, Tillie was a welcome distraction.

When she looked across the table, Kaitlyn caught her eye, brows raised.

Nick engaged Ed from his other side, something about a new water trough for the corral. Her arm brushed Ed's as she lifted her spoon. She caught his warm gaze.

She took in all the sights, all the whispers between the children's bent heads. A big family around a table. This was what her heart had wanted all along.

"I'm the better speller between us, anyway." David's response to Jo's last whisper boomed out. "Boys always are."

The whispering stopped as Jo raised her head. She stared straight at Rebekah. "Didn't you beat Isaac at a spelling bee back in school? Uncle Nick said so."

Rebekah's face heated as silence fell over the table, all eyes on her. She felt Ed still at her side, the spoon frozen above his bowl.

"Rebekah used to beat everybody." Isaac waved a hand in dismissal.

Ed shifted in his chair. "I was there when she won the award for the best poem. Beat out the entire school."

Isaac let his spoon clank in his bowl, turning in Ed's direction. "I was there when the teacher asked her to stand and read Shakespeare because she did the best dramatic reading. No one else read aloud that day."

Drew and Nick shared a glance, then shifted their attention back to where she sat between Isaac and Ed. Ed had leaned over to send Isaac a side-eye. Rebekah squirmed a little in her chair, not sure how to deflect the attention of the table from her.

"Well, I remember when she beat everyone at marbles." Ed moved forward, glaring at Isaac. "Or what about when she tagged you in that game of blindman's bluff?"

"Speaking of school days," Rebekah interrupted, "I remember when Ed won the horseshoe contest at the Fourth of July picnic."

Ed blinked in surprise. Rebekah was aware of the entire table watching her watch him.

Isaac cleared his throat. "I think he still has the ribbon."

The moment was broken, and murmurs of conversation started up again.

She tried to keep her focus on her food but felt Ed shifting in the chair next to her. Under the table, the soft pressure of his boot pressed against hers from the side.

The basket of biscuits made its way to Isaac. He reached in to grab the next to last one. Ed had his hand out for the basket, but turned to Nick to answer a question. In a quick motion, Rebekah reached for the last biscuit. Everyone else was distracted, and Rebekah slid the biscuit, still warm in her hand, onto the edge of Ed's plate.

"Pass that basket this way." Kaitlyn called from the other end, and Isaac handed it off without looking inside.

Ed's shoulders slumped until he turned to his plate. His eyes darted up to hers, questioning. A blush flooded her face as he mouthed a thank-you that sent a warm, pleasing sensation through her.

"How long is Rebekah staying?" Tillie pushed the chunks of venison around her bowl.

"As long as she needs," Ed piped up from beside her, answering before she had a chance. His expression reminded her of their confrontation about the interviews. All the protectiveness of Ed rolled over her as he leaned out to focus on Isaac. "How long could it take to track down a single outlaw?"

Isaac stirred his stew around, refusing to meet Ed's stare.

"Not sure I'm the one to ask." His spoon scraped against the side of his bowl, a disjointed sound.

Something in his answer unnerved her. This wasn't the man she'd known, even from afar, all those years ago. And yet she sensed it had nothing to do with her or her letters.

Ed focused on her as if no one else were there. "When do you plan to get back to the paper? We'll plan for a way to get you there safely."

Warmth filled in the cold cracks of her heart at the thought of going back to town. Ed hadn't asked her to give up working at the paper. He knew how much it meant to her.

Conversation had dwindled and Drew stood. Ed pushed away from the table. When Drew called to him, he offered a quick "I'll be back" and followed his older brother out the front door.

"We'll go draw you some water for the dishes." Nick nodded to Kaitlyn as Isaac grabbed the wash buckets and followed Nick outside.

Rebekah and Jo cleared the table, then Rebekah helped Kaitlyn wash up the dishes. As Kaitlyn finished putting away the last of the bowls, Rebekah took the dishrag out to wipe off the dining table. Isaac sat in a chair at the end, watching the children on the other side of the room.

When Tillie summoned him with a wave, he shook his head.

He rose to move as he saw her approach.

"I need to talk to you." Her fingers trembled in time with her insides as she pushed the rag over the table. This was her chance to set things straight.

He shifted. Uncomfortable?

Boots shuffled on the front porch. She'd best speak quick before they were interrupted again.

"You never answered my last letter." She rushed on without waiting on him to answer. "I think I was . . . letting my imagination get the better of me. Although you wrote me those beautiful letters, in person there's no spark between us."

Meeting his gaze was difficult, but she forced herself to do it. It was the first time he'd really looked at her since she'd arrived at the ranch.

The front door opened, and she was aware that the time for this conversation was over.

"I've never been one to put stock in writing letters."

She smoothed her apron with shaking hands. No stock in writing letters? She'd expected more than that. Disappointment surged. He had written such lovely sentiments. Did he feel nothing for her now? Was it so easy for him to accept she didn't want him? It was better that he wasn't making things difficult, but somehow, things still felt unfinished.

Drew's and Ed's voices filtered into the front room as they entered. Rebekah lifted her eyes. Ed's watchful gaze caught hers. What had been a smile on his face faded to a frown. Just then, Kaitlyn called Rebekah back into the kitchen.

Was something wrong?

"Uncle Ed, come with us. Please." Tillie held up an empty

jar that Kaitlyn used for canning. Rebekah stood just behind her. "We're going to catch fireflies."

"I don't know, Tillie girl," he hedged. He cut his eyes away, unable to keep away a flash of memory of Rebekah and Isaac in a serious conversation, only a few minutes ago.

Part of him wanted to confront Isaac, who'd already slipped away from the family gathering.

Tillie's plea gave him the perfect opportunity to escape outside and talk to Rebekah. But Rebekah's smile slipped the longer he hesitated.

Nick coughed to cover a grin, keeping his head low as Ed stood to join Rebekah and the children. Ed combed a hand through his hair, trying to shake off the awkwardness.

"If you don't need my input for a bit, I'll get some fresh air," he said to Drew, who nodded.

His desire to talk to Rebekah must be more obvious than he liked to think. At least the children had been making enough fuss. Maybe Rebekah hadn't caught all the glances exchanged by his brothers.

He stepped forward to hold the door open, thankful no one knew how his stomach flipped at the words he rehearsed in his head to tell Rebekah.

Tillie yelped as the children tumbled outside and off the porch, scattering in their pursuit of the glowing bugs. He hung back near the house, close to Rebekah. A million stars shone in the night sky, competing with the lightning bugs for attention.

"I've got one!" David let out the first holler from the other side of the house, and the girls rushed around to see.

Rebekah started down the steps of the porch with Ed,

the edge of her skirt gently brushing against his legs in the light breeze. "The children seem to have fully recovered from the poisoning."

Ed sidled away, putting a foot of empty air between them. "I'm grateful for all you did that day."

Rebekah didn't comment, keeping in step with him as they slowly walked beside each other. Not far away, the children's shapes were shadows in the darkness.

She tilted her head to face him. "Can we talk?"

"I need to tell you—" His words had come tumbling out at the same time as hers.

Her nervous laugh wrapped around him. David's shout rose and the girls' laughter rang out as he caught them running by the clothesline.

"I saw you talking to Isaac." He hadn't meant to say that. He was supposed to confess about the letters. Saying the words aloud brought a beat of the old pain. Isaac was always between them.

Rebekah tipped her head to look at the stars. "There was something I needed to settle with him."

He couldn't decipher her quiet tone.

Had Isaac seen the light? Realized how amazing Rebekah was?

"Did you get the matter settled?" He choked the words out.

Before she could answer, the children's figures drew closer in the deepening dark, running in a breathless clamor from the clothesline toward Ed and Rebekah.

"We caught five already." Jo held up the jar.

"Excellent work." Rebekah caught his eyes over Jo's head.

She wore a serious expression until one corner of her mouth kicked up in a partial smile.

One that made Ed's heart thud with hope.

"I see more by the tree. Over there." Tillie squealed and pointed, then huffed to catch up with Jo and David.

If Rebekah still wanted Isaac, Ed's heart would be broken. But wasn't it better to know?

Who knew how long before the kids would interrupt again?

He drew in a breath, praying for the right words. "There's something you should know about those letters Isaac sent you."

"Have *you* ever thought of getting married?" Rebekah asked quickly.

Ed blinked. *What?*

She stepped closer, her eyes on his face. Curious and serious and . . . "Kaitlyn told me—"

"Miss Rebekah, you have to come see!"

The chorus of voices made him want to howl.

Rebekah sent him a chagrined smile and traipsed in the direction the kids had called from. He followed.

Kaitlyn had told her what? About his feelings? About the letters? The questions chased around his brain as Tillie and Jo swarmed them in their impatience to reveal the surprise.

"It's a frog." Jo opened her hand. The frog jumped away as Tillie screamed in delight. Both girls ran after it.

"I caught another one." David's call came from near the porch, causing Jo and Tillie to leave the frog and run in his direction.

Ed saw his chance.

"Why don't we walk out by the barn? We can still keep an eye on them from there." He'd never get the words out this way.

She nodded, then looped her arm in his, her warmth so close, creating goosebumps on his skin despite the mild night. They outpaced the children, the voices becoming hushed. The darkness offered an intimacy that made his heart race.

As they stopped close to the corral, Ed looked over his shoulder to see the children still chasing fireflies near the house. Rebekah unwound her arm from his and leaned on the railing, giving him her profile. The night air filtered between them, making him suddenly cold.

"When you delivered that ad for Isaac, I tried to control everything. The letters, the ones I gave you the other day, they were from the other women. I . . . I hid them. I figured if he didn't get any other letters, things would have to go my way."

He heard the hint of shame in her voice.

"Rebekah, I—"

"Let me get this out."

Ed swallowed back the words he'd worked so hard to push forward.

"I thought I wanted Isaac, tried to bend the circumstances to suit me, but it turns out that I don't want to marry him after all." Her speech that had begun so strongly had fallen to a whisper. Her eyes held his gaze for a long moment, then dropped.

"You don't?"

She shook her head.

He reached out to touch her arm, letting his hand slide down to cup her elbow. If only he were more eloquent like she deserved. If he knew what she wanted him to say, he'd say it.

She rubbed a hand across one arm as if she were cold, trembling as she did. He stepped closer, close enough to kiss. Her head tilted. The look he'd wanted from her for so many years captivated him—if he wasn't mistaken in his interpretation. He hesitated, then slowly lifted his hand to cup her chin, tilting it further, closer.

Maybe we shouldn't have done that. The words from five days ago filtered through his mind.

"I don't want this to be a mistake," he murmured.

Rebekah leaned up toward him on tiptoe. The warmth of her breath kissed his chin right before her lips met his. So tender and soft. He wrapped her in his arms, pulling her closer as goosebumps prickled his neck. This beginning felt more right than his stolen kiss before. His heart raced all the quicker from their closeness.

Rebekah had kissed him. She didn't want Isaac.

He let himself linger in the glory of their kiss, then pulled away. He needed to tell her the truth. Words that might ruin everything.

He slid a finger across her cheek.

He had to clear his throat before he could speak. "Rebekah, I have to tell you something." His mind was spinning with joy. It was hard to think what to say. What if he messed everything up?

A rush of commotion descended on them.

"There you are." Jo careened to a halt, placing her hands on her hips, with Tillie close behind her.

The kids. He'd lost track of them.

Rebekah stepped away, smoothing out her skirt. What he'd give to pull her back to him . . .

"David put a May beetle and a frog on Tillie's head."

"Jo slugged me." David approached them in the dark, rubbing his forearm.

"Because of what you did to Tillie."

"Where is Tillie?" Rebekah put a hand on Jo's shoulder, moving away from Ed as she did. But he caught the warm glance she aimed his way.

"Here." A whimpering Tillie stepped out from somewhere behind Jo. She beelined for Ed, arms outstretched.

Tillie was almost too big to be carried anymore, but he reached out anyway. With her head on his shoulder, legs wrapped around him, Ed placed one hand around Tillie's waist to secure her. With the other, he rubbed David's head.

The moment with Rebekah was broken, the children serious. The jar of lightning bugs was nowhere in sight.

"Next time, stop after the bug."

David shrugged and grinned, reminding Ed of a much younger Drew. Rebekah shot Ed a bit of a glare over David's head for encouraging him, but her eyes sparkled. Ed reached out to tug a strand that had fallen loose from her bun, just like in school, earning him a wide-eyed look of stern reproach that only made him grin.

"Let's get you all to the house."

This time, there was no holding Rebekah's arm. Jo walked between them, complaining about her brother. Rebekah led the weary troop to the porch, then opened the door so that a rectangle of light fell on them.

Inside, she stopped to give Kaitlyn an explanation of the children's argument before turning back to Ed.

"How about a cup of coffee? Rebekah?" His hands went clammy as everyone gave him a questioning look. "We could . . . visit . . . a bit more."

In the lamplight, the shadows beneath her eyes showed her weariness, even as she settled a soft smile on him. She'd told him she hadn't slept.

The children made a ruckus behind them as Kaitlyn shooed them upstairs to get ready for bed.

"Time for me to head to the bunkhouse." Nick rose to grab his hat.

"It is late." Kaitlyn's gaze wandered between Ed and Rebekah.

"Never mind," he said quietly. "We can talk tomorrow."

"Talk?" Nick teased in passing.

"Goodnight, all." Ed bade Kaitlyn and Drew goodnight, still standing close to Rebekah. He never took his eyes off her. "See you in the morning."

"In the morning." She dipped her head, a shy smile beaming right at him.

Ed made his way to the door, casting a final glance over his shoulder. Rebekah looked back over at him as she followed Kaitlyn upstairs. His heart filled to bursting, but as he tromped outside, the jarring feeling returned—the very one he'd felt when he'd seen Rebekah and Isaac talking after supper.

She'd kissed him. But he still had to tell her the truth. He'd written those letters. What would she do then?

Sixteen

NOW THAT YOU'VE TALKED TO DREW about your carpentry, will you get to the bakery as soon as I'm settled with Mr. Sullivan at the newspaper office?" Rebekah paused by the boardwalk as Ed helped Tillie and Jo from the back of the wagon.

His hand rested on Tillie's shoulder protectively. He lifted his gaze to Rebekah. "Will you be all right for a bit on your own?"

"I'm sure I'll be fine once I'm inside the newspaper office. You will take the estimate by, won't you?"

She wanted nothing more than to see him succeed in this and had told him as much on the ride to town. If she only had the courage to tell him to go on without seeing her into the newspaper office, but the more she worked to still her hands from trembling, the more her knees shook. It'd all started the moment they'd driven past the edge of town where they'd walked off the boardwalk that day.

"I will." Ed rounded the wagon to stand near her, appreciation written all over his face in the most delightful way. "As soon as we get you settled." He scanned her, squinting as if he'd picked up on her anxiety. "And after I help Tillie and Jo pick out a gift at the general store for Isaac's birthday."

"And those candies for Ma." Tillie bounced on her heels, oblivious to the tension between the two adults.

"I don't know how some candy is going to help her stomach." Jo crossed her arms.

Ed flicked Jo's braid. "Don't grouch about it."

"She's still not totally recovered from the well incident?" Rebekah began the walk toward the newspaper office with her arm looped in Ed's, the girls close beside them. The tension in her shoulders eased as he crowded close to her, still scanning the street.

"Kaitlyn's stomach upset comes and goes . . ." His voice trailed off as he stilled in front of the cracked-open door of the newspaper office. "Mr. Sullivan here?"

Rebekah couldn't understand for a moment as he held his arm to block her entrance. "Not supposed to be. He should be soon though." She spied the splintering in the door, as if it had been forced open. "What—"

She looked past him. Her desk lay on its side, papers strewn everywhere.

Tillie and Jo had crowded in close, and Jo gasped while Tillie cried out.

"Don't look," Ed ordered.

Behind him, a knife protruded from the door, stuck in a newspaper article.

Ed turned to follow Rebekah's line of sight. He put his shoulders between her and the knife. "We need to get the marshal."

Rebekah gulped for air. How was this happening? Where was Mr. Sullivan? Tillie moved close, and Rebekah wrapped an arm around her, reaching her other one out to pull Jo close too.

Ed pushed the door open the rest of the way. The familiar bell never jangled. Instead, it lay broken on the floor. Ed bent to pick it up, scanning the ransacked office.

Everything was silent except for the sound of her harsh breathing in her ears.

"Whoever did this is gone."

"Uncle Ed?" The rise in Jo's voice held a mountain of nervous questions.

Tillie's eyes were huge in her face.

"Why would someone do this?" Her desk had been turned on its side, all the drawers opened and pillaged. Pencils lay scattered across the floor.

He reached to pull her back from the doorway. "I need to get you to the marshal's."

"Mr. Sullivan—" she started, but Ed interrupted.

"I don't think whoever did this cared about Sullivan."

She stood on her tiptoes to see the headline. Her head-line, from the Cheyenne paper. "Mysterious Tattoo Clue to Bandit."

She pressed her fingers to her forehead in an effort to stop the pounding. She'd written that story. And now someone had broken into the office, the wood by the handle marred where they'd busted the lock.

"Rebekah, come on," Ed said gently. "Let's go to the marshal."

The back door opened, and Mr. Sullivan stared across the expanse of mess.

"What happened?" he demanded.

"I don't know," she breathed.

"The door was ajar when we arrived," Ed added.

Mr. Sullivan's feet crunched in the glass strewn across the floor. He paused and bent to examine the press, lying on its side, smashed. Tears smarted Rebekah's eyes. They were supposed to go to print with a new issue tomorrow.

As Mr. Sullivan approached, he looked at the article still pinned to the door. "You wrote that article? While I was away? That's not what I hired you for."

The words felt like a blow. Ed's hand rested on her back.

Mr. Sullivan pivoted away from them, knocking his hat off with one hand and burrowing the other in his thinning hair. "My livelihood. Destroyed."

"The press can be repaired," Ed offered.

Mr. Sullivan glared at him, then turned his focus to Rebekah. "You've painted a target on the back of both of us," he spat.

"I—" She couldn't argue. Not when he was right. It seemed her article had brought the bandit and destruction right to Mr. Sullivan's door.

From where she stood, she saw the pulse pounding in Mr. Sullivan's throat. His shaking hand at his side.

"Are you afraid?" she asked.

"Of course I am," he shouted. "I promised him—"

Ed went still behind her.

"Promised who?" she asked.

For one moment, his eyes looked like a wild animal's. Trapped and terrorized. And then a mask slipped over his features. "The bank. I signed a promissory note. How will I repay the mortgage now?"

"The marshal—" Ed started.

"The marshal can't do anything," Mr. Sullivan growled.

"Is someone threatening you?" Rebekah pressed.

"Stay out of it." Mr. Sullivan's glare landed on her. "You're fired."

Rebekah froze.

"Get out."

Ed tugged her arm. In stunned silence, she let him pull her out onto the boardwalk.

Tillie was sobbing with loud gulps, probably from Mr. Sullivan's shouting. Rebekah froze. Even the glances from passersby on the street didn't touch her.

Mr. Sullivan had fired her.

With his arms wrapped around their shoulders—the girls on one side and Rebekah on the other—Ed led them down the street. He handed the girls into the wagon, then clasped Rebekah's hand. "We'll go see the marshal. Then figure out what to do."

His steady presence helped calm the storm inside her. For the second time, he was protecting her. Caring for her.

She wasn't alone.

Ed exited the marshal's office ahead of Rebekah, scanning the boardwalk for any signs of danger as he held the door. Only the usual shopkeepers and pedestrians were on the street, but he couldn't let his guard down.

He'd dropped Tillie and Jo off at his cousin Merritt's house earlier, and it was a relief to know they were safe.

"Thank you for coming with me." Rebekah had her arms wrapped around her middle. She looked lost, staring at the buildings across the street.

He wanted to punch Mr. Sullivan.

"Let's grab the girls," he said, reaching out to touch her arm. "I'll take you to the Boutwell place."

She seemed to shake herself out of her thoughts. "I just want to go home." The wind fluttered her skirts. "I mean . . . I want to go back to the ranch with you. But what about your shopping?"

"It'll wait."

Her lips firmed. "But your business with the bakery won't."

The estimate he'd worked up rustled from where he'd wedged it beneath a stone on the wagon seat. And then blew out of the wagon to land near Rebekah's feet. He moved, but not before she snatched it up. "Got it."

Her smile faded as her eyes fell to the page. He saw her freeze.

"I know this handwriting." Her whisper cut through him.

Rebekah was smart. Of course she would figure it out if given the chance.

The curls around her face bounced as she shook her head. "This can't be." The paper lowered, her eyes peered into his. Questions, disbelief, all of it on her face. "Ed, tell me this isn't true. This is the handwriting that was in every letter from Isaac."

He tried to push the words out. But they stuck behind his breastbone.

She stared at him, realization dawning. "You weren't surprised. When I told you I'd written him. I thought . . ."

It was as if she read the answer in his face. "Those weren't Isaac's letters at all. They were your letters." Her eyes fell to the estimate again, and more words rushed forth. "Were you—poking fun at me behind my back?"

"No! It wasn't like that." He swallowed hard. "You admitted you had a plan to win Isaac. Well, Drew and Kaitlyn masterminded the plan to find Isaac a wife. The ad."

She shook her head slightly. He pressed on.

"I didn't want any part of this. Not at first. But when I read your letters, everything changed. Writing to you—I started having feelings for Ree. Don't you see?"

She slapped the estimate against his chest. He brought his hand up to cup hers, but she jerked her hand away, and he was left holding the paper.

Her eyes lit with fire as she talked through gritted teeth. "I admitted everything to you, and *you* didn't say a word."

Everything in him spun, slowing his responses and muddling his brain. How could he make her understand?

"Rebekah, just listen—"

She spun away when he reached for her.

Her nostrils flared, eyes filling with tears. He was cut to the bone. Rebekah never cried.

"I suppose you were laughing when you read my . . . proposal to Isaac."

"Your what?" His head buzzed. His limbs froze.

She'd proposed to Isaac.

Because she'd always wanted Isaac. And Rebekah was never afraid to go after what she wanted.

"Is everything all right?"

He hadn't even heard the marshal come out of the jail. Her steely gaze took in everything.

Rebekah was silent.

Ed cleared his throat. "We were about to head home."

"I'm not going anywhere with you," Rebekah snapped.

The marshal looked between them. "I can see Rebekah settled at the boardinghouse. Set a patrol."

"Thank you." Rebekah held her chin high, not meeting Ed's gaze. She fell in beside Danna, already moving down the street.

"Wait—"

"I have nothing left to say to you." There was a finality to her words.

And then she was gone, and he was left to grasp the side of the wagon bed with both hands, unsteadiness leaching through his bones.

He'd tried to explain everything . . .

All he could see was a memory of the tears standing in Rebekah's eyes. *I have nothing left to say to you.*

He'd ruined everything by keeping secrets. But would it have mattered if she'd listened? She'd proposed to Isaac.

Always Isaac. Why couldn't Ed be good enough?

Seventeen

TWO DAYS AT THE BOARDINGHOUSE IN town had only served to fray Rebekah's nerves.

She finished pinning up her hair, then bent to lace up her boots. The marshal had insisted Rebekah stay in town. Insisted staying out at the Boutwell farm wasn't safe, was too far away from the nearest neighbor if the bandit came after her.

She'd barely slept, waking often from nightmares of that knife on the door. As Rebekah slipped down the steps, hoping to leave without notice, a board creaked beneath her feet.

Mrs. Thorton poked her head out of the kitchen. "Would you like any breakfast this morning? I'm about to clear the table."

The way Ed had beamed at Rebekah when she'd saved him a plate that morning at the McGraw homestead flashed across her mind. His surprised gratefulness had touched her. Made her want to save him a plate every day. But now? Thinking of it made her stomach hurt.

"Not this morning. Thank you." Rebekah hurried down the stairs and out the front door, ignoring the woman's tsk.

The smell of the dirt packed by rain settled in her nose as she started along the boardwalk to the newspaper office. These last few days, she'd half expected a note or a message sent from Ed.

She'd reacted badly. She could admit it now that the anger and humiliation had faded. If he asked, could she forgive him for his deception? She didn't know.

As she neared the office, Billy nodded at her from the other side of the street. What would he do if Mr. Sullivan followed through with his threat to shutter the paper?

Just ahead, Danna strode toward her. Rebekah slowed her steps. The marshal made a show of cutting her eyes in all directions.

"You out by yourself?" There was a slightly accusatory tone to Danna's voice.

Rebekah had been trying to tell herself not to be nervous, but the marshal's words reminded her that this wasn't over. "I'm on my way to see Mr. Sullivan about getting my job back." Surely he'd have repaired the press by now.

"Things are still dangerous." Marshal O'Grady nodded to a man passing by, then focused back on Rebekah. "I thought I was closing in on the bandit. We tracked him to a hideout near the county line, but he disappeared."

"I appreciate the warning," she said tightly. "I'm sure I'll be fine."

Danna couldn't expect her to stay sequestered indoors forever, could she?

"Be careful."

Rebekah tried not to let the marshal's concern worry her. But as she walked down the familiar streets that made up the town that had been her home for years, every shadow between the buildings was a threat.

A shout from the saloon turned her head. She faced the splintered door to the newspaper office, her body poised to run. She took a long breath, straightened her blouse, then let her fingers press against the door. It opened slowly. A shadow moved inside. It had to be Mr. Sullivan.

She let her eyes adjust to the light. He bent over his desk, riffling through papers, stuffing his personal belongings in a satchel.

Her gaze lingered over the mess. The desks were righted, but all the papers were cluttering the front in an odd array of haphazard stacks. Metal letters were strung out on the floor along with pieces of the broken-up stand for the printing press. Her job. Her dreams. All lay scattered in a hundred pieces across the floor.

"How can I help?" Her voice trembled with emotion.

"Go away. You're not supposed to be here." Mr. Sullivan spat out the words, not even stopping his mad rummaging through his desk.

She stood, jutting her chin. "I love this job, you know."

He gave a humorless laugh. "What job? There's no paper anymore. See this mess?"

"You can rebuild." Hadn't Ed said the press could be repaired?

Sullivan shook his head. He found the ledger in the drawer.

Desperation rose inside her. "You can't just give up."

He fixed her with a wild stare, making her glad for the desk between them.

"It's not safe," he rattled. "This—this was just a warning."

"Whose warning?"

He shook his head, moving around the desk, heading for the door.

"Quade?" She caught the truth in his eyes as he moved past her. "If he threatened you—"

"Remember Frank Jones? I can't go to the marshal. Even if I could repay the money, everything I've worked for is ruined." His expression wore both fear and resignation. "I'm leaving. Going to live with my daughter. Start over."

"You mean take the coward's way out."

"Watch yourself," he said sharply. "Words can get you into trouble."

The door slammed behind him. He was gone. Out the door and past the large window overlooking the board-walk. She stared after his retreating figure until she lost track of time.

But you can't control everything. You'll end up miserable, and it won't work.

Kaitlyn's words from weeks ago ran through her head.

Rebekah had tried, hadn't she? Written that article, chased leads. And look what had become of her job. The paper.

There had to be something here she could do.

Her foot rolled over a piece of metal on the floor as she

took a step forward. A letter she used for typesetting reflected the stream of sunlight from the window. She bent to grasp it from the dust, dropping it in her pocket. Then grabbed up a handful close to the other. They were scattered all over.

She held up her skirt in front of her to create a fold to place more letters in. Rebekah dropped to her knees in the dust and grime, running her hands along the floor in search of her beloved letters. Silent tears of exhaustion flowed as she scoured the wooden floorboards. Finally, she rocked back on her knees to swipe at her face. Holding up the fold in her skirt, she began sifting through the letters. There were so few compared to what she needed. She'd never be able to make the words with these.

She pushed up to place what few letters she'd salvaged in their tray, which lay on the desk close to the press. As she rose, the fabric of her skirt moved, allowing letters to spill out. They hit the floor with a clink.

Tired and spent, Rebekah gripped the edge of the desk. All her letters, her dreams, lay broken and scattered. Just like her relationship with Ed.

A loud bang from outside made her jump. She shouldn't stay here.

She needed to write to Aunt Opal and Uncle Vess to tell them all that had happened. Without the paper, her income was gone. She might have to go back east after all. Surely they'd insist on it. And to think of all she'd done to get here in the first place.

The ache in her heart ran so deep that her tears dried up. She stumbled forward to grasp the tray for what letters were left. In a desperate move, she splayed them in their tray. None of them organized, just heaped in the slots.

"I can't fix any of this."

She'd been believing a lie. She'd never really been in control of her life. But even if she had been, she certainly wasn't now.

Ed slammed the posthole auger into the dirt and twisted.

Only ten more posts to set to finish the extra fence project Drew had asked for. With a twist, he spun the auger until enough dirt built up on top to dump it near the hole, then started the process over again.

Clang.

He wanted the effort that was tiring out his body to tire out his brain, but it wasn't working. Drew's promise to give Ed more time away from the ranch duties hadn't come to fruition. Ed was letting Mrs. Wilson down. He'd promised to bring in a chair for her to look at.

Ed tossed the dirt to the side again, then dropped the auger back in the hole.

Clang.

How did a man keep the promises he made when they were dependent on others keeping theirs? Something Drew hadn't done, even if his reasons were legitimate. Sweat dribbled down his back. He didn't look forward to the next drive to town. It meant a discussion with Mrs. Wilson that he didn't want to have.

At the thought of town, Rebekah's face invaded his

thoughts. Was she safe? Was she eating? Were nightmares plaguing her again?

The remembrance of her tears made him want to howl. His body ached, but his soul ached worse.

Clang.

I have nothing left to say to you.

Clang.

The desolation in Rebekah's eyes as she'd spoken haunted him. Always would. Even as he shoveled out another spot to start the auger. He pressed the shovel below the weeds with his boot, stopping to wipe the sweat off his face with the back of his arm. His mind might never stop going back to Rebekah.

A distant shout interrupted his musings.

"Dinner's ready. You comin'?" David didn't even bother to come the whole way. He stood at the edge of the fence-row, hands cupped around his mouth as he hollered.

Ed lifted a hand to wave him off. He didn't want to face his family. Not after all their hopeful teasing.

He would have kept working if it weren't for his grumbling stomach. He slipped into the house through the side door to the kitchen. In the shadows of the corner, he bent over the washbasin. He splashed the water over his face and neck, then reached for the soap. As he did, a happy birthday chorus filled the house. They were singing without him?

Ed shifted from the shadows to peek into the dining room as he scrubbed with the soap. Isaac sat stone still. Tillie's and Jo's faces were shining. David was leaning to whisper something to Nick.

Ed ducked back into the corner, replacing the soap to

rinse his hands off. Hearty laughter filtered in from the dining table as they finished the song. If Rebekah had been here, she would've insisted they wait.

"Uncle Ed." Tillie's voice came from the doorway of the kitchen. When had she stepped this way? "You missed the song. Hurry or you'll miss the cake."

She rushed forward, gripping his hand before he'd finished drying it. With a tug from Tillie, he gave in to following her.

"Happy birthday." He paused long enough to grumble out the greeting to his brother.

Isaac's gaze cut away.

The table quieted. Kaitlyn wore a sort of pitying smile as she exchanged a glance with Drew. Nick raised a brow as he finished a sip from his glass, as if studying him. But only Isaac's concentrated stare unnerved him.

Ed stopped at his place, then halted when there wasn't any silverware.

"I'll get you a fork." Kaitlyn pushed up from the table.

"Don't bother. I know where it's at." He huffed to the kitchen, pulling out a drawer from the kitchen safe a little too hastily. Silverware jangled as he did.

As Ed picked up a fork from the drawer, his eye caught a strawberry cake. Kaitlyn must have baked it for Isaac's birthday. Figured that the night they had cake, it'd be strawberry. If he ate it, he'd break out in hives. But Kaitlyn didn't know. She'd only been part of the family for a few months.

He reached for the cookie jar, intending to grab himself a bit of dessert. He'd tuck it into a napkin, pull it out as the others ate the cake. Where did Kaitlyn store the napkins?

He jerked open a drawer, but instead of the napkins, he found the bundle of letters he'd stashed there a couple weeks ago. He ran his hands through his hair, remembering how he'd hidden all the letters from the other women who'd answered Isaac's ad there after Rebekah had come to the ranch looking for Isaac. With a jerk, he pulled open the lid to the kindling box and shoved the bundle to the bottom, right where they belonged.

Another burst of laughter echoed from the other room, bringing with it memories of Rebekah at the table with them the other night. The brush of her shoulder against his, the sparkle in her eyes.

I suppose you were laughing when you read my ... proposal to Isaac.

He dropped the fork back into the drawer.

His shoulders drooped as he slid the silverware drawer closed, casting a quick glance back at the happy celebration before he turned to slip out the lean-to door.

Eighteen

FROM ONE OF THE STALLS IN THE BARN, Ed pitched a forkful of manure into the wheelbarrow he'd stood in the aisle.

He'd lasted all of ten minutes in his silent cabin, haunted by memories of Rebekah and her admiring gaze fixed on him. From the corner of his eye, he caught the familiar saunter of his brother approaching. What did Isaac want?

"Fine sunset." Isaac spoke low. He stood in front of the wheelbarrow.

Ed grunted. His brother should have stayed inside for his birthday celebration.

"You didn't have any cake," Isaac said.

Ed tossed the next forkful of manure at Isaac's feet. Missed, but only by an inch.

Isaac's eyes flashed. He grabbed a pitchfork and stepped into the next stall. "I didn't ask for a strawberry cake."

When Ed didn't respond, Isaac flipped dirty straw over

the stall wall. It ricocheted off Ed's leg. Ed's shoulders flexed as he tossed another load of manure into the wheelbarrow.

Isaac flipped more straw over the barrier. He was doing it on purpose, but Ed didn't react.

He tried to ignore his brother completely, focus on the pull in his muscles, the task at hand.

Isaac matched every stroke, filling up the wheelbarrow in double time. "Something eatin' at you?"

Ed gritted his teeth, felt the pinch of long-standing hurt.

With his next pitch, the fork slipped from Ed's hand in a clumsy maneuver. All the pressure inside him exploded. He kicked at it, sending it toppling into the pile of clean hay at his feet.

Isaac stilled.

Ed turned away, unable to bear his brother's scrutiny.

"Unless you'd like to talk about whatever is eating at *you*, I'd like to finish this alone." He grated out the words, his voice rough.

There was a beat of silence.

Isaac growled, "I'm not going to talk about that."

"Then do you mind?"

"Maybe I do mind." Isaac stepped into the aisle, and Ed let his anger get the better of him.

He followed, his hands fisting at his sides.

Isaac eyed him. "Did it help last time?"

The bruises from their last fight had lasted for days. Ed deflated. He dusted his hat against his leg.

"Never did work to come against you," he mumbled. He took in a deep breath, then straightened. "You were always stronger. Smarter. The conquering hero."

Isaac scoffed. "What are you talking about?"

The utter disbelief on Isaac's face eased a bit of the tension still tightly strung inside Ed.

Isaac let out a snort as he went back to the stall to shove his pitchfork into the straw again, slower this time. "I'm no hero."

There was a darkness in his voice.

Isaac paused. "If you're feeling unappreciated—"

Ed's turn to snort. "Try invisible."

All those missed meals. Rebekah had been the only one who'd noticed. He pitched the next load too hard, and it overshot the wheelbarrow. Great.

"You're not invisible to God." Isaac didn't stop his work. "You know what Ma always quoted from the Bible about being knitted together in our mother's womb? How God sees us and thinks of us?"

"I know Psalm 139." His mother's sweet voice as she'd quoted the verses ran through Ed's memories. Did he really know the truth of those verses in his heart?

It said he'd been wonderfully made. He was who he was supposed to be. Not his brother. The man God had made. The man God saw. How could he be invisible?

Isaac considered him. "When everyone was sick, you saved the day."

Ed waved that off. Anyone would've done it.

"You kept the herd together through that terrible snowstorm two years ago. This ranch would fall apart without you. Drew knows it. We all know it." He paused. "But maybe we don't say it enough."

Ed let Isaac's words sink in deep, like a salve to his insides.

His family saw him too. His throat burned. "I want to do carpentry."

After having said it to Drew, it was somehow easier to say again.

"So do it."

"Pa always talked about the family legacy." Ed sighed deeply. When Isaac had left to join the U.S. Marshals and Nick had gone to normal school to train to be a teacher, Drew and the kids had desperately needed help. Things might be different now, but Ed wouldn't forget that. "Drew has worked so hard to keep this ranch together. How am I supposed to just walk away when I'm needed here?"

Isaac scuffed his boot along the dirt floor. "If you run yourself ragged, burn yourself out, how does that help the ranch?"

Ed shook his head. He didn't know.

They stood staring at the back of the barn, shovels stilled.

"What happened with Rebekah?"

I suppose you were laughing when you read my ... proposal to Isaac.

"I messed up," he confessed, though the words threatened to choke him. "Besides, you're the one she really wanted. Did you even read her letters?"

Isaac shook his head. If Ed wasn't mistaken, a hint of red was creeping up his brother's jaw. "Can't you fix things? She loves you."

"What?" Ed blinked, jerking back his head in disbelief.

"Oh, let's see now." Isaac held up his hand, lifting one finger to count on. "Rebekah is all smiles when you come into the room." He ticked off another finger. "She makes sure she sits real close to you." Another. "The last biscuit is saved for you by who? And what about that late-night walk? We all saw the stars in her eyes when you came back to the house."

With each tick of his brother's fingers listing those moments with Rebekah, a bit more hope swelled up in him. Only to crash around him.

"I lied to her. About the letters." He crammed a hand in his pocket, suddenly feeling the cooling of the evening air.

"So keep apologizing until she forgives you."

He lifted his eyebrows. "And if she won't speak to me?"

"You wrote all those letters. You'll figure out what to say." Isaac held Ed's gaze for a few beats. For the first time in a very long time, Ed felt like he had his brother back.

And then Isaac bent his head back to his work.

His brother was right. He'd only be failing if he didn't try.

Whether Rebekah wanted to listen or not, he had to find a way.

Rebekah ambled down the boardwalk with Merritt, heading back to the boardinghouse on the way back from the bank. It'd been nearly a week since Rebekah had seen Ed. Danna still hadn't found the bandit, and Rebekah's anxiousness about that fact had grown the longer he remained a free man.

"I'm sorry you weren't able to get the loan." Merritt looped her arm in Rebekah's as her shoulders drooped.

Rebekah swallowed the bitter disappointment. "Some men can be so old-fashioned," she muttered. With Mr. Sullivan having fled town, she'd hoped to secure a loan for a new printing press and the rent for the newspaper office. As a single woman with no collateral, she had been refused, the banker shooting down any hope she'd had this morning.

Yesterday, she'd wired her aunt and uncle about losing her job. Now she couldn't seem to keep her thoughts in order. She realized her friend was speaking of one of her former students only when Merritt stopped talking.

Rebekah smiled wryly. "I'm sorry for my distraction. I'm worried about Uncle Vess's ranch."

"Are things really so dire?" Merritt asked.

Rebekah suspected they were, though she'd wait for a return wire before she knew for certain.

"Will you really have to leave us?" The genuine compassion in Merritt's question tugged at Rebekah's heart.

"I don't see how I can stay." A heaviness settled in her chest.

They passed by the bakery, where Rebekah could see Mrs. Wilson bustling about inside. Had Ed pursued the estimate? In her distraction and the upset emotions of the past days, no one had told her and she hadn't asked.

She missed him.

Merritt nudged her arm. "I'm worried about you. You aren't acting like yourself."

"Sorry," she said again.

Her anguish tightened inside her as they neared the newspaper office. The brown paper covering the broken window made her want to cry all over again, as did the Closed sign hanging on the door.

Merritt stood silent beside her.

Whoever had destroyed her beloved paper was still out there.

All of a sudden, she couldn't hold back the torrent of words inside her.

"I've tried too hard to keep things perfect—just the way they should be—ever since that ad arrived. And I've only managed to make everything worse."

Merritt let her stew in her thoughts for a long moment— or maybe she was thinking of what to say.

She began slowly. "I've been where you are. I tried to hold on so tightly to my idea of right . . . but God had a better plan for me. He brought me Jack. I had to let go of my idea of how things should be."

"I don't know if I can do that," Rebekah admitted.

"Have you tried? Given over your will and asked for what God wants for you?"

She hadn't. From the beginning, she'd only gone after what *she* thought was best. She hadn't even seen Ed, hadn't considered him a friend or a suitor until they'd been forced together by circumstances she certainly wouldn't have chosen.

"If I let go of how I had my life planned, I'm afraid. Afraid of whether I'll like how things go," Rebekah confessed.

Merritt was sympathetic. She'd been Rebekah's friend for a long time. She knew why Rebekah had come west, all of it. "What if God has other blessings in store for you?"

What if . . .

Rebekah had never considered it before. New tears filled her eyes as she stared at the brown paper blocking the windows. Surely God wouldn't ask her to leave the newspaper. Leave Uncle Vess and Aunt Opal.

She didn't know if she was strong enough for that.

"You can trust Him with your plans," Merritt said. "He is a good God."

The words settled inside Rebekah. Merritt was right. God was ultimately in control. All Rebekah's striving had gotten her nowhere. It felt frightening, but right, to give control to the One who had created all things.

She knew it. She'd known it since childhood. But a new acceptance settled over her.

"I know you've been in love with Isaac for a long time—"

"I've never been in love with Isaac." Rebekah read the shock on Merritt's face. "Anything I ever felt for Isaac pales in comparison to my feelings for Ed."

"Ed?" Merritt's surprise was obvious.

Rebekah had been too ashamed of having written under a pretense and hidden the other letters to tell Merritt what had really happened. Now everything was a mess.

"What if things can't be patched up?"

Rebekah turned her head from her friend's stare, unable to bear Merritt's scrutiny in this moment. Fingering that place where the paper had been torn on the newspaper windows, she could not resist the urge to have one last look. Rebekah bent her knees until level with the peeled back bit of brown paper. She peered through the torn-out hole to take in the inside of the newspaper office. The empty shell of what had once been her whole life.

She scanned the office, but, no—

Someone had been inside. There were tracks through the mess.

Ignoring Merritt, she lowered herself once more. This time she let her eyes slow to take in every detail. Amidst the mess, an area had been cleared out where someone had been working to repair the frame for the press. Her pulse pounded in her ears as tears threatened.

Rebekah jerked upright again, then started for the door.

"Wait." Merritt pulled at her sleeve, but Rebekah shook her off.

"Please be open." She whispered the words as she wiggled the knob just so. A trick she'd seen Mr. Sullivan use occasionally when the lock jammed, appearing locked when it wasn't. A quick click and the door opened.

Merritt was close behind her.

With hurried steps, Rebekah moved to the frame. The frame for the printing press had been disassembled. The pieces lay in neat rows. There was a pile of new wood and tools organized on a table nearby. Even the metal letters had been swept up and placed in a bucket.

In the midst of the sawdust were footprints. She placed her foot inside one as her heart leaped. Silly, but some part of her knew, just knew, she was standing in the spot where Ed had been. It had to be him. Who else had the skills to repair the frame to the press?

A new hope sprang up inside her, washed over her with a renewed longing. A letter sat atop the frame, propped there with her name on the front. The familiar scrawl warmed her as she reached out a trembling hand to pick it up. Merritt's footsteps tapped across the floor as she drew closer, but

Rebekah didn't care. Heart pounding, she tore open the envelope, then pulled out the letter. Her eyes drank in the familiar handwriting.

Dear Rebekah,

I write this letter to ask you to forgive me. These days without you near have been the loneliest ever. I never knew how much our friendship meant until it wasn't there. I never knew how much you meant to me until you weren't there.

I never should have written to you under a false pretense. Once I realized the letter writer was you, I had already fallen so in love with you I didn't dare risk losing you. Please tell me I haven't lost you now.

If you find this letter before I'm done fixing the frame, know that I'll be back to finish what I started. Your printing press will run again. One way or another.

As always,
Your Wyoming Rancher
Ed McGraw

"Who is it from? Ed?"
She nodded, fearing to speak. If she did, her emotions

might burst out. Every nerve tingled. She ran her hand along the wood. As she rushed to the door, she tucked the envelope in her skirt.

"I have to go."

"Wait." Merritt trailed behind her. "Danna thinks it's still dangerous."

Hesitation warred with determination. Rebekah couldn't wait.

"I have to go to Ed."

"Then I'm coming with you."

Nineteen

E D SPUN THE PENCIL IN HIS HAND, darting his focus to the clock on the mantel for the dozenth time.

He'd only come home from town to grab a specific tool for the printing press repair. He'd been heading back to the road when Drew waved him inside.

His brothers sat around the table, sipping coffee. For once, Ed didn't care if he missed out. There was still time for him to make it back to town before nightfall. He'd beg for Merritt and Jack's mercy and a place to stay. If only Drew would stop talking.

"We'll need to bring in the wheat, starting next week. Nick will round up a few extra hands if he can." Drew nodded at Nick, elbows propped on the table, then directed his gaze to Ed. "The lean-to needs repair."

Isaac shifted.

Ed caught his eye from across the table, and his heartbeat ratcheted up. "I can't do it tomorrow."

"Can't?" Drew's brows rose.

"I'm going back to town to finish fixing the printing press." He couldn't say the rest aloud. His plans to find Rebekah. Win her back. His hope was too new. "I'll need another day later in the week to work on a table for the bakery too. But I'll fit the lean-to in."

A frantic knock sounded at the door before it burst open. Merritt stood there, hair tousled, panting as if she'd been running.

"What are you doing here?"

"What's wrong?"

A chorus of voices rang out as the brothers jumped up from the table.

"Rebekah and I were riding this way." Tears filled her eyes.

Rebekah? Rode out here? Worry spiked.

"A man overtook us." Merritt gasped out the words, leaning into Kaitlyn as all the brothers crowded around. "He had a bandanna over his face. He pulled Rebekah off her horse."

Everything in the room slowed around him. Ed couldn't think clearly. He barely heard the rest of the conversation as he tried to will his feet toward the door. But it was as if he were trudging through molasses.

"I didn't have—I was unarmed. They galloped off, and I was too scared to go after them." Merritt sobbed out the words.

Isaac kneeled beside her, his voice steady and low. "Where?"

The fog in Ed's brain cleared. He settled his hat on his head as he pushed past them and out the door. His heartbeat pounded in rhythm with his hurried steps.

Rebekah needed him. She was in danger.

He passed Merritt's horse, spent and covered in sweat, then rushed into the barn and looped his hand through the bridle hanging on the wall. Footsteps sounded behind him as Isaac gathered his tack.

"They weren't far from the Boutwells'. Up at the fork in the road." Isaac had the saddle on Bullet, cinching it down as Ed finished saddling Lightning.

Ed was already in the saddle when Nick emerged from the bunkhouse with a couple of rifles. "Here." He held the rifles out to them. "I'll catch up to you."

Drew ran out of the house, not far behind Nick.

Ed turned to Isaac. "You're the best tracker I know. Help me find her." His desperation rang out in his words.

Isaac nodded, mouth grim.

Ed urged Lightning forward. He couldn't think about the ranchers who had been beaten. What if they couldn't reach her in time?

He leaned low over the horse's neck and asked for more speed.

Please God, keep her safe.

At the fork in the road, another rider approached from behind in a cloud of dust. Ed's pulse ratcheted up a notch. He fingered the butt of the rifle, ready to pull it from the scabbard, when the horse slowed.

Isaac reined in and pointed to tracks leading off the road as Nick thundered past, heading toward town. Hopefully to get the marshal and bring help.

A nicker sounded from nearby. Isaac slowed his horse, shoulders going tense. A dark-brown horse was half hidden behind a stand of trees in a field a hundred yards ahead. Riderless.

Isaac scanned the surrounding field, then kept moving, Ed trailing as his brother swiveled back and forth in the saddle, on the lookout for any motion. When they neared a wooded area, Isaac held a finger to his lips.

Ed dismounted when Isaac did. Both took their rifles with them and drew nearer to the edge of what appeared to be a steep drop-off. Voices echoed from below. With his hand, Isaac motioned for Ed to drop low.

The undergrowth tickled his face. Isaac halted in front of him. Ed moved in beside him, slow and easy, to peer over the rise. A rough sort of clearing came into view.

Rebekah was slumped on a wide tree stump, her hands tied in front of her. She was alive!

Ed's breathing went shallow as a man—the bandit?—stood over her menacingly. The man faced away from Ed, and he couldn't make out his features, but a bandanna was hanging down around his neck.

It had to be the bandit.

Ed's breath caught in his chest as he took a longer look at Rebekah and saw the red mark on her cheek.

He couldn't let anything happen to her. Not his Rebekah. For whether she wanted him or not, that's what she'd always be. And nothing in life would ever be the same if she were taken from him.

"Tell me where he is."

"I don't know." Rebekah's voice was stubborn and angry.

"You know. You just won't tell me." The man let go of her and straightened to his full height.

"He must mean Sullivan," Isaac said.

Ed hadn't paid much attention to the exchange. All he cared about was rescuing Rebekah.

The outlaw drew his gun.

Isaac was ready. He had his rifle aimed into the gully.

Ed laid his on the ground, right at hand.

"My boss wants to see him." The bandit aimed his gun at her. "Where is he?"

Ed's heart threatened to explode.

"Take the shot," Ed urged.

But Isaac was frozen beside him.

"Isaac," Ed pushed.

Isaac's fingers remained clasped around the rifle's stock. His eyes darted wildly, as if he couldn't find his focus.

And then Isaac relaxed his grip, breathing hard as if he'd been running at full speed. "I can't."

"You have to. He's gonna shoot her." Ed pushed the words out with force as his chest clenched.

Isaac shook his head, his hand still wrapped around the stock.

There was something terribly wrong with Ed's brother, but this wasn't the time to deal with it.

"You're just as good. You take the shot."

What choice did he have?

Ed leveled his rifle at the man who was threatening Rebekah. There was no time for more thought. That revolver could go off at any moment.

He closed his finger over the trigger. And took the shot.

A shot rang out.

Rebekah jumped, the sound reverberating through her chest.

But she felt no pain.

Thump!

She hadn't realized she'd closed her eyes, but they flew open now to see the bandit fall to the ground. Blood seeped through his fingers where he clutched his arm.

His gun had been knocked away. It lay in the grass nearby.

Dirt and rocks rattled loose. A man was scrambling down the rise.

Ed.

Fear swelled inside her and overflowed as tears filled her eyes. He rushed forward to spring on top of the outlaw. The bandit saw him and rolled toward the gun.

"Ed, watch out!" Rebekah kicked at the bandit.

Ed launched at him, threw a punch that knocked back the bandit's head. Their tussle pushed close, and she was knocked off the tree stump, falling hard on one shoulder.

She couldn't tear her eyes from where Ed followed the outlaw as the man tried to run away, then wrenched his arm so that the outlaw cried out.

"I've got him," Ed called out.

And there was Isaac, only steps away. She hadn't even noticed him coming down the hill.

Ed quickly handed off the man and came to help her sit up.

"I thought we were going to be too late." A huskiness filled his words.

She could feel the wobble in his hands as he worked to untie the ropes on her wrists.

He pulled her close. She went willingly, felt his still-frantic breathing under her cheek. She leaned into his strength, letting his warmth flow into her.

He'd come for her.

Ed slid his hands from her back to hold her arms, lifting her away from him with a gentle strength. His face grew stern as he surveyed her bruised wrists. "Are you sure you're okay?"

"Yes. What about you?" Unashamed tears streaked her face as she reached up to touch the blood trickling from his brow. "You're bleeding."

Ed barely seemed to notice. "He must've gotten in a lucky punch."

All the while, he ran his hands down her arms, tracing over them for any signs of injury.

More tears slipped free. "You came for me. After everything."

Such depths of tenderness lingered in his eyes as he moved his hand to gently cup the side of her face. He turned her jaw slightly, examining her cheek. It'd been hurt when she'd tried to get away. From the purse of his lips and the working of his jaw, she must have gotten a bruise.

He met her eyes again with intensity. "Of course I came. I'll always come for you."

Her hands cupped his jaw as she leaned up to let her lips meet his. His hands closed around her waist. This was what she'd always wanted. She let herself lean into him. She was home in his arms.

"Ow!" The man howled as Isaac jerked a rope tight around his wrists.

Rebekah pulled back from Ed's warmth.

She caught Isaac ducking his head in an awkward bend while wrangling the man, as if to avoid intruding on her moment with Ed. Once he had the bandit subdued, Isaac jerked the man to his feet.

The bandit let out a grunt, eyes on Rebekah. "You and that story you printed made too much trouble for my boss. You turned me into a wanted man." He spat at the ground. "I should've been a better shot when I had you in my sights in town."

Ed took a step toward him but stopped when Rebekah touched his arm.

Isaac jerked up the man's sleeve to reveal a tattoo. The very one Rebekah had sketched at Quade's ranch.

This was the man. He'd attacked both Mr. Billings and Mr. Jones. Admitted to shooting at her in town. They'd caught him.

The man tried to wrestle away, but Isaac held tight.

"Let's go." Isaac glanced at Rebekah. "You okay?"

She nodded. Overwhelmed, she watched him move off, prodding the bandit forward to where the horses must be waiting. She blinked and turned her head to see Ed watching her.

His eyes tracked to Isaac and back again.

His mouth was set in a thin line, but it was the vulnerability in his eyes that hit her hard. "If you still want—"

"I don't want Isaac. I only want you." Tears stung behind her nose as she reached out to touch his arm. "You're my hero."

She caught his flare of relief and the recognition and connection that followed.

He moved to pull her close again, but she stayed him with a hand on his chest so that they were inches apart.

Ed tilted his head. "I'm sorry for not telling you sooner about the letters—"

"I'm sorry too. If I hadn't been trying to control everything…" Her breath escaped in a quick sigh as he gathered her hands, then intertwined their fingers.

"What were you thinking?" he chided gently. "Riding out when there was still danger."

A breathless hope rode on his words.

She dropped her eyes to focus on his work-hardened hands. "I was coming to see you. There's something I have to tell you."

She lifted her eyes to study his dear face. His brow wrinkled in question.

"I know now. It's you I love. It's always been you. From the very first letter."

A light dawned in his eyes. He darted his gaze across her face as if trying to decide where to land. "I've had feelings for you for a long time."

"Not good ones." She suppressed a giggle.

"Actually, I couldn't even admit it to myself." His eyebrow quirked, his gaze intensifying. "But I liked you from the start. And I love you even more now."

His smile softened as he leaned in. She felt the pull of his arms around her waist, drawing her closer. She slid her hands around his neck and wove her fingers into his hair, enjoying its softness. The scent of him filled her nose. All sweat and sawdust and everything Ed.

His lips met hers. Fireworks erupted inside her. Her left foot lifted back in a little kick while their kiss deepened.

Another contented sigh filled the space when his lips left hers.

She tilted her head as his forehead rested against hers. She never wanted him to stop kissing her this way.

A shrill whistle echoed out from the top of the rise where Isaac now stood.

"Drew's up here. David too. You guys coming?"

Rebekah let her hand slide down Ed's arm as she stepped in the direction of the hill, but Ed tugged her back.

"You've taught me the importance of asking for what I want. What I need." He spoke with an urgency. "Rebekah, I need you in my life. Will you marry me?"

While all her dreams for the paper were teetering, this dream was unfolding before her anew. The best dream of all.

"Yes, Ed McGraw. I will."

Twenty

WE THANK YOU, LORD, FOR FAMILY and friends, especially for Ed's new wife."

Ed's head bobbed up unbidden at the phrase rolling off Drew's tongue.

Ed's new wife.

He squeezed Rebekah's hand, and she squeezed his right back, sending an overwhelming wave of anticipation through him. It'd only been three weeks since he'd popped the question. And now they were sitting together at the table, surrounded by family.

"Bless this marriage and this food. Amen."

Ed kept hold of Rebekah's hand as he opened his eyes to look at her. She smiled as she sat there in that delicate-looking blouse she'd sewn to go with her navy skirt. One with those puffy sleeves he didn't usually care for on women but loved on her as she lifted a shoulder with a twinkle in her eye.

Rebekah leaned close. "I haven't told you yet how handsome you look."

He cleared his throat, hoping the heat he felt in his cheeks didn't show. Not much into fashion, he'd nevertheless donned his best Sunday shirt and pants along with the boots purchased after the sale of another table to the bakery.

If all the family weren't sitting around the table, he'd lean over and wrap her in his arms for another kiss. But there would be time enough for that later tonight, after they finished their celebration with the family at the main house.

"When do we get cake and raspberries?" Tillie fidgeted in her seat, her grin rivaling Rebekah's as chuckles erupted around the table at her outburst.

"As soon as you finish with your dinner, little lady." Drew winked at her as he passed a plate to Kaitlyn.

Nick leaned close to David, holding up a hand to get Jo to stop chattering long enough for him to hear her brother. All while Isaac stared off, barely breaking a smile at Tillie's antics. No doubt remained for Ed that Isaac wished him and Rebekah the very best. He'd been more relaxed around Rebekah since the whole letter mix-up had ended. But the old Isaac still lay hidden under the depths of whatever plagued him.

Ed could only guess what had happened to make Isaac so withdrawn. If he couldn't shoot at a man, it was no wonder he'd left the marshals. But it hadn't affected his ability to manage his tasks around the homestead since he'd come down from his cabin. Drew and Nick didn't need to know that Isaac couldn't shoot until he saw fit to tell them.

"What kind of cake is it?" Rebekah leaned forward to tease Tillie, as if she hadn't helped Kaitlyn with the baking yesterday. If her aunt and uncle had been back, Opal would no doubt have had that honor. Her aunt's latest letter held not only the good news that Vess's treatments were working but also that they hoped to return in the fall. Rebekah couldn't wait to see them both.

The conversations echoed over the table as everyone laughed and smiled while passing plates of carrots, green beans, mashed potatoes, gravy, and fried chicken.

"I haven't had this much food since a certain picnic." Ed wiggled his brows at Rebekah.

She blushed before scooping up another mouthful of potatoes. The picnic she'd been planning to surprise him with had taken place after they'd seen the bandit safely locked away in the Calvin jailhouse. In fact, she'd brought food out nearly every day he'd been working on his cabin the last few weeks. So much that he'd had to loosen his belt a notch for the wedding.

"Now that Ed's lean-to is done . . ." Nick's words faded as Tillie and Jo squabbled across the table.

His brothers had been eager to help him add a lean-to onto his cabin for his carpentry. Once done, he'd managed to move his work out there and scrub away all the sawdust just in time for the bright yellow curtains Rebekah had brought over to hang in the front windows.

Platters of food made their way around the table for second helpings amidst the joyful celebration. Ed let his focus fall on his new wife once again as her laughter filled the space beside him. Everything in him wanted to keep her happy for the rest of their lives.

"Will you build me a cradle for Prudence?" Tillie's request burst into his thoughts.

"Your doll doesn't need a cradle." Jo glared at her sister.

Drew cleared his throat. His shoulder was pressed close to Kaitlyn's. "There's going to be a need for a full-sized cradle first."

There was a moment of silence and then a chaos of congratulations.

No wonder Kaitlyn had been pushing food around on her plate without eating much. Tillie bounced in her seat. Another McGraw would be arriving soon.

"Is it time yet?" Tillie pushed her carrots around her plate, causing two glasses to bump together, and Kaitlyn reached to steady them, breaking the mood after the big announcement.

Kaitlyn turned to raise her brows at Rebekah. "Want to help me cut the cake?"

Rebekah dabbed her napkin to her lips. "I think this is the perfect time for it."

As Rebekah pushed back her chair, her cheerful countenance flooded Ed with joy once again. He lifted a hand to clasp hers, then slowly let it go as she moved away from the table. He caught Kaitlyn watching them with a wide grin on her face. As Rebekah rounded the table to join her, Kaitlyn looped Rebekah's arm in hers.

The two had grown thicker than ever. Kaitlyn had invested part of her inheritance to help Rebekah rent the space for the paper in town. A silent partner. After Mr.

Sullivan had skipped town, the bank had been eager for any renter.

"I'm so glad we're finally sisters." Kaitlyn's whisper met his ears. "I knew it all along."

Tillie pushed back from the table to follow them, Jo close at her heels.

As they disappeared into the kitchen, Ed shifted his attention to the low conversation between his brothers.

"Did you get the second part of the contract for the bakery?" Drew rested his arms on the table and leaned forward.

Ed had intended to spend more time in town next week converting the area above the newspaper office into an apartment to stay in while Rebekah worked on the paper each week, splitting his time between town and the homestead. "I can turn it down. Won't you need more help around here with Kaitlyn in the family way?"

The old worry slipped in. Things were changing.

"Isaac and I have it covered." Nick shared a glance with Isaac. It was good to have him back in the physical form. If only their brother were back to himself.

"David's already stepped in to take on more chores too." Drew settled the look of a proud father on David, who lifted his lips to form a faint smile. A lot for the boy who emulated his stoic Uncle Isaac.

Ed eased back in his chair.

"Did you hear the latest on Quade's bandit?" David interjected the question, no doubt wanting to join the talk of the men he admired.

"Heard he refused to talk. Marshal O'Grady's hands were tied since Rebekah was the only one who saw him on Quade's ranch. There wasn't enough proof to connect them."

"Did they talk to Isabella?" As Ed spoke, David started to speak but bit his lower lip.

"She wouldn't give them any information, not even an interview." Even as he spoke, Drew turned his focus to hear what had David drumming on the table as he waited to speak.

"I mean about him dying," David said.

"Dying?" Ed scanned the faces at the table. His gaze landed on Isaac, who stared out the window, the muscle in his cheek twitching. Ed glanced back at Nick and Drew. Concern radiated between them.

"The marshal went in to retrieve the dishes after the bandit finished his supper one evening only to find him dead." In his rush to tell the news, David appeared oblivious to Isaac's silence.

The brothers exchanged another knowing look.

"Quade's gonna be elected as president of the Cattlemen's Association." Nick pulled a frown.

Rebekah had printed the truth of his connection with the bandit, but public opinion still favored him. Folks didn't believe he'd paid the man to do his bidding. Especially after prior articles Mr. Sullivan had printed in Quade's favor. Articles that Quade had paid Sullivan to write. It had hurt Rebekah to the core to imagine her mentor accepting a bribe, until she'd discovered Mr. Sullivan had offered to pay it back after his daughter recovered. But Quade had threatened to ruin his reputation.

"He managed to work the whole bandit story around

for his good." Drew picked up his glass for another drink, then replaced it.

"Did he make another offer to buy us out?" Isaac asked, voice grave.

When Drew shook his head, Isaac muttered, "He ain't done with us yet. He'll try for the land again."

"We'll be watching for whatever he tries next," Drew said. "And keep trusting God's plan."

Isaac's eyes were banked with a smoldering fire. "We may have to fight."

Tillie burst into the room, interrupting the men's serious talk. "It's ready."

Kaitlyn rounded the corner with plates of cake in her hands.

Thoughts of Kaitlyn and Rebekah partnering to run the newspaper hit Ed in the gut. Rebekah always wanted to print the truth. Her other articles had put her in danger with the bandit. What might lie ahead?

Balancing more plates of cake, Rebekah followed close behind Kaitlyn, cheeks glowing. Ed kicked the negative feelings away as she moved closer. There'd be plenty of time for dealing with Quade later.

The faint scent of Rebekah blended with the sweet aroma of cake and berries as a loose ringlet of her hair spilled over her shoulder. Her eyes held his, and he'd never been more seen. Never felt more full of joy and life and laughter than in this moment.

Something swelled inside of him. He'd never ask her to give up what she loved. He'd do everything he could to protect her. From this day forward.

The palpable tension between the men surrounded Rebekah as she settled a plate in front of Ed.

He kissed her cheek to no doubt ease the questions in her raised brows. *I'll explain later*, he mouthed.

A new sensation of warmth filled her. There were no secrets between them anymore.

"Aren't you going to take the first bite?" Tillie wore an expectant look, no doubt finding it hard to wait.

After breaking off a bite of cake with her fork, Rebekah looped her arm with Ed's as they fed one another the first bite. A rousing cheer rose from the table while Tillie shoved in her first taste of the cake. It'd obviously taken every ounce of willpower for her to hold off eating.

Rebekah reached her napkin up to brush a crumb away from Ed's cheek, and he caught her hand to kiss her fingers. She could get lost in his eyes. For years, she hadn't given him a chance. God had known better. And brought them together.

As everyone finished their cake, the children hurried off to go play. A low conversation ensued among the adults, but little of it registered with Rebekah as she focused on Ed's profile. He glanced over at her and smiled. A smile that spoke more than any words could say.

Scanning the other faces at the table, she noticed one person had gone missing.

"Did Isaac leave already?"

Kaitlyn frowned. "He left a while ago."

Drew reached out for his wife's hand. "Seems our plan to draw him back in didn't work quite like we planned."

A heaviness settled over the room. Kaitlyn had confided in Rebekah about their worries for Isaac. She shared in the feeling, a sisterly concern.

A gentle tug from Ed's hand brought her hand to his mouth. He kissed the back of it, his eyes meeting hers as he did. "I'm not sorry the plan failed."

He winked, and heat rose up her neck.

"He's grieving." Nick fiddled with his fork.

"I still say a woman's presence in Isaac's life could bring the softness he needs." Kaitlyn shared a look with Drew.

"Too bad there weren't any other letters," Drew said absently.

"There were." Ed's voice broke the silence.

Rebekah's eyes shot up to find Ed's searching for hers. They locked, allowing unspoken words to pass between them. As if he were reassuring her that her secret was safe with him. The echo of Tillie's and Jo's murmurs could be heard from above, where they'd run off to play.

"I never answered any other letters. Rebekah's were the only ones that mattered to me." His eyes never left hers. "The last time I saw the letters, I shoved them at the bottom of the kindlin' box in the kitchen. I'm done meddling in Isaac's life."

"I second that." Nick frowned, a silent reminder he'd never agreed with the plan in the first place.

"I've no interest in answering any other letter now, but at least our plan worked to get one of my brothers a wife." Drew winked at Ed.

Kaitlyn rose from the table, circling it to stand beside them. She bent to embrace Rebekah in a hug. "We are so glad you joined the family. I can't think of a better sister to have."

Drew slapped his knees, then rose from the table. "Let's all move to the other room for some games and singing."

It wasn't long before the children rejoined them. As the evening wore on, Ed slipped beside Rebekah, weaving his arm around her waist. He leaned close to whisper in her ear.

"Are you ready to go home?"

She turned her face to his, so close she could kiss him, and the memory of their first kiss flashed across her mind. There would be many more. Her lips turned into a grin as she nodded. With the family engrossed in singing, he led her by the hand to the kitchen and out the back door.

Ed playfully bumped his shoulder against hers. "I've got a surprise for you."

Rebekah held back from asking what it was, relishing the secrecy of it.

With her hand looped in Ed's as they cut across the field, she let their arms swing together in time with their steps, occasionally brushing up against one another. This was her husband. Joy bubbled up in her, mixed with a tingle of anticipation as he gave her hand a squeeze.

"Think you'll be happy here?" He shot a questioning glance at her as they drew closer to his cabin, their steps slowing.

Butterflies danced in her stomach double time.

"I will." A flush rose up her neck as she leaned closer to him, sliding her hand out of his and looping it around his arm. "I'm sorry about all the extra work with you caring for my aunt and uncle's place until they return."

He ducked his head closer. "It's not a burden. You know I'd do anything for you."

Rebekah lifted up her face in time to plant a quick kiss on his cheek. A gentle breeze swept over the surrounding field, bringing with it the promise of a summer shower.

As they neared the porch, Ed moved to walk backward in front of her. "Once we're on the porch, I want you to close your eyes."

"You what?" She couldn't keep the grin off her face.

"The surprise is inside." He took her hand to lead her up the familiar steps to his front porch, leaving tingles flowing through her fingertips. Then he placed his broad shoulders between her and the door. "Ready?"

She closed her eyes as she tilted her head, letting out a giggle. "I'd follow you anywhere you lead, Ed McGraw."

His shirt rustled as he brushed past her and stepped behind, placing one hand over her eyes. She could make out a bit of what was in front of her as he reached around to open the door, but her attempts at peeking were cut short when his other hand fell over her eyes as well.

His warm breath tickled her ear as he moved closer to her. "Take a step. Another."

She shifted her feet in time with his commands, completely trusting him to guide her. Inside the cabin, he spun her back toward the fading light in the doorway. It was all she could do not to turn back around and look. What could he be planning to surprise her with?

"Don't turn around while I light the lamp."

The sounds of him lighting up the lamp were followed by the whiff of burning kerosene.

"Can I look?" Her own voice sounded giddy as it hitched up an octave.

His hands covered her eyes again as he spun her around, then lifted. "Now."

In the middle of his freshly swept cabin stood a bookcase. Her breath caught. She'd never seen such fine workmanship.

"How did you ever find time for this?" The words tumbled out of her as she took a step forward. The light from the lamp glowed across the newly sealed wood. With slow steps, she wound her way around the bookcase, her hand running along its smooth surface.

"I've never seen anything so fine before." Her words were threatening to clog in her throat. "It's perfect."

A tear meandered down her cheek as she tried to choke out more words. She quickly swiped it away, not willing to miss a second of this moment. "My father's books are on the bottom shelves. That's what you were hiding in that crate in the wagon."

Ed stepped near, slipping his strong arms around her waist to pull her closer. "Mm-hmm."

"But why is the top shelf empty?"

"That shelf is for your books." The warmth of his breath mingled with the depth of his belief in her.

"Mine?"

He'd saved a shelf for her books.

"You're a good writer. I believe in you. I've no doubt your

book will be published. And many more." Ed turned her around in his arms to face him.

She had no words. This man . . . her husband . . . being so close to him, the joy inside her threatened to explode. His slight movement forward drew her like a magnet. Their lips met in a sweet kiss. Breathless, she yielded to his movement as he pulled back from their kiss to touch his forehead to hers.

"Whatever made you want a guy like me, anyway?"

Rebekah slid her hand down to reach into the pocket she'd sewn into her skirt. There she held a precious reminder of their love. She slipped the two metal letters from the printing press into his hand and closed it.

A question spread across his face as he shifted to uncurl his hand and reveal the letters. XO. His eyes lifted to meet hers as she clasped her hand over his.

"Don't you know? You won me with your letters."

"Jo, this is your worst idea yet," David whispered. At fourteen, he didn't want any part of whatever plan Jo had concocted.

She kneeled on his bed as murmurs from the adults, still visiting, filtered through the closed door. Anyone could amble into his bedroom next to the kitchen and catch them.

This letter business had already caused enough trouble.

Jo's braid swung over her shoulder as she riffled through the handful of letters on the bed between them. She must have been listening from the top of the stairs as the adults had talked about the letters. It was the only way she would have known where to find that bundle. He'd heard every word from his room.

"You do this and I swear I'll never tell Pa what really happened to his best knife."

She was blackmailing him?

Jo squinted her eyes at him, cementing the threat.

Staring right back, his stomach knotted as he weighed the consequences. Pa had been looking for that knife for a week. David didn't feel good about lying to him, but he'd taken the knife without permission.

And lost it somewhere in the barn.

Would she really tell? Most likely. The knife incident was too much to let out in the open. He broke the stare-down. He had no intention of testing her on this one. Even if he did have a few secrets of his own she might not want him to share. Jo always did get her way.

"What do you mean to do with these silly letters, anyway?" He shrugged at her, trying another tactic. Maybe she'd change her mind about this. "And why do you need me?"

"You know good and well what I want you to do. My handwriting is too bad to pass for a man's." Jo pursed her lips as she squinted again. Must be her latest trick for getting her way with Tillie.

But he wasn't Tillie. And he didn't like being bossed around by his younger sister. He'd had enough of that. He crossed his arms over his chest and waited.

She pulled a face. "You heard Pa. Uncle Isaac is still sad."

He'd heard all right. He hadn't meant to eavesdrop, but

they'd both overheard Ma and Pa talking while they'd been cleaning up after the party. Their voices had been full of worry.

"We have to get Isaac a wife." Jo's lips scrunched up as she widened her eyes. The look she always used when she was determined to get her way.

David placed his hands on the quilt covering his bed and leaned forward. "No way. A grown-up woman ain't gonna believe I'm Uncle Isaac. Not if I answered one of those."

As Jo jumped on the bed, landing on her knees, she threw a punch to his gut. He doubled over, stifling his yelp. He didn't want the adults in here. Didn't want to be in trouble again for something Jo had started.

"Uncle Isaac needs us." She twisted his ear, and he barely held back a yelp.

David pushed her face away with his palm, earning a grunt.

She came right back, and he swatted her away.

"Uncle Isaac has to have a wife." Jo gritted her teeth. "If not, he'll never be happy again. Is that what you want?"

It'd be nice to see Uncle Isaac smile again. David thought about how Isaac was always serious now. The haunted way he stared at the horizon. His uncle was hurting.

"Ma knows it would bring him back."

His heart pounded in his ears as Jo switched to a softer tactic. Even knowing how she worked to get her way, the words hit him in the gut harder than her punch. "All right."

He'd barely mumbled the word, but Jo already had the letters fanned out in her hands.

Jo chewed at her bottom lip as she flipped through the

letters. Her fingers grasped at an envelope. As she worked to pull it out, a faint scent of roses filtered into the air. Jo wrinkled up her nose. "This can't be it."

"Why not?" A gnawing started in his stomach. He wished she'd get on with this.

"If her letter smells like that, what is she gonna smell like?" She tossed the letter to the floor.

"Don't you think Uncle Isaac wants a girl that smells pretty?"

"I've smelled pretty. That ain't it." Jo fingered the stack again, landing on another letter.

The apprehension grew larger in his stomach as he caught the gleam in his sister's eye. She yanked at the envelope, pulling it triumphantly from the pile.

"*This* is the one."

Bonus Epilogue

Are you are a member of our new releases newsletter? You can receive a special gift, available only to newsletters subscribers.

This Bonus Epilogue to *A Secret Heart* will not be released on any retailer platform—it's only available to newsletter subscribers.

Find out what happens next with Ed and Rebekah. Scan this QR code to subscribe and get your free gift. You acknowledge you are becoming a Sunrise Publishing, Wendy Klopfenstein and Lacy Williams subscriber. Unsubscribe from any newsletter at any time.

THANK YOU

Thank you again for reading *A Secret Heart*. We hope you enjoyed the story. If you did, would you be willing to do us a favor and leave a review? It doesn't have to be long—just a few words to help other readers know what they're getting. (But no spoilers! We don't want to wreck the fun!) Thank you again for reading!

We'd love to hear from you—not only about this story, but about any characters or stories you'd like to read in the future.

Contact us at www.sunrisepublishing.com/contact.

READ ON FOR MORE FROM THE

Wind River
MAIL-ORDER BRIDES
SERIES

JOURNEY ONCE MORE WITH OUR MAIL-ORDER BRIDES WITH OUR FOURTH ROMANTIC WIND RIVER MAIL-ORDER BRIDES STORY, *A DANGEROUS HEART* BY LACY WILLIAMS AND WENDY GALINETTI.

Former U.S. Marshal Isaac McGraw wants nothing more than to forget his past and live in isolation on the family ranch. But his meddling family has cooked up other plans—plans that include matching Isaac with a mail-order bride who has two young boys in tow.

There's something about Clare Ferguson that bothers Isaac... more than the haunted look in her eyes and the way she's constantly glancing over her shoulder. Against his will—and better judgment—he finds himself drawn to Clare and her cheery disposition.

When Clare's secret past and relationship to an infamous outlaw is revealed, Isaac must break free from the chains of his past to keep his new family safe...

This sweet historical romance is perfect for fans of the following tropes:

*lawman hero

*ready-made family

*heroine on the run

*grumpy/sunshine

*redemption

One

"Y OU CAN'T CATCH ME!"

Shrieks and laughter from young voices carried on the early-autumn breeze as Isaac McGraw strode through the yard between the barn and the original family homestead—now his older brother Drew's home.

His six-year-old niece Tillie had sprouted up while he'd been gone on his last mission for the U.S. Marshals. Eleven-year-old Jo had grown lanky and awkward and looked more like her mother every day. But when Isaac looked at them, sometimes he saw the little tykes they'd been before.

Isaac's younger brother Nick trailed the girls toward the barn. He was within shouting distance but only raised his hand in a wave.

Isaac returned it half-heartedly and continued toward the main house.

He steeled himself and slowly pulled in air through his nose, the smell of damp hay and musky horses mingling in the fall air—familiar scents that now felt suffocating. A low-hanging fog clung to the grass and the bottom rails of the paddock as Isaac trudged through the mist and climbed the steps. The aroma of freshly brewed coffee greeted him as he crossed the threshold. He stalked to the dry sink, reached for a cup on the shelf above, and snagged the tin pot from the stove.

"Were you out all night, Uncle Isaac?"

Isaac had seen his nephew David stacking plates in the corner as soon as he'd come inside. It was too much to hope the fourteen-year-old would keep his silence.

Isaac nodded, setting the coffeepot down and turning to lean his hips against the counter. He lifted his cup to take a sip but avoided looking directly at the boy. It was too hard. David reminded him of another boy, one who hadn't lived to see his fourteenth birthday.

"Are you going again tonight? Can I come with you?"

David's questions tumbled over each other. The boy had idolized Isaac since they'd pinned the marshal's badge to his chest. And even now, when Isaac had given it up.

"No." Isaac hadn't meant to growl the word, but there it was.

David went quiet, subdued.

Drew hadn't asked Isaac to keep watch, but it gave him an excuse to keep his distance, and it felt like penance for not having been here when the well had been poisoned a few months ago. According to their middle brother Ed, the family had been so ill they might've died.

Voices carried from the adjoining living and dining

room, along with a husky laugh that belonged to his new sister-in-law Kaitlyn.

Moving to the doorway, he caught sight of Rebekah, Ed's wife of only a few weeks.

Two of his brothers had settled into marriage recently. It was another sign he didn't belong here anymore. He preferred the isolation of the hill country, his only companions a few varmints and a herd of cows.

But the ongoing feud with their neighbor made the solitude impossible. For now.

Isaac knew that any man willing to poison and kill wasn't going to give up easily. That's why Isaac needed to keep watch. Heath Quade wasn't going to give up, not when the McGraws owned the best water in the county. Quade had made that abundantly clear as he'd bought out two more neighbors over the past weeks. It wasn't enough for him to own the biggest ranch in the county. He'd bought or finagled nearly every piece right up to the McGraws' property lines.

Isaac's chest cinched tight at David's disappointment. He moved into the dining room to join Ed and Rebekah and Drew and Kaitlyn.

"What's this?" his brother Ed asked, bewildered. He was looking down at a white piece of paper on the table. Rebekah stood behind him, hands on her hips.

"It came to the mail-order bride postbox addressed to Isaac, postmarked a week ago. I found it in the mail when we were in town yesterday." She narrowed her eyes on her husband. "I thought I was the only one you were writing to."

Isaac watched color rise into Ed's cheeks, and a tiny part of him liked that his brother's new wife was sassing him. Months ago, Ed and Drew and Kaitlyn had cooked up a plan to find Isaac a bride—without bothering to ask him if he wanted one. The letters that were exchanged after the family had placed the mail-order bride ad on his behalf had caused a mess of trouble—and resulted in a match between Ed and Rebekah.

It gave Isaac a perverse kind of pleasure to see his brother squirming from the consequences of meddling in his life. Isaac was still angry.

"You are the only person I wrote to," Ed said.

Rebekah softened. "Then why does this Clare Ferguson say she's arriving on the train tomorrow?"

Isaac went still.

There was a jerky movement in the doorway at Rebekah's question.

"Hold up, son," Drew said at the same time as Isaac swiveled his head.

David stood in the open doorway, guilt written clearly on his expression. The kid had no poker face. He was trying to edge away unobtrusively, but Drew's focus was legendary.

"Why don't you come in here and tell us what you know about this letter." There was no room for disobedience in the command.

David hung his head, barely stepping inside the room. "Jo made me do it," he mumbled.

"Do what?" Ed asked.

Isaac's skin prickled at the sideways glance David shot him.

"Write a letter," the boy said hesitantly. He rubbed the back of his neck. "To get Uncle Isaac a wife."

Kaitlyn choked on her coffee.

It seemed that once he'd started, the words just tumbled out. "We heard you all talking at Uncle Ed and Aunt Rebekah's wedding. About Uncle Isaac. I told Jo it was a bad idea, but she—" His gaze flicked to Isaac. "We don't want Uncle Isaac to be sad anymore. So we picked one of the extra letters and wrote back to the lady who sent it."

Isaac's skin stretched too tight over his bones. No one in the family knew what had happened. There was no way David and Jo could know the well of darkness he'd descended into. But their innocent desire to help him—when he didn't deserve it one whit—hit like a punch to his solar plexus.

Isaac saw the guilty looks his brothers exchanged and Drew's glittering gaze.

"How many letters did you write?" Kaitlyn asked.

"Only two. Back and forth. They were good, long letters though. She's a really nice lady from a farm in Missouri. We paid for her train ticket from Jo's egg money and my savings."

"Why would you do that?" Drew demanded.

Ed had color high on his cheeks. Rebekah was hiding a laugh behind her hand.

David tilted his chin stubbornly. "Well, it worked for you and Uncle Ed."

Isaac turned to leave. He wanted no part of this.

But Ed said, "You'd better stay."

Anger flared. His brothers were still meddling in his life.

"I don't suppose you want to meet this woman?" Rebekah asked quietly.

Isaac ignored her completely.

Drew spoke to David. "Apologize to your uncle."

"You can't just mess with people's lives." Kaitlyn's words overlapped with her husband's.

David's chin was still jutting out. "Pa and Uncle Ed did."

Drew placed his hands on his hips and glared at his son. But he couldn't quite put any heat in his argument. "You're gonna have to fix this," he said. "You're gonna ride to town tomorrow and tell this woman to go back home."

"What? But Pa, she's coming to marry Uncle Isaac!"

The outburst was so unexpected from the usually even-keeled David that for a moment, the room went still.

Isaac felt the weight of the look Drew and Kaitlyn shared, the careful way Ed averted his eyes, Rebekah's hand on his arm.

"I'm not marrying anybody, kid," Isaac's voice grated. "Not ever."

David spun and ran from the room. The banging door punctuated the awkward silence that permeated the room.

Drew cleared his throat. "We'll make this right."

"You taught him to meddle," Isaac said coolly. "I want no part of this."

He left without looking back.

"Aunt Clare, are you really gonna get married to a cowboy?"

Get-ing marr-ied, get-ting marr-ied.

The train chugged and clacked, its wheels singing Clare Barlow's future.

She looked down at her eight-year-old nephew Ben, who gazed up at her with a wrinkled nose and an expression filled with curiosity. He had his mother's soft brown eyes and ready smile, always seeing adventure around every corner of life.

"What do you know about being a wife?" On Clare's other side, twelve-year-old Eli had his chin jutted at a stubborn angle and his arms crossed. His feet swung out into the aisle as if he couldn't sit still. A trait he came by honestly, from her side of the family. The Barlows were always on the run.

When he wasn't scowling, Eli was a handsome boy. Already more handsome than his father, with his intense dark-brown, almost black, eyes framed by thick lashes, and a square jawline that hinted at the man he would become. Not like his father, if she had anything to do with it.

Noth-ing, noth-ing.

Clare found a reassuring smile for both boys. "Yes, I'm really getting married. And he's a rancher, not a cowboy."

She would have to be enough. She'd gambled everything on this escape.

It wasn't the courtship most young women dreamed of—marrying a complete stranger. But Clare's belief in fairy-tale endings had been shattered years ago by her father. She'd learned a harsh truth that many girls never grasped: every fairy tale contained a villain, and sometimes that villain was a part of one's own family. A father. Or a brother.

"Can I be a cowboy too?"

Sweet Ben. Clare slid her arm around his small shoulders and pulled him closer. She whispered a reminder in his ear.

"Of course. And remember, you're to call me Ma."

"Okay," he whispered back.

She'd waited until now to tell the boys about the plan. Too much was at stake. She'd been too afraid of being found out before they'd left Missouri. She'd spent the first hours of their journey constantly looking over her shoulder, certain that Victor would find them.

Her outlaw brother would kill her for running away. Doubly so for taking his sons.

She knew what she'd done wasn't properly legal. She had no papers, no official claim to Ben or his brother. But she'd promised her late sister-in-law Anne in those last days before she'd passed. She could still hear her breathless plea. *Take them. Keep them safe. Make sure they don't grow up like him.*

And Clare couldn't break that promise.

The scenery out the window showed the Laramie Mountains in the distance.

Al-most there. Al-most there.

Calvin, Wyoming, was the next stop.

Absently, Clare noted the portly gentleman in the row in front of them getting up out of his seat. Before she'd fully registered it happening, Eli had slipped his scrawny arm between the seats and snatched it back with something clasped in his hand.

Clare caught his wrist in an iron grip.

"What is that?" Her whispered hiss and tightening grip had Eli revealing a fine gold watch with a broken chain.

She glanced over her shoulder at the man halfway to the hopper toilet at the back of the train. He hadn't even registered the watch was missing. No one else paid them a lick of attention.

It was a valuable piece—gold-plated and everything. It would be so easy to slip it inside her pocket. The man wore a fine suit. No doubt he could buy another. Clare and the boys had little funds. Her past whispered to her: easy pickings.

She took the watch from Eli's hand and dropped it back on the seat in front of them.

"We aren't Barlows anymore," she told him in a low, steady voice. "Remember the things your mama taught you. Thou shalt not steal."

Eli shoved back into the seat. He crossed his arms over his chest and jutted his chin in defiance. Gone was the older brother eager to help with his baby brother. Now she saw an echo of Victor, his father. Anne would have known better what to say, how to reach him. Clare didn't.

Her stomach clenched with grief over missing Anne. Through every hardship, Anne's faith had been a beacon. She'd changed Clare, brought light and truth into the world of darkness Clare had been born into. Clare had to continue Anne's legacy for her boys.

"Calvin, Wyoming!" the conductor announced as he passed down the aisle. As the train slowed, Clare's heart pumped faster. Ben sprang to his feet, gripping the seat back in front of him and lifting his boots off the floor to get a better view through the window of the row in front. Eli remained affixed to the seat, his mouth screwed tight.

She prayed he would keep his mouth shut and not give them away the first moment off the train.

The train braked and rolled to a stop. Clare rose from her seat, heart pounding, knees trembling. She smiled tightly at the boys.

At the front of the train, the steel-haired man with a wide, neatly trimmed mustache, around the same age as her pa, was the first passenger to stand. After a grand stretch, he donned his fancy black Stetson. She'd made him when he'd first entered the compartment. He had the sharp eyes and that certain shrewd manner of a man who lived outside the law.

Ben's hand slipped into hers. She dropped her eyes, turning her face away from the oily gaze that made her skin crawl and focusing on keeping the boys at her side as they disembarked.

A brisk breeze swept over the boardwalk, stirring up dust as Clare stepped off the train. Her skirt flapped against her legs as she surveyed the town. Behind the rooftops, the hills were dotted with trees, their green leaves on the verge of turning gold and amber with the cooler fall weather.

The streets were wider than the ones back home. Wide enough for two large wagons to pass. Wide enough for the herds of cattle that ranchers would drive into town and load onto trains headed for Chicago. Isaac had written in his last letter that she would arrive in time for the roundup. And wouldn't that be something?

She passed a young woman, carrying a toddler on her hip, who seemed to all but disappear into the arms of a hulking man in overalls. Clare froze and pressed sweaty hands together, struck by the realization that she hadn't considered how to greet her new groom. Would he anticipate a warm hug?

Where was Mr. McGraw?

She scanned the area and caught on a lone cowboy near the corner of the platform away from the rails. Dressed in dark trousers and a light-blue canvas shirt topped with a black vest, he stood rigid, shoulders squared, chin slightly lowered. He had that watchful look—steady and unblinking. His fingers even twitched at his side, a gunman ready to draw.

For a moment, she recoiled. Then she noticed what was missing—no gun belt, no pistol. Still, he glanced around, alert as any lawman.

No one else waited on the platform. Other folks were walking away. This had to be Isaac McGraw.

She took a few steps in his direction, her breath catching at the heat of his intense stare. If this was him, then her intended groom was an exceptionally handsome man, with his high cheekbones, vivid green eyes, and square jaw softened by a dimple. But why was he scowling at her?

They met at the far corner of the platform. She was aware of Ben and Eli trailing behind her. Eli muttered something to his brother that she didn't hear.

"Mr. McGraw?" Was that her voice? Breathy and trembling?

She saw the minute flare of his nostrils. Other than that, he was totally unreadable. He nodded.

"I'm Clare."

Ben shifted his feet, and the handsome cowboy–rancher's eyes flicked over Ben and moved to Eli. His frown tightened.

Her stomach dropped. She hadn't told her intended groom about her nephews. She hadn't wanted to give him any reason to reject her.

She glanced away. Saw the train porters unloading wooden crates. One crate caught her attention with the flash of a familiar name—*Hercules Powder.* Explosives?

She blinked, drawing her gaze back to the rancher, who didn't look any happier to see her. This man was nothing like the man in his letters, who'd written so fondly of the ranch and his family. Unease twisted in her belly, like when one of Pa's plans went awry.

She put a hand on Ben's small shoulder. "This is Ben. And this is Eli." She raised her other hand to Eli's shoulder.

Isaac's scowl deepened, but he didn't outright reject them. His gaze traveled to the street, past the crowd on the boardwalk, and landed on the man in the Stetson, standing several yards away, still on the platform. Stetson was talking with two other men who must be in their forties, wearing dusty trousers and vests over their shirts. Ranchers?

Isaac McGraw stiffened, and his eyes narrowed. She needed him to focus on her.

"Will we be going to the parson's house first?" Clare pressed, trying for a soft smile. "Before we go to your ranch?"

Isaac's eyes snapped back to her, distraction gone. "Miss—there's been a mistake. I didn't send for you, and we are not getting hitched."

His words didn't register at first. When they did, she felt

that knot in her belly twist tighter. "What do you mean?" she asked. "A mistake?"

He didn't answer directly. "It would be best if you got on that train and went back where you came from."

Ben's hand fisted in her skirt. Eli made a scoffing sound. She could feel the boys' nerves ratcheting higher. Or maybe it was her own.

"That won't be possible." There. She'd kept the tremble from her voice.

But Isaac didn't soften.

She was aware of curious gazes from people milling about the platform nearby. She couldn't afford to give Isaac more time to argue. "I don't understand. You sent for me so we could be married."

"I didn't send for you."

He'd said that before, but it didn't make any more sense this time. His voice was low and urgent and made her think he wanted her to be silent.

It only agitated her more. She reached into her skirt pocket and pulled out the folded envelope. "I have your letter right here. You promised we'd marry!" Her voice pitched higher and louder than she intended.

Heads turned from the crowd on the platform, especially Mr. Stetson and his two companions. Their gazes were like nettles on her skin. She and the boys were too exposed out here in the open. She stepped closer to Isaac McGraw. Close enough to see the tight lines around his mouth and hear his breath catch.

"Is there somewhere more private we could go to straighten out this misunderstanding?" she asked softly.

Ben chose that moment to yank at her sleeve. "I'm hungry."

Isaac glared at her. "We are not going anywhere," he ground out. "You're getting back on that train."

Her plan was unraveling before her eyes. Since she'd stepped foot off the train, nothing had gone right. Victor was behind her. There was no returning, not after what she'd done. She couldn't give up. "You gave your word. We're getting married."

A shadow fell over her. "Is there a problem here, miss?"

She didn't notice until she looked his way that it was sharp-eyed Mr. Stetson from the train.

She was close enough to see the subtle change in Isaac's expression, the way his back bristled. He turned a stony face to the interloper. "No."

The man ignored Isaac, his calculating eyes on Clare. He puffed out his chest and tipped his hat toward Clare. "Heath Quade, president of the Cattlemen's Association and a citizen of this fine town. And you are?"

"None of your business, Quade," Isaac growled.

Ben butted his head into Clare's side, jolting her. She'd been so caught up in the tension between the two men that, for a moment, she'd lost track of both boys. Panic flared as she turned—until she spotted Eli, quietly watching Quade. Relief rushed through her.

"I thought you were getting married." Ben chose the worst moment to pipe up.

Heath Quade's shrewd eyes darted between Isaac and Clare. "That true?"

The muscle in Isaac's jaw jumped, but he remained mute.

Quade turned a calculating glance toward Clare. "You one of those mail-order brides? The McGraws sure do like them."

Clare didn't know what he meant, but it was clear his words stirred up something in Isaac.

"This ain't your concern." Isaac stepped in front of Clare and the boys, partially blocking her from Quade's view. She was surprised by the protective gesture after his earlier scowl.

Isaac's head turned, and she realized the two other men had stepped over to flank their friend Quade. With her feet at the back of the platform, it felt a little like being trapped. Her gaze darted all around as she looked for an escape.

One of the men addressed her. "This man botherin' you?"

She shook her head.

Apparently, the moment of distraction meant Quade had stepped to the side, around Isaac. He addressed Clare.

"I couldn't help but overhear—"

"Stay out of it, Quade." There was something dangerous in Isaac's tone. Couldn't everyone hear it?

Quade didn't. "As an upstanding citizen of Calvin and a duly elected official, it's my duty to come to the aid of a lady who finds herself abandoned at the train station."

Isaac blocked Quade when he tried to step closer, keeping his lean, muscular body between Quade and Clare and her nephews. Almost like he was shielding her.

Her chest tightened. Had anybody ever stepped between her and danger? She didn't think so.

"Did I hear you say you had a letter? A written promise to marry could be considered a binding contract."

Clare's fingers gripped the letter tighter. She wanted to shove it back into her pocket. But that would be too obvious now.

Quade spoke to the man closest to him. "What do you think, gentlemen? It'd sure be a shame if one of Calvin's first homesteading families got sued for breach of contract."

Isaac's shoulders tensed, and his stance grew more rigid.

The other rancher looked uncomfortable. "If McGraw can't keep his word, the circuit judge can sort this out when he comes to town."

Something passed between Quade and Isaac. She wished she could see Isaac's face.

Quade said, "Maybe we should just walk over to the marshal's office and see what Marshal O'Grady has to say about this."

Eli, a statue throughout the whole exchange, began to shake. His fists were clenched at his sides, and he was standing on the balls of his feet, ready to run.

Clare gripped his sleeve. "That won't be necessary," she said quickly to Quade. "I'm sure Mr. McGraw and I can come to an equitable—"

Isaac turned toward her. He motioned to the stairs off the platform. "The wagon is thataway. Get a move on."

The command in his voice grated on her last nerve, but she also had a sense that this was the only offer he was going to make. And she needed to get off the platform, away from so many prying eyes. Eyes that could report back to Victor if he ever sent a scout looking for her here.

She grabbed Eli's arm with one hand and Ben's hand

with the other and followed Isaac's long-legged stride off
the train platform.

Acknowledgments

Many thanks to everyone at Sunrise Publishing for taking a chance on me. And to the teamwork of all the authors working to bring the stories of the four McGraw brothers to life for readers to enjoy – Wendy Galinetti, Martha Hutchens, Traci Summeril, and Lacy Williams. Lacy deserves a huge round of applause for her investment in all of us.

A special thanks to Erin Mifflin, Kristi Woods and Lori DeJong. These ladies helped me iron out the premise for the audition to write this story. I am so grateful for their help and friendship.

Thanks to my sister, my son and daughter-in-love for their unwavering support. You guys are the best!

Saving the absolute best for last – thanks go to Jesus. He made this happen. I never could have done it on my own.

Also by Lacy Williams

Christmas Bells and Wedding Vows (anthology)

Wagon Train Matches
A Trail So Lonesome
Trail of Secrets
A Trail Untamed
Wild Heart's Haven
A Rugged Beauty

Wind River Hearts series
Marrying Miss Marshal
Counterfeit Cowboy
Cowboy Pride
The Homesteader's Sweetheart
Courted by a Cowboy
Roping the Wrangler
Return of the Cowboy Doctor
The Wrangler's Inconvenient Wife
A Cowboy for Christmas
Her Convenient Cowboy
Her Cowboy Deputy
Catching the Cowgirl
The Cowboy's Honor
Winning the Schoolmarm
The Wrangler's Ready-Made Family
Christmas Homecoming
Heart of Gold

USA Today bestselling author **Lacy Williams** is devoted to bringing her readers heartwarming love stories about cowboys and the women that tame them. She is the author of over fifty-five books, including the acclaimed Wind River Hearts and Sutter's Hollow series. Her books have been nominated for the RT Book Reviews' Seal of Excellence as well as finaled in RT's Reviewers' Choice Awards. She has been a puppy parent almost her whole life and often writes with one of her dogs snuggled in her lap. She is a mom of four and spends her non-writing time buried under piles of laundry and dishes.

Learn more at lacywilliams.net.

Wendy Klopfenstein enjoys sunshine, sweet tea, and a good book, preferably all at the same time. Having always loved creating stories as much as reading them, she now puts the ones wandering around in her head on paper for others to enjoy. When she's not sitting on the porch reading or helping clients in the family business, you can find her working on her next novel.

Discover more at wendyklopfenstein.com.

Wind River
MAIL-ORDER BRIDES

USA Today Bestselling Author *Lacy Williams*

Martha Hutchens, Wendy Klopfenstein, Wendy Galinetti, Traci Summeril

In the wild and untamed landscape of old west Wyoming, the McGraw brothers navigate the challenges of ranch life, unexpected love, and the transformative power of second chances. As each mail-order bride enters their lives, these steadfast men discover that love can bloom in the most unlikely places. Love comes softly in Wind River...

We solve the problem of what we read next.

Available on Amazon

BLOOD OF KINGS: LEGENDS

Award-winning author

JILL WILLIAMSON

with Andrew Swearingen,
Kelly Fernlake, & Niki Florica

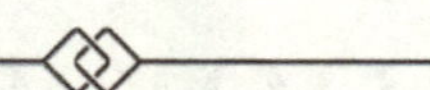

Return to the world of Er'Rets in an epic
fantasy series brimming with richly woven
tales of loyalty, love, and sacrifice...

YOU MAY ALSO LIKE...

When a blizzard strikes Deep Haven and Megan is overrun with catastrophes, it takes a former Ranger to step in and help. But the more he comes to her rescue, the sooner she'll move out... Come home to Deep Haven in this magical tale about the one who got away... and came back.

Still the One **by Susan May Warren and Rachel D. Russell**

Grace Howell leaves her life as a ballerina and returns to Heritage, Michigan, to heal. Teaching dance is just a temporary gig, until she finds herself unexpectedly charmed by small-town life and her growing attachment to Seth Warner, a man from her past with a troubled history of his own.

You're the Reason **by Tari Faris**

Dani Sullivan is determined to revive Jonathon Island's fading charm and reunite her fractured family. Her plan? Reopen the Grand Sullivan Hotel. But without the funds to restore the hotel, Dani's forced to accept help from Liam Stone—a big-city hotel developer whose sleek, modern vision is everything she's trying to avoid.

Meet Me at the Grand **by Lindsay Harrel**

We solve the problem of what we read next.   Available on Amazon

**WHERE EVERY STORY IS A FRIEND,
AND EVERY CHAPTER IS A NEW JOURNEY...**

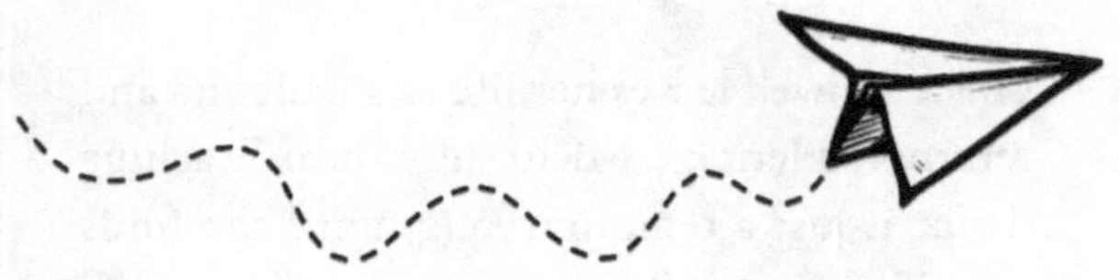

Subscribe to our newsletter for a free book, the latest news, weekly giveaways, exclusive author interviews, and more!

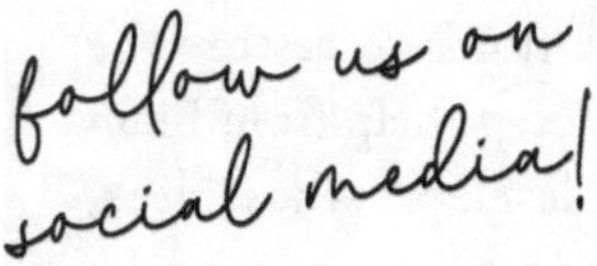

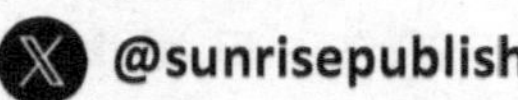

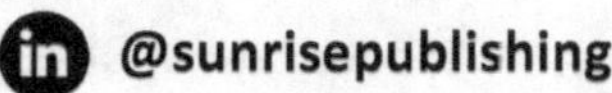

Shop paperbacks, ebooks, audiobooks, and more at
SUNRISEPUBLISHING.MYSHOPIFY.COM